I CALL HIM DADDY TOO

I WISH SERIES

MARIAH KINGSLEY

I would like to dedicate this book to everyone that loved I Wish You Were. It's because of you that I even thought of writing this book. I hope it is everything you want it to be.

Copyright © 2021 by Mariah Kingsley

All rights reserved.

No part of this book may be reproduced in any form or by any electronic or mechanical means, including information storage and retrieval systems, without written permission from the author, except for the use of brief quotations in a book review.

❦ Created with Vellum

PREFACE

This book is part of a series. The stories run side by side they should be read in conjunction with each other. Book one is called I Wish You Were.

1
EBONY'S

The music was blasting in my car as I drove down Coldfax. I was starving. Today had been another long day; Ty, my boss, had meetings all day, the last one just ending half an hour ago. I put the music on loud so I wouldn't fall asleep before I got something to eat. It was common for Ty to have late meetings, especially on a Friday night, but the city wanted an update on the building we were buying and with all of the red tape, I wondered if she was going to be able to buy it.

I was going to call Sierra and ask her to meet me for dinner, but I remembered the text from her saying that she was going on a date. I rolled my eyes at the thought of another date for Sierra; I know in the morning, I am going to get a call telling me about this one. In the last month, she had been on fourteen—yes, I said fourteen. All a disaster, all were worse than the last one. I would tell her that it's her, but she is not ready for that come-to-Jesus meeting yet.

I was great at giving advice about relationships; I was better at giving advice about sex. It was my specialty. I helped men and women find their inner sexual being. Years ago, I got tired of my homegirls telling me that a guy was great, and then they got in the bedroom and it was horrible. So I started a service where I helped men, and oftentimes women, learn the techniques to please even the freakiest of partners.

It was my side hustle; honestly, I could quit my job for Ty and do this full time. I was in such a demand that my weekends were filled with requests for my services. I charged a ten thousand dollar retainer fee, and in that fee I listened to dates, I observed the client in the act, and then I taught them how to please their partner. I had several successful marriages to my credit. Women that wanted ball players, hedge fund brokers, and men that made the kind of money that made women search for my services. I've even had several marriage offers, but it never crossed my mind to even consider the offers. Some were from clients, some from boyfriends.

Boyfriends were not really my thing; no matter how honest I am about what I do, they always want me to quit. The thought of my teaching sex ruffled their feathers. I got it, I even could see how that could be an issue, but when the right man came along, he wouldn't care about my side hustle.

Honestly, I couldn't remember the last time I felt free in a relationship. I don't remember the last time I was in love. I don't think I have ever been in love, and I don't think I have ever truly been loved by anyone romantically.

Sure, they loved the idea of me—I was a freak, I was pretty, and I don't say that to be full of myself; I was pretty. Men fell all over themselves to be in my face, and truthfully, women did too. Ty was the first woman that I knew was gay that didn't hit on me. It was refreshing.

I pulled into the parking lot of Ebony's; it was a new

place that I had visited a couple times in the last month. It was classy, and one of the few places that served upscale soul food. Before driving here, I'd looked at tonight's menu and saw that they had seafood, and I couldn't pass that up. The other thing I liked about this place was that every booth was private, you were cocooned in your own little world, and tonight, I was happy for that.

I was going to take off my shoes and put on some flip-flops, but I watched the people walking into the restaurant and they were dressed to impress. I always took pride in the way that I looked. I never left the house without a little makeup and a pair of heels. But I had been on my feet all day, and although I was used to high heels, this was getting painful. I looked at my flip-flops longingly on the passenger seat, but decided to leave them there.

I closed the door to the car and walked into the building. The lights were low tonight, I had never been there that late; I either called in my meal or came for lunch. Every table had a candle on it, a small bouquet of flowers sat in the center, and the place was packed. There was a low rumble of conversation as I approached the hostess. She smiled brightly at me.

"Welcome to Ebony's. Do you have a reservation?"

Shit, I didn't have a reservation. I looked around the room and saw that it was packed. My eyes stopped on a man sitting to the back, and his eyes were on me. His gaze a caress, making my skin prickle. I felt heat at my cheeks, and I suddenly wanted to fall into him. The hostess cleared her throat, and I looked to her, feeling a loss with just my eyes moving from his.

"Sorry, I don't have a reservation."

And I was sorry, I wanted to look at him some more. He was handsome, older than me, but his body was strong. His face was partly hidden in shadow. I looked back to where he was to get one last look at him as she told me that it would be an hour wait, but he wasn't there. Was he a figment of my imagination? As tired as I was that wouldn't be a stretch. I gave her my name and number and went to walk away when I turned I saw a broad chest. He wore a beautiful dark blue shirt and tie. I looked up, and up, and there were those eyes that warmed and thrilled me. His deep voice caressed me.

"If you don't mind sharing a meal with me, I have a table alone."

I was never lost for words, but right then I couldn't find a word in all the words that I knew. I just nodded my head; he took my hand and the warmth of his engulfed me. I was in six-inch heels and I didn't even reach his shoulders.

I vaguely heard him ask for a menu and then he turned us to the dining room. I watched him walk, commanding the room. I felt eyes on us, but I soaked him in, wanting to remember every inch of the walk to the table. He maneuvered me in front of him like we had been dancing. The stranger let his hand glide to the small of my back as he pulled out my chair, placing me in the seat with ease. I enjoyed his short walk to his chair and then he sat. He had a glass of wine on his side of the table. His food had not been delivered yet; he handed me the menu while speaking.

"I'm Robert, by the way, and you are Lisa." I looked at him with puzzlement. Had I told him my name? He read my face and said, "I overheard you tell the hostess your name."

I smiled at him and did something that I rarely did; I gave him my correct name. "Alesia." No one ever said it correctly anyway.

"Alesia, such a beautiful name." And the way that he said it, it was very beautiful. I felt heat touch my cheeks and looked down at the table.

I wasn't this girl; I wasn't some shy speechless woman who blushed. I was a warrior; I was feisty. I had to snap out of it. I taught women how to not be a shy woman; I couldn't believe that I was feeling this way.

I pulled myself together after that thought. Reached for the menu and looked it over. I didn't need it; I knew what I was going to eat. Deciding what to eat was an excuse to look down so I could pull myself together. My eyes roamed over the menu and, out of my control, I looked at Robert. His eyes were dancing, his smooth ochre skin gleamed as he flashed a tantalizing smile with large full lips. I suddenly had the urge to kiss those lips.

"So, Alesia, have you decided on dinner? You have been examining that menu for a while now." He picked up his wine and put it to his lips. I watched the simple movement and my mouth went dry.

"I was thinking the salmon. Have you had it?" I choked out.

Robert placed the glass on the table and spoke to me while looking at me. "I think I have tried everything on the menu; the salmon is good. You should try it with the crab cake."

That sounded great, and I smiled at him. When I did, his tawny eyes got intense, and I felt that heat hit my cheeks once again. Before I could say anything, the waiter came. He asked if we were ready, and we told him what we wanted.

"Alesia, what do you do?"

My wine had been placed in front of me and I took a sip. "I am an assistant to a real estate firm." I didn't tell him about my other job, but I didn't tell many people that. I didn't want to give him the wrong idea about what I could do. Okay, let me be real, I would fuck him with no hesitation.

"What do you do, Robert?"

"I own an investment firm."

I could see that he commanded a room. His presence alone had eyes all over the dimly lit room drawn to him. "Do you always draw attention?"

He smiled and his eyes swept the room then came back to me. "Beautiful, I do believe they are looking at you."

I gaped at him; his deep voice calling me beautiful did things to my lady parts.

He continued, "That pink dress is holding your curves like it was made for you. And the shoes are simply beautiful."

I smiled at him, secretly happy I'd left the flip-flops in the car. I wore a soft pink bandage dress, one that fit so tight it felt like skin.

"From the moment you walked in the door, your presence was known. I don't think I've looked at the door since I sat down, and this isn't the best light for people watching, but when you walked in, every eye here was on you." That was sweet, and I liked that he felt that way. "I wasn't the only man that was sitting alone to get up, I just got there first."

I hadn't noticed any other men; I only had eyes for him. Those eyes roamed his face, and all I could see was sincerity.

"You are very handsome, Robert; how old are you?"

That was a very rude question; he screamed mature, but his body was powerful. His massive chest tapered down onto a slim waist. No beer belly for him. He reached out his hand and took mine.

He took a sip of wine, and the waiter came back with our food, asked if we would like a refill. I needed all of my faculties so I declined, just asking for water.

"I'm fifty-five, I have a birthday in two months. How old are you?"

"Thirty two next month." I thought about the age difference; it isn't a deal breaker for me. In this moment, there wasn't much he could do that would be a deal breaker. He didn't dress like an old man; he didn't give me dirty old man vibes either. I got those a lot.

"Is the age difference going to bother you?" he asked me as he took a bite of food.

"Why would it bother me?"

"Because I would like to see what's under that dress."

I smiled at him boldly. My eyes staring him up and down.

I leaned into him, lifting my ass off the seat. "There is nothing under this dress, Robert. And the thought of you finding out what I have to offer turns me on in a way that I haven't been in a long time."

He also leaned forward after I finished. "I really want to kiss you."

"What's stopping you?"

He leaned closer to me, taking my mouth with his, and fire rushed to my core. We were in a crowded restaurant, but he took his time savoring me like I was the finest thing he had ever tasted. My eyes closed feeling his tongue against mine, stoking that fire deep inside of me. When the kiss broke, I sat back in my chair on shaky legs. It took some time, but words came back to me, and I spoke softly.

"I want to do that again."

His eyes sparkled and lips tipped up in a sexy way. "Eat your dinner, and I will give you more than that."

My belly flipped as I sat back in my seat. My body began heating all over.

Our conversation flowed, and we talked about our jobs. I

told him about the long day I'd had and how I was happy that I'd stopped in. I was happy he was excellent company.

"Would you like dessert?" Robert asked, but the way he said it made me think he was not talking about what was on Ebony's menu. His hungry eyes glued to mine made my skin heat. I bit my lip, and his gaze intensified.

"Yes, I would love dessert, but to go."

He smiled at me and ordered a brownie with ice cream on the side.

The waiter came back with the food and check, and I pulled out my wallet. He gave me a look so sharp I drew in a breath.

"I invited you to sit with me, I have enjoyed your company, please put your wallet away." He pulled out a shiny black Amex and laid it on the check. Next, he pulled out his phone. "Are you staying with me tonight?"

My common sense told me that I shouldn't; I should make him wait. But I never listened to that side of myself.

"Yes."

He pulled out his phone, hit a few buttons, and spoke into the phone. "I would like a suite for tonight."

I also pulled out my phone, texted Sierra, and told her I was spending the night with a man name Robert. I also told her that I'd just met him. I would call her in the morning. I didn't think he was a killer, but we made a promise that I would always tell her if I had a one night stand.

It didn't happen often—well, not anymore—but it could happen.

"We have reservations at the Ritz," he said while signing the check. I was happy that he was looking away because I was very surprised. In the old days, a room by the hour was good enough to get my rocks off, but the Ritz was not a place you got your rocks off and left. You stayed a while; you enjoyed the room. I wondered how much it cost.

I didn't ask that question. When his eyes met mine, I smiled at him and said, "Pulling out all the stops."

What he said next made my heart stop. "You're beautiful, Alesia; you deserve to lay in the lap of luxury while I please you in every way I know how. I hope to learn your body. In order to do that I must make sure that body is comfortable; I might need to feed you, and I can't do that and stay close at the Motel 6. I want this to be a night to remember."

He didn't have to worry about me remembering; I was going to keep this night in my heart. Rarely do men with money not flaunt it. He could have taken me to Motel 6; as turned on as I was, he could have taken me in the backseat of my car, although his tall frame wouldn't be comfortable. I was into public sex, so it wouldn't bother me. What struck me was that he called ahead to make sure that I not only enjoyed his body, but he took the time to make sure that I enjoyed where we were staying the night.

He didn't asked to go to my place, and I was happy; it was one of my rules. I could count on my fingers how many lovers I've had in my home. It could get tricky. I didn't want some stranger knowing where I lived, and I wasn't a fan of going to the homes of the men I met either. I was cool with the local pay by the hour room, just to have privacy. But the Ritz...that got me excited. I had never been to the one in Denver. Ty had taken me to a few when we went out of town, but never in Denver.

"Thank you for thinking of my comfort."

He smiled at me inclining his head and started to get up. I found my purse, and he helped me out of my seat. We walked out of the restaurant weaving through the tables, his hand on the small of my back. When we reached the door, he clasped my hand in his and walked me to the parking lot. I beeped the lock to my red Mini Cooper and started it.

I watched him lift his hand, and then the lights flipped on to a pearl white Rolls-Royce Ghost. *Father in heaven.* My steps faltered, and I wondered how I'd missed it when I pulled in. It was beautiful.

"That is sexy," I said under my breath. He heard me and chuckled. After walking me to my car, he opened the door and held it while I got inside.

"Do you know the way?" I didn't so I shook my head no. "Follow me, in fact, give me your number in case we get separated." He handed me his phone and I put in my number. Closing the door, I waited for him to get to his car, which was a few rows away. I didn't hear it start, but I saw him pull out just enough for me to be behind him.

My phone rang from a number that I didn't recognize, but I answered it anyway. "I need to stop at CVS for condoms," Robert's voice said over the speaker of my car.

"I have condoms in my trunk," I said this before I thought about the implications. I kept condoms for clients; many didn't know their size and complained about them being too tight or too loose. I also had dental jams for safe sex during class. Along with at home HIV tests. They were a little pricy, but it was worth it.

"I love a woman that is prepared."

I let out a breath I didn't know I was holding. I'd had many lovers that were not as nice about me having a trunk full of sexual aids.

"Okay, baby, I'm going to let you go; stay close to me so I know you are safe. Call me if you get lost along the way."

I held my breath again. People didn't do these kinds of things for me. Men just didn't check and make sure that I was okay. No matter if this was only for tonight, I was going to enjoy it.

"You got it, honey."

We disconnected, and I drove in silence. Usually I needed music to hype me up. Hell, two hours ago I was dog tired. The possibility of being with Robert...and I was wide awake. I looked at the clock on the dash and it said a little after ten. I thought that I would be asleep at this time. But from the looks of it, sleep wasn't in the cards.

2

THE COMPANY WAS BETTER

The sun was shining and my body was sore; I had just dosed off to sleep, and now I was awakened by soft voices. Robert kept me up through the night. I lost track of the number of times I came from his mouth or his fingers, and Lord, his cock was amazing. Everything about last night was spectacular! He made me scream out his name so often my throat was a little raw. I have never met a man that made me lose control. I'd had many lovers. Some were great, but none like him. He could be demanding in bed, rough even, and then he could be so tender tears leaked from my eyes. The way he explored my body with his hands and mouth was out of this world.

The door opened slowly and he walked in; the fact that he could still stand after nine—I looked at the clock—no, ten hours of love-making made me envious. He looked at me in bed and smiled a bright smile.

"Good morning, beautiful. I am so sorry if I woke you; breakfast is here."

My stomach growled at the sound of breakfast, but my body was warm in the bed. This wasn't my first all-nighter.

Well, it had been a while and never had I had an all-nighter with one man—maybe three—but I couldn't feel my legs, and I was afraid if I stood I would fall.

"I don't think my legs are up for moving yet."

He laughed softly, his eyes roaming my face. "I can carry you if you need me to."

He might have to carry me; I wiggled my toes, and even that was tiring. I watched as Robert gave me a cocky smile, his eyes moving from my toes. He walked to the bathroom door, going behind it and pulling a robe from the back of the door then walked to my side of the bed. He wore the clothes from last night, but they looked casual somehow. I remember from last night how good they'd looked on his incredible body. Now as he walked to me, pants hung low, shirt only having two buttons done, I liked what I saw. Smooth muscled chest, I remembered the taste of him, the feel of his chest rising and falling. I found myself wanting to feel that again. He reached for me, and I went to him, my body protesting just a bit. My legs felt like jelly under me. My arms went through the sleeves, and he wrapped the robe around me. When he was done, he kissed the tip of my nose.

"You okay?" he asked me gently. His eyes were so damn soft. And a piece of me that I had never felt peeked out to see what this man was offering. Was he offering something? I shook my head.

"What can I do to make you okay?" *Damn, this man was something else.*

"I'm okay, I was just thinking something crazy. Don't mind me, I am fine, I promise."

I was fine; I had woken up in a bed with many men. Hell, many women as well, but not once did they ask if I was okay. Once my body had pleased their body, I was an afterthought. A fond one I was sure, but an afterthought nonetheless.

I turned away from him on my jelly legs, having to escape the emotions I was feeling. Emotions that I had longed to feel for a lifetime. I walked out to living area, looking at the spread of food. There was French toast and coffee, but there was also fruit, yogurt, and so much damn food that I would never be able to eat all of it.

I felt him again, right behind me, his arms going around my middle. And that part of me that wanted someone to love me deeply peeked out again. I wanted to push him away.

"Can I ask you something, and you'll tell me the truth?"

He hugged me then spoke, "I will always tell you the truth."

In my vast experiences with men, they never told all of the truth. I snorted, a habit that I got in Detroit. I had a friend there—I don't even remember her name, but I did remember her spunk—and the day she snorted, we were in a crowd of people; they all were talking bad about me, my clothes, my mother, and she had my back.

My mind came back to the room. "Is there a wife wondering where you are?"

"I have never been married. I don't have a live-in girlfriend. I don't have a girlfriend. Six months ago, I broke up with a woman because she valued my portfolio more than she valued me. I am generous, you would think after all these years I would learn not to show my wealth so early, but it's who I am."

As he spoke he walked me to the table, his hand resting on the small of my back; through the robe I could feel his heat and strength. He helped me sit in my chair and then went to his. I watched him; he was fun to watch.

He sat down and gave me a small awkward smile, something that I hadn't seen in the short time we'd been together.

"What's wrong?" I might not have seen that look on his face, but I had seen that look, and it made my stomach uneasy. Honestly, if he was ready for me to leave, breakfast was great but unnecessary. I hid my uneasiness and took a French toast off the platter. The table held fruit and French toast, and the smell of the coffee said that it would be the best coffee that I'd ever had. I vaguely wondered how much this room was a night. Maybe I could do this as a treat for myself?

"Can I ask you a question?" I looked to him; he hadn't touched his food. His eyes stared across the table at me, and he was uneasy as well.

"I guess we can make this the question and answer portion of the morning." He smiled a little, and I poured syrup over my food. Not really wanting to eat, wanting to face this head on, but I didn't want to look defensive, so I fixed food I wasn't sure I was going to be able to eat.

"I looked in your bag." Well, that was nosy. "I was looking for more condoms so I looked in the bag."

Yeah, he would have questions after looking in that bag. There were all types of toys of the male and female variety. Handcuffs, ropes and sexy videos. Along with dental dams and condoms of all sizes and variety.

"And the question would be?" I didn't want to give too much information. I mean maybe he wanted to use some of the toys in there. I would be down for that. "Why do I have a bag like that?" I could say a lot of things—a girl has to be prepared, or simply tell him to mind his business. I was about to do that when he spoke.

"Alesia, I like you, I won't judge if you are a hooker. We

can talk about it, and I don't judge. I know people do what they have to do to make it. I would just like to know."

His face was sincere, his eyes pleading, and I just stood there. I wasn't into prostitution. Yes, I sold sexual services, but I wasn't selling sex per say. I decided to go with the truth all of the truth.

"I am not a hooker, or a call girl. I teach men and women how to please someone sexually. I started back in college when an ex was in love with a woman that couldn't please him in bed; he asked me to teach her. He paid me well, and it all started from there. I have a private client list; I am available by word of mouth only. I charge a retainer fee and usually just watch, coach, and teach. My clients can be businessmen and women, as well as professional ball players. I work twice a week; in fact, I have a client tonight."

And I did have a client. Richard and his wife Susie. They had a great marriage, but the sex was lacking on both parts. Many times, I just watched the way people had sex and critiqued the interaction. Honestly, halfway through their evaluation, I stopped the trainwreck and started working with them. In three months, the sex was sensual and beautiful, and honestly, tonight I was going to tell them they didn't need me anymore. They paid well, like all the others, but I would miss the downtime that we had together. After their sessions we talked, had a snack, and I listened to the life that they have out of the bedroom.

"You teach people to have sex?" he said in disbelief; he wasn't condescending, just asking a question. I smiled at him and cut into my French toast.

"Look, there is a lot of bad sex out there; there was a need, I just filled the void. My client can be married or engaged, sometimes they are single. I don't have sex with all of them, but it has happened. I charge for my time because in the beginning it's a lot of talking and explaining.'

I took a bite of my food, and my eyes rolled in delight. It was perfect. I looked over at Robert and saw that he too was eating his food. I continued, "I even set up some of my clients; so far I have been invited to ten weddings. I hooked up eleven, and the last one has been dating for a little over a year. I have high hopes for them."

"So you are telling me that last night I made love to a sex guru?" He said that in a teasing voice, but the words *made love* made me stop chewing. Before last night I had never felt anything like what we shared. I fucked, and I did it well, but I had never made love. Robert insisted on eye contact and kissing me with long deep strokes. If I could teach a class on fucking, he could definitely teach a class on love-making. I pushed those thoughts away, chewed, and spoke.

"You damn right, and that wasn't all my tricks." I winked at him.

He smiled at me and looked satisfied. In my experience, this conversation could go really bad; most men would insist I stop my business or they were out. Well, all were out at that point. Others would stare at me in disbelief, then tell me all the reasons I was too good for the job, and how my career choices affect them. How they didn't want people to know what I did; they didn't want people to know they dated a hoe. Yes, I had been called a hoe on more than one occasion. I watched Robert eat, seemingly not having a care in the world. Maybe he knew that this was a one night thing, and he didn't have to deal with the fallout of my career.

"What time is your class tonight?"

He called it a class, and I liked that. "It starts at eight tonight. Honestly, the last two sessions have gone so well, I think I am going to graduate them tonight."

They were doing great, they communicated beautifully, they communicated well in everyday life, but when it came to the bedroom, neither wanted to be in control. After months of assignments and talking through their issues, we'd worked though all of that and were able to get to a point where they both enjoyed sex, and if I say so myself, they were getting hot.

"I need to work a little today. I wanted you to stick around. If you agree, I would like to have a masseuse come up to the room. All I need is an hour, and in that time, you could have the massage and then I would like to take you to an early dinner."

He didn't want this to end, and neither did I. I wanted to be in his presence, which was different. With most men when I was done, I left. I had my own bed and liked it very much. But the thought of being in that big bed suddenly made me feel lonely. "I don't have anything to wear for dinner here; I can go home and get something to wear."

"If you tell me your size, I could get you something from a boutique I know of."

I don't know I felt about him buying my clothes; I was particular about what I wore.

"You don't know me well enough to buy clothes for me. I don't mind going to get what I like. If you say it's close, I can put on the clothes that I brought with me and go find something for dinner."

I was done eating, but he wasn't, his fork paused mid-air as he gave me a perplexed look. I leveled my eyes on him; I was serious about this. I couldn't be bought. I made really good money for an assistant, and I made even more money on my side job. My house was paid for, so was my car. I had little overhead. I could afford a boutique dress. It was a nice offer, but it seemed that he needed a lesson as well. I know

I Call Him Daddy Too

he was used to showing off his money, and honestly, this was an issue that most men had. Many women wanted that, the expensive bags and shoes, and some needed that. I wasn't one of those women. I could do what I needed for myself. "The offer was sweet, but unnecessary. I will take you up on the massage because I am a little tight, but I can buy an outfit."

He moved slowly to pick up his glass of water and took a sip. I watched him, then he spoke. "The boutique is across the street; would you like me to call and get you an appointment?"

"I would like that very much. I would also like for you to tell me where dinner will be so I can find a dress that goes with the environment."

He sat back in his chair, amusement in his eyes. "There is a private dinner club in the mountains, and since you have other plans for later tonight, the fastest way to get there is via helicopter. I thought we could leave about five, see the sunset over the mountains, that's if you are not afraid of helicopters."

"I have no issue with air travel, but just for your memory bank, I'm afraid of snakes, not too fond of clowns, and needy men give me anxiety."

He laughed at the needy men comment, and I took a sip of my coffee. Through his laugh he said, "I will remember all of that, and will endeavor not to be needy."

"That would make me very happy. Now let me get ready, I need to shower and get ready for the day; if you are a good boy and quick with making that appointment, I will let you dig in my bag of tricks and meet me in the shower."

He threw down his napkin and reached for his phone, pushing a few buttons, and then put it to his ear. "Hello, Veronica, I have a friend that will be in your shop in two hours, she will not be using my account, she will be paying on her own. Please wait on her when she gets there." He ended the phone call as I walked to the back, pulling off my robe as I went. The shower was divine, the company was better.

3

FLAT ON THE TABLE

I made my way out of the Ritz and thought I definitely had to come back, maybe not the penthouse, but I would see what else they had to offer. Downtown Denver was alive and well; I didn't need the boutique, Cherry Creek mall was just down the way, and if they didn't have my style at this place, I would take an Uber to the mall. When I walked into the store there were three women there, all stylishly dressed, and they all smiled at me. Robert timed it just right, it had been two hours on the dot since his call.

"I am supposed to see Veronica," I said to the room at large; taking in the clothing, I hadn't decided if it was my thing yet—some of the clothes were for older ladies, ones that had real money. I was into flash; I had the body so I flaunted it. Veronica smiled at me extending her hand and told me to come in.

"So what's the occasion?" she asked with a smile.

"We are taking a helicopter to dinner in the mountains. I also need shoes, I think."

I had a classic pair of black pumps in my car from last week that I hadn't taken out. Let's be honest, my car had an emergency supply of shoes for all occasions. I wasn't sure that I didn't have a pair that would work, but I would look while I was here.

The store was beautiful, chandeliers all over rich golds and blacks on the walls. This is a place that Ty would take one of her women, not that those gold diggin' hoes deserved it. But I liked the store. In the front the store had very conservative clothing, but bold and sexy was in the back. I was drawn to this blood red dress, low cut, form-fitting, and I had to try it on.

"I would like to try on this one." I pointed to the dress, and Veronica smiled brightly. She asked my size and I told her. She showed me to the back of the store where there were very spacious dressing rooms. There were mirrors to show every detail of the dress. I looked at the price tag and blew out a breath; it was over nine hundred dollars. It wasn't the first time that I'd spent that kind of money, but I wasn't expecting that. Then I put the dress on and it fit like a second skin. Gliding down over my ass, stopping right at my knee. I wanted it in every color. I walked out of the dressing room, and Veronica clapped when she saw me. "That looks so good on you. Please take a photo and tag us in it. You look amazing."

I felt amazing. I took the dress off and went into the shoe section, finding a red sling back shoes that went great with the dress, and they were on sale for five hundred. Veronica took the dress and shoes out of my hands and took me to the register. My MasterCard was smoking, but I smiled when I got the bags.

I decided that I needed to go to my house to get some things. It didn't make since to buy new hair products for one night. My house was just out of downtown; Ty let me buy it for a song, and I fixed it up the way that I liked. My house was over three thousand square feet on one level. It was a four bedroom, but I used only two as bedrooms. The other two were an office and a playroom. I hadn't used the playroom in a long time and was really thinking of turning it into a library. I was getting into reading and had quite a collection. I walked into my closet and got an overnight bag, putting hair products and perfume into it, I also got my thank you notes and pretty pens to thank my couple that would graduate tonight. I like to remind them of where they were and how far they had come. I always reminded them that they could always call me if they found themselves in trouble.

It didn't take me long, I had to get back for my appointment with the masseuse; driving back, Sierra called and I took it. "Hey girl, how was your night?"

"Girl, this man brought his mother on the date; she asked me all kinds of personal questions including when my period was."

I laughed. "So, I can assume there won't be a second date?"

"That is a correct assumption. You met someone new last night?"

"Yes, and I like him; the sex was amazing. I'm headed back to the hotel now. We have a dinner date before I meet my clients tonight."

I pulled onto the freeway and waited for my friend to speak.

"You always meet all the good ones."

I smacked my lips. "Girl, did you forget about the guy that wanted me to let his friends run a train after he found out about my business? How about no job Josh? That man spent more time in the mirror than I did. Robert is cool, he's older than me, but he can keep up. He's working right now and says that he has never been married. The best part is when he found out about my clients, he didn't sweat me about it. Made reservations for dinner early so I could be back in time to meet them and asked me to spend the night with him again."

"You never do two nights in a row, and you don't sleep in a bed with a man that you just met; he must be something."

I laughed again. "Girl, I only slept in that bed because I couldn't get out. The sun was up when he was done, and baby, it was amazing. He got me up a few hours ago and fed me, fucked me real good in the shower, and told me to come back for a massage. I'm on my way back to the hotel now. I just stopped by the house for clothes and stuff that I would need."

I wasn't ready to talk about how we spoke softly between the sex, how he kissed me so tenderly. How he ran his hands through my hair and put me to sleep. I couldn't say out loud that I enjoyed that more than the sex.

Sierra was talking in my ear, but I didn't hear a word she said.

"Girl, my phone went out what did you say?"

"Oh, I was just saying make sure you get his number; you might go through a dry spell. And when is this party for your company?"

I was hoping to hook up Ty and Sierra; I have been dropping hints about them for months. The only thing was I didn't know how to tell Sierra that Ty was a woman. She wasn't as open as I was about dating. They were perfect for one another though.

"It's Saturday, and the drinks are free, so make sure you are ready to party." *And ready to meet the love of your life.* I couldn't say that to her; she is all about finding Mr. Right, but honestly, I think she is bi-sexual. She's always making comments about a woman's body. She even looks at some women with lust. She is lying to herself, and I was about to make her see the truth.

"Okay, girl, I am at the Ritz…"

"The Ritz!" she screamed. "The best I could get was the Palace Inn."

The Palace Inn was a by the hour hotel, it was clean, but it was not something to brag about.

"Yes, the Ritz, and I plan to rent a room here soon; you can come with me when I do."

"Yes! Let's plan that visit soon! Okay, girl, love you and don't forget to call Mama. She said she hasn't heard from you."

Sierra's parents were like my parents; they took me in when I was a kid and still treated me like I was their child. I loved every piece of them. "I will call her as I am getting ready for dinner."

We ended our phone call, and I parked in valet like Robert requested. Going up to our floor with my bags for the night, Robert had given me a key, and I used it to get in. That room was breathtaking; Robert was standing at the windows talking on the phone. He was quiet on his end of the phone, so I walked to him, putting my bag at the end of the sofa. When I reached him, I put my hand on his back and kissed his cheek. I went to walk away when his arm came around and pulled me into him, kissing me soundly on the lips. I could hear the other person on the line talking to him. He didn't seem to care; he kissed me like it was his last chance. God, I hope it wasn't the last time.

He mouthed to me to give him a moment, but as he said it, there was a knock on the door. I went to it and opened it to the masseuse. He was huge and oh so beautiful Creamy skin, dark blue eyes, and arms as big as tree trucks. He wore all white and stood at the door with a bright smile. I let him in doing my best not to stare; I mean I was here with Robert, and he hadn't flipped out when he'd learned about my side job, but I didn't want him to see me openly gawk.

"My name is Brad; where would you like me to set up?"

I looked to Robert, and he was still on the phone but looking in my direction. I pointed to the middle of the room, and Robert nodded his head, turning back to the window.

Brad set up and asked me to change. I went into the other room and changed into the robe the hotel provided. When I was done, I walked out, and Robert was getting off the phone. He came to me, kissed me on the lips, and told me to enjoy. I walked to the table, took off my robe, and laid face down on the table. The lights were turned down low, and then I felt heavenly hands on my body; Brad started on my neck going down slowly. As he worked, I heard soft music start to play, and then the sound of keys working over a keyboard. When he got to my back, I blocked everything out and started to drift to sleep.

Robert called my name softly, and I mumbled, "Huh?"

Robert asked, "Can he give you the full treatment?"

I didn't know what the full treatment was, but I did know I didn't want him to stop, so I nodded my head and drifted back to sleep.

I woke when I felt his hands so close to my pussy that if he went an inch to the left, he would be right in the middle. I held my head up and looked at him; he didn't seem to notice me, but Robert saw me. And then Brad touched my clit as Robert's eyes were on me. HOT eyes. Brad robbed me of speech when he hit my clit just right, and I moaned. Robert got up from his seat and walked to me.

"How is it going, baby?"

I Call Him Daddy Too

I didn't know what to say. I could only moan when Brad's slick fingers entered me. Robert kept up his questions.

"Would you like to ask Brad to stop?" At that exact moment Brad found my G-Spot. I cried out, and my mind went blank. Robert's mouth went close to my ear. "Did Brad turn you on when he walked in? Did that tight pussy contract, with the thought of him inside of you?"

Brad was doing wonders with his fingers in my pussy. I couldn't speak, just moan my answer to Robert.

"Can you be my dirty girl?"

I nodded my head; I could be all of that.

I started to pant, my orgasm so close I could taste it. The feeling hit me, and I grabbed the legs to the table and screamed with pleasure. Robert's mouth came down to mine kissing me softly. I kissed him back liking the way he tasted.

Brad continued the massage like he didn't just have me singing high notes and worked on my legs and feet. And I again fell back to sleep. I felt hot towels replace the ones on my back, and I further relaxed. As the towels cooled, I became vaguely aware that Robert and Brad were talking. Soon the towels were cold, and Brad was back removing them and helping me up. My body was loose, and I was completely relaxed.

"I hope my services were up to your standards," Brad said, and I smiled at him.

"This is definitely a massage that I will never forget."

He leaned in and helped me off the table, and Robert was there with my robe. He helped me put it on and pulled me into his arms. I hugged him back, standing on jelly legs.

4

CAN I SEE YOU AGAIN?

Robert and I got ready for dinner; we shared the bathroom like we had been doing it for years. He might have had this experience, but I hadn't. I had never lived with anyone, could count on one hand how many men I had stayed the night with. Every once in a while, I would catch him watching me, like he was intrigued by the motion of me flat ironing my hair. He would lean in and kiss my neck as my hands were over my head trying to straighten the very top.

He was almost dressed, and I was still applying makeup when I had to ask a question.

"So, you like to watch sex?"

He smiled a brilliant smile at me leaning against the counter in the bathroom. "I like to watch, yes. I like other things as well."

"You have me intrigued; I enjoy watching as well...as other things." I smiled up at him, spraying on Miss Dior and loving the smell. "Just a small thing we should discuss, I enjoyed this afternoon, but in the future if we are going to get adventurous, we should discuss our limits. I don't have many, but I think we should discuss things before we start. I don't think we need a contract, but I don't want you to bring back some random person and we have sex with them. Without talking about it."

His eyes were hungry, and I think that he liked the idea of us bringing a person back and both of us fucking them. I stored that in my memory bank. He spoke and his voice was low and husky. "Are you telling me that you don't mind fulfilling some of my fantasies?"

"I'm telling you that I want to explore both of our fantasies as often and as thoroughly as possible, but we have to communicate what we want as well as what we won't do. I don't have a lot of limits, but I think you should know that I do have some." He nodded his head and I continued, "I don't do anything with bathroom functions, if you get my drift."

He chuckled and said, "I'm not into peeing on people." That was good because he could hang that one up with me. "I am into squirting. Nipple clamps and light bondage." My nipples got hard, and his eyes flared. "I also am into swinging; I enjoy watching good sex. I would like to explore all those things with you. I know I'm coming off forward, but I am too old to play games, and I am not looking for forever. I don't think that is in the cards for me."

His declaration of nothing long term was fine for me; I don't think there is just one person for me either. I had to ask a question that has been in the back of my mind since he said it. "I know you have never been married, why is that?"

He seemed to think about that question and answered, "I have had all kinds of women in my life, but I have yet to find a woman that wasn't playing games. One that said what they wanted and didn't change when work got busy, or my children needed me. I want to spend my time with someone that has their own things going on, and not someone that spends their days shopping and bitching about what they don't have."

"You know part of this is your fault." He looked perplexed, so I continued, "The first thing you offered me was a shopping spree, you brought me to the Ritz and didn't get a regular room, you got the room with the butler. You showed your wealth and also showed that you were willing to share it just by meeting me. I didn't have to work for it or prove that I deserved it. Men like you are a gold digger's paradise, and they don't have to invest one ounce of emotion or loyalty."

"I see your point, and it's not like my friends haven't told me this, it's just my way. I'm not staying at the Red Roof Inn. I like expensive clothes, and I like for my woman to look that way too."

I smiled at him. "Did you like my outfit last night?"

"Yes, it was spectacular."

"I got it from Fashion Nova; for what I spent last night on that one dress, I could have had a wardrobe at Fashion Nova, shoes included." I look at him gently. "Robert, I don't even know your last name, and I am here with you, in all this fabulousness, and I don't even know your last name. And you don't know mine either. Honestly, I don't know if you want to just meet up for hookups or not." I paused and reached for his hands. I held them in mine. "I want to know you, but I don't need to be spoiled with riches." To lighten the moment, I added, "Now if you were ugly, maybe." And we both laughed.

"So, we should skip the helicopter ride?"

"We could, we could go to El Pollo Loco." His face said no to that idea. "My point is, for the next woman, go slow."

I didn't want to say that the thought of there being a next woman gave me a little ache. But I wasn't the girl that thought it should be me. In all my years, I was rarely chosen to have something beautiful. And Robert was beautiful, almost a dream.

He looked at me with soft eyes and nodded. I let his hands go and started with my makeup.

"Just so you know, that little piece of information would have cost another man."

He laughed. "So you charge for these gems?"

Through the mirror I saw him and looked back at myself to put on mascara. "Men don't just come to me for sex advice, but to figure out where they went wrong. My classes are not on the perfect sex positions; I talk about what to do after sex is over. How to be a good listener and a good partner. Sex is maybe ten percent of what I teach; I teach them how to be open and honest about what they want and need. And to listen to what their partner wants." I stood back and looked at myself in the mirror, liking how this mascara looked. My makeup was coming along nicely.

Robert leaned down behind me, looking into my eyes through the mirror. When he spoke, a shiver ran down my spine. "Alesia, I really like you, and I don't want tonight to be the end. And my last name is Howard by the way. I think it's too soon to talk about being exclusive right now, but I don't want you to write this off as a one night stand. I want to see you again."

My heart leaped; I wanted the same thing. I couldn't say anything, I just turned around and kissed him softly on the lips. Pushing the emotions that I felt aside, I got ready.

5

THINGS HAD TO GET DONE

Monday morning came too fast, and I was already in the office when Ty got there. She was dressed in a light grey pair of pants and tailored aqua button down. Her face was done up, and she wore a nude lipstick; she was beautiful.

"You, my dear friend, are absolutely stunning." She stopped walking and looked at me. I wore all black, with a bold red lipstick.

"So are you, Lisa. How was the weekend?"

I thought about my weekend, the helicopter ride over the mountains at sunset, the beautiful candle lit dinner and the conversations. And the feeling of longing after my last session with my clients. Their love making was too beautiful to watch, so I left them to it, leaving a handwritten note on a table outside of their bedroom.

"My weekend was one for the books, but we can't talk about that; we have a meeting in ten minutes. You also have dinner reservations with your family tonight. It's in your calendar for work, and I confirmed it this morning. The building on Lennear has inspections today, and honestly, I don't know if it will pass. That new contractor is behind schedule, and I have two coming in this afternoon to see if we can hire them. You have lunch with Lizzie about the designs for that new building she sent them over, and they don't match what I think you wanted for those offices. I circled where she went against what you asked for. And last but not least, your conference call is at three with Davis Popov. I would offer to take it, but you don't pay me enough. He is a real douche nozzle. I only blocked off ten minutes, and I will come get you so you can say no, sooner than later." I took a breath and handed her the mail, which I'd already gone through.

"Isn't your next performance review coming up?"

"It is next week, and I asked for a raise of eight dollars, but I am willing to negotiate."

She was looking through the mail and said, "I will take the raise and offer another week of vacation. If you take the Davis thing."

Davis thought that women were mindless creatures who did what he said; he never asked for anything, he told you what you were going to do, and he always got a no from Ty. He wouldn't be happy talking to me, and that made the offer sweeter.

"Great, we can take that off of our schedule for next week and make it a lunch for celebration."

She nodded her head and walked into her office.

My phone dinged with a text, and when I looked down, it said "Old Man." I smiled, Robert may have been older, but he wasn't an old man. He was a great man. I smiled at the message; he told me to have a great week and that he would be out of town for business from tomorrow until Friday night. I worked late and had told him that last night. Ty usually left around four, but I was here later. And when I got off work, some nights I had clients. Ty planned to retire in five years, and when she retired, I was going to as well. Ty had irons in many fires, and so did I. Most millionaires have seven streams of income. I had two, but they were both doing well.

None of my other friends made the kind of money that I made; my bonus last month was five figures alone. I worked hard for Ty, and she recognized that. I sent Robert a quick text back telling him I would see him on Friday. Then I went back to work; things had to be done.

Robert

I had dinner plans with my children tonight, and I was sitting in a meeting not paying attention at all; my mind was on the vixen that held me hostage in the helicopter last night. Alesia introduced me to the mile high club on the way back from dinner, giving me the best blow job of my life. She was a dream come true. I wanted to send long stem roses, but held back. I thought about what she said, and I knew she was right. My phone dinged in my hand and a simple text said, "See you Friday." That was it. I was used to women being upset that I was unavailable during the week. My phone dinged again and it was Tyanna's mother. When I saw her name, my eyes rolled. Trina was long gone from my life, but I felt that she didn't understand that piece of information.

In the text she asked if I would send her to France for a week to shop. And by shop, she means that I pay for it. I told her years ago that the answer would be no, but she didn't mind asking. What she didn't ask was how our daughter was doing. She also never asked a thing about her, unless it was close to her birthday and she wanted Ty to send her money.

Trina was beautiful—no, I mean stop traffic beautiful. I had to have her, and when I got her, I wanted to give her back. She was a headache to say the least, and if gold digging was a sport, she would have the gold medals for it. The woman was over fifty and had never had a job. When I met her in New York, she was trying to be a model, but the size of her tits made that impossible. However, I was all over that. We dated for a few weeks before she told me that she was pregnant. She made me sign a contract saying that after the baby was born, I would fix all that the child had done to her body.

Trina didn't have a maternal bone in her body; she didn't change diapers, didn't feed her, and hired a nanny to take care of Tyanna. I kept the nanny and got rid of Trina. That didn't mean that through the years Trina didn't pull shit like she was pulling today. She demanded child support, even with no child. She demanded that I keep her in the lifestyle that she'd had while we were dating, and even took me to court for it. That was denied. What she never demanded was to see her daughter.

Tyanna is the spitting image of Trina on the outside. Thank god she was nothing like her on the inside. When Tyanna started making her own money at thirteen, she sent her mother money all the time. It broke my heart; now that she was grown, she never talked about Trina. I can't remember the last time she even said her name, but Trina was a hurt that my baby girl never got over.

I typed Trina a message back, thinking of what Lisa had said the night before. I wrote back, "Trina, as our daughter is in her thirties, I don't owe you shit. I also don't want you writing me again, after this I will be blocking you. Treat me like you treat Ty, don't have anything to say to me."

I hit send and proceeded to block her from calling and

texting me. I had a soft spot for her; she gave me my baby girl. And I wanted to show my appreciation, but I gave her a gift as well. Ty was spectacular, she was the best person I knew, and to know that I made such a great person made me poke my chest out daily. My boys were good men, but they all had mothers that loved them with everything that they had. I co-parented with my other children's mothers well. I just didn't have that with Trina.

I had to concentrate on this meeting. I was building a resort in The Bahamas, and I needed to know where my money, my family money, was going. Tonight during the dinner with my children, we would be discussing what is going on with the build. I've watched over this project, but today was the first day that I was not really paying attention. The resort held three hundred resort style rooms, right on the beach, and the hoops the government had made me jump through were crazy, but it would be open next summer and all the hard work would be worth it.

My children and I had several resorts all over the world; the one in Bora Bora turned a pretty penny this quarter. I was happy that we were doing well; even in a recession, we made money with our resorts. I thought often about moving closer to at least one of the islands, but I wanted to be closer to my babies. Well, they were not babies anymore; they were grown, and thriving. I sent a message to all of them in a group text telling them that I love them. I got a message back from Brent saying that I was getting soft in my old age. Alexander said that he loved me, but damn, did we have to discuss it? But my baby girl wrote, "I love you too, Pop, and you are not old, you are like fine wine." My baby girl knew how to be so sweet, and then she asked Brent if the Viagra worked that she'd sent him. I chuckled. Brent then went into detail about his latest girlfriend and

I Call Him Daddy Too

that she could tell her that his penis worked just fine, thank you.

Ty sent him back a response saying that let her have a go at her and see how well she liked him after. This started the fight. You see, Ty was a lesbian, and I gave not a damn. My girl always had a beautiful woman on her arm, but she hadn't found the one yet. I was hoping that all my children found love, but I wanted it more for Tyanna; she was looking for the one thing, and I sent a silent prayer that my baby girl would find it.

As on cue, my phone rang and it was my best friend Carson. I answered, "I was about to call you. I can't make golf this Thursday; I will be in Bora Bora for a meeting."

"Damn, you know what? This is your third cancellation. I'm getting a complex."

"If you must know, I can't stand to look at your ugly ass that long."

He laughed, and I stopped to sign a contract I had drawn up that my secretary had. Carson was far from ugly, in fact he put himself through school by modeling. He was from Samoan heritage, very tall and very muscular, and if you were looking at him, you would think he was a player. He wasn't, he had been married over forty years and thought that his wife walked on water. They were cute together, and deep down I wanted that for myself.

"I met someone," I said out of nowhere. I didn't even intend to say anything about Alesia.

He took a deep breath. "Of course you did, and let me guess, she's beautiful and has no personality at all. She likes to shop and wants to be a model."

Okay, I will admit, that is most of the women that I met, but I was going to surprise him. "She is beautiful, she also told me that I show women my wealth too fast." He pulled in a deep breath, but I continued, "Told me she could buy her own dress, and went to the boutique and paid for it with some shoes. She is by far the best lay I have ever had and didn't worry about messing her hair up while we had sex."

"And where is this unicorn this morning, packing for Bora Bora?"

"She is at work, left me last night saying she had an early morning, told me that she would text when she could, and I texted her that I was going out of town and she said, 'Okay, see you when you get back.'"

"You mean to tell me you met a woman that you were attracted to that went to work after a weekend with you, and then hasn't called or texted you saying she needs a pair of shoes?"

"Nope, told me that for the price of the dress that she bought from the boutique, she could have gone to Fashion Nova and bought a whole wardrobe. Didn't ask once to drive my car, and didn't order room service. Actually suggested we go to El Pollo Loco, for dinner. While she wore a dress that cost more than a car note for some people."

"El Pollo Loco!" Carson screamed, then he called for his wife, "Mia, Robert met a woman that apparently has her own money and suggested they eat at El Pollo Loco. She told him that he gave too much too fast and the kicker—she bought her own damn clothes."

I rolled my eyes; Alesia had done all of this, and it never happened ever.

I couldn't hear what Mia had to say, but I could imagine. "How old is she?"

See, that's where it got tricky; Alesia was younger than Ty, but she was wise.

"Younger than Ty," I said hesitantly.

To my surprise Carson said, "Look, if she can keep up

with you and help you keep your money in your pocket, I am all for it. How about we meet her in a week? Let's see if this is a game she is playing. Mia will be able to sniff it out real fast."

Mia hated every woman I ever dated, and had no issue telling me all the ways that I was a fool. For the first time ever, I was looking forward to Mia meeting a woman.

"I will ask to meet her Friday; I don't want to wait. I think Mia will like her. She is very blunt, in a nicer way than Mia is."

"Mia heard you, by the way, she gave you the finger."

Yeah, Mia most likely gave me the finger. When Carson and I were in college, I was dating Mia. We went on three dates, and then she asked about Carson. Told me that we didn't have anything in common, but my best friend was a better bet for her. And Carson and Mia have been together for years. At first I thought it was because of his looks. It wasn't. It was because he was sweet, and he thought the sun rose when she woke up. Mia was also blunt; she was the reason I had thick skin. She told me that I was the richest dummy she had ever met. Called my girlfriends glorified hookers, to their face. Mia could be a lot, but she was good to my children. She'd offered to beat the shit out of Trina more than once. Told me to get her a good lawyer and she would fix the issue.

Carson and I did our usual and said we would meet on the golf course the following weekend. We planned to have dinner the following Friday so they could meet Alesia. It was strange calling her Lisa. After she'd said that so many people called her Lisa, I wanted to be one of the few that called her by her real name. It was a beautiful name.

Today was a full day, I had another meeting this afternoon, and tons of phone calls to make, I was looking forward to the day being over. As soon as dinner was over with my children, I had to hop a flight and sleep on the plane to be ready for a meeting at nine in the morning Bora Bora time. I had two luxury apartments going up and needed to make sure they were up to my standards.

Pictures didn't always tell the whole story, and I didn't depend on anyone's eyes but mine when it came to my buildings. For the first time in a long time, I didn't want to go; I wanted to call Alesia and see what she had to do this week and take her with me. I couldn't do that. She'd made it clear that her job was important to her. She was an assistant to a real estate mogul and she seemed to like him. I most likely knew him, but didn't want to ask his name. I didn't want to mess things up with her, told myself that I would take this slow, at her pace. I was holding myself back, because when you find something rare you keep it. You watch it grow into something. And that's what I was going to do with Alesia—keep her.

6

CHILDREN

I had been dodging calls from Trina all day; she'd called the office fifteen times, and I'd declined all the calls. My receptionist called in three times and told me that Trina was making her day hell. Not in those words, but I got her point. Soon I would have to offer her a raise for dealing with my crazy ass baby mama. And we didn't even have a baby, we had a grown woman for a child. I told her the next time she called to tell her I was in Bora Bora and wouldn't be back until late next week. That finally made her stop calling, and I was happy about that.

I had a driver pick me up and take me to dinner; I returned phone calls while riding. It was Brent's turn to pick the restaurant, and he always picked Cuban. No place in the city was as good as his mother's cooking, but this would have to do. I should call her and catch up. She was now married to a nice man that didn't mind that I sat at his table and ate her food. Gloria was a beauty, and after she had Brent, she wanted to get married. I didn't want that, so we went our separate ways. It was rocky in the beginning but as

Brent grew, the love as friends grew as well. We went on family vacations together, I helped her with her salon, and eventually she bought me out and opened three more luxury salons in Colorado. She married a welder when Brent was fourteen, and she had two daughters that called me Uncle.

My children were all over the world working, but they all came home for our monthly dinners. It was usually on Sunday, but Brent was in Spain designing a garden for a park there. He was invited to Spain after he designed a garden for a billionaire in Romania. He traveled the world doing what he loved. When he was younger, I'd worried about the boy; he didn't do well in school, but he was always in the garden with the landscaper doing odds and ends. When he was ten, he asked if he could go with him to do other houses. I agreed, and that was the best thing I could have done for him. Brent had an eye for rare flowers, and took real time and care learning about them. I forced him to get a degree and he got it in Botany. Two weeks after he got his degree he came to me with a plan, and I helped him start his business. He didn't cut yards, he designed gardens and he did well for himself. It took him three years to pay me back two hundred thousand. He was now very wealthy, having taken his passion to the next level.

Brent also had stake in my company business and designed all of the gardens for my builds. People came for the landscaping alone. Even in the middle of a busy city, I made plans to have a garden. Not because I wanted my son to have something to do, because he was extremely busy, but because I could charge people just to visit them. There was a staff there just to make sure that no one picked flowers, as that was a big issue when little children visited.

I was let out at the front of the building and told Claud he was welcome to join us for dinner. Claud had been with me for over twenty years. He had seen the world; he also was never married and had no children. He treated my children like his own; he and Marcus were really close. I thought when he retired he would spend his time watching over him.

I got out of the car and was greeted by one of my twins. I couldn't tell them apart when I first saw them, only their mother could. It wasn't until one of them spoke that I knew which was which.

"Hey, Pop." It was Alexander, his voice was deeper than Johnathan's.

"Hello, son, how was your week?"

"Long, and it's only Monday. I have a case with the IRS this week; my client had someone else do his taxes. This is going to be expensive. I'm just happy I asked for my money up front."

We both laughed. Alex did all of my accounting, and how he found time to do that and take on customers that weren't family was beyond me. The boy was a workaholic; honestly, we all were. They got that from me, but we made time for important things like family.

We walked into the restaurant where there was a buzz of Latin music, and people were dancing. I saw Brent with a beautiful Latin woman with long curly hair in a fire red dress that clung tightly to her body. Brent was salsa dancing with her, swinging her around, and she was having the time of her life. That was my son the dancer, he danced with that woman like he'd known her all his life. For all I know she could be his date to dinner. The song was ending and he had a little sweat on his brow. Many of the dancers had stopped to watch them move, and as he twirled her around, the song ended and he dipped her at the last beat. The crowd erupted in cheers and the girl in his arms came up from her dip and kissed and hugged him. Brent had a huge smile on his face, twirled the woman out, and took a bow. His mother would be proud that he moved like that.

Brent looked around the room and saw Alexander and I standing watching him; he whispered in the woman's ear. She made a pouting face, and he walked away, people patting him on his back as he went. "How's it going, Pop?"

He said this with a smile as he gave me a hug. I was glad that my sons didn't have barriers about showing me love; they hugged me no matter where we were, even boardrooms. "Doing good, not as good as you I see. That was one pretty girl you were dancing with."

He looked back at the dance floor and now the girl was surrounded by three other woman, all of whom were giving Brent a seductive look. I didn't see what he did, but all of them smiled broadly.

Alex and I followed Brent to the back of the restaurant. We had a private section and when I got there, I found that Johnathan and Tyanna were arguing. Something that had been going on for as long as Tyanna could talk. She loved her brothers, but she could dish out the shit better than anyone I knew. She kept them in line, she was also the first person they called when they were having trouble.

Brent spoke to his brothers and leaned in and kissed Tyanna on her head, then he went straight to his laptop. I swear that boy lived on that damn computer. I bought his first one at six, and by the time he was fourteen, the government had hired him to hack into Russia. I didn't know what he did now, I just knew he had offices all over the world. We, as his family, were always targets of some type of hack, but he kept us safe. He was retiring in a few months and I wondered what he would do after this.

"My God, I made some pretty babies."

They all looked at me and the room brightened with their smiles. Tyanna got up and ran over to me, hugging me tightly. "Hey, Pop. You look good."

I smiled at my baby girl, looked into her sparkling green eyes. Gauging her mood, I could always tell how she was doing just by the color of her eyes. I also could do that with her mother. Tyanna was everything to me, and I wish that Trina saw her more.

"Hey, Daddy's baby. You look happy."

"I didn't have to talk to Davis Popov today. My assistant took that job. It cost me a raise and extra vacation time, but it was worth it."

Brent spoke up, "I don't know why no one will let me hack into his system and put a worm there. It would be fun."

"We are not doing that," all of us said at once.

Davis was an issue, he had shady business practices and none of us liked the rumors that he had swirling, but we didn't attack people we didn't like. However, if he crossed us, all bets were off. Davis had come to all of us individually and as a group to do business with him. He'd even approached Claud to get to me. I shut that shit down real fast, but it seemed he couldn't just leave well enough alone.

I took a seat at the head of the table as Claud walked in, sitting next to Marcus. Dinner was loud and crazy, and I loved every moment of it. I often wondered how Alesia would fit in. If she would like my children, if they would have an issue because of her age? Or would they just see her as a person that was good for me? I wondered how much time I should invest before I brought her to meet them.

Johnathan asked Marcus, "Where is Lizzie?"

Marcus' face turned sad, and my heart stopped. "We broke up over the weekend. I asked her about children, and she told me that she never wanted to have them. I loved our life together, but children are something that I want. It's her right to say she doesn't want children, and I don't want her to resent them if we did have them. We decided that we would be better as friends."

He looked at all of us, and I was in shock. Lizzie was a great woman, hard-working and loving. To know she didn't want the joy of having children was saddening.

"Son, it's better to know now then down the road, and you two could still be great friends. You will find someone, son, and when you do, this time will be a blip on your emotional radar. Some breakups are for the best. You are loving, my dear boy, and if you want to give some of that love to a child, I think you would be an excellent father."

Marcus looked at me; his eyes held tears. "Coming from you, Pop, that's a high compliment."

"Each and every one of you are special, each of you have gifts that should be shared with the world. And if you want children to share that gift with, I would be proud to have the privilege of being those children's grandfather."

"Can you imagine Pop being called granddaddy?" Jaxson questioned.

The table erupted with laughter; even Marcus had a smile. "I would totally be good with granddaddy. I would love to hop my grandchildren up on candy, buy ridiculous gifts so they could have all they ever wanted. In fact, I started saving for that a while ago, and let me tell you, the interest on that account is sizable. All of you are playing with these women's emotions; I want grandchildren and I would like them before my back goes out. Piggy back rides are in my future."

Through the chuckles, Tyanna asked me, "Would you do it over again?"

I looked to her and the table went silent. "Do what again?"

"If you met the right woman, would you have more children?" I thought about Alesia; what if she wanted children? Could I do it again?

I looked at all of them, different in so many ways, but they all had one thing in common.

"I loved every moment of your childhoods. I loved the nights when you woke me up and couldn't sleep. I loved when you got in trouble, knowing that you would come to me, knowing that you all trusted me with you hearts. I would do it five more times, knowing that in the end I made the world better by having my children in it. If I met the right person, and they wanted children, or even had children, I would do it all over. I might not have been lucky in love, but when it came to you guys, I hit the lottery."

My children all had soft expressions looking at me, then Brent spoke. "Damn, Pop, now you got me wanting to have a baby. Let me go find that chick I was dancing with, she might be ovulating tonight." This boy here—Lord give me strength.

They all laughed and I shook my head.

"You know what, Marcus, why don't you and Claud go down to Houston, he could drive you, I don't really need him with me."

Marcus gave me a small smile, and Claud clapped him on the back, saying, "I love Texas women."

Marcus gave him a smile, and I knew he would be okay. If I couldn't be there, Claud was the next best thing.

Dinner was over way too early, and I had to get to the airport. I had a private plane to take me, but I still had to be on time. I hugged and kissed all of my children and told them I would text when I got there.

On the plane I went straight to bed, wishing Alesia was with me. Dreaming of her heavy with my baby.

7
BABY MAMA

My private chef placed food on the table and I thanked her, not looking at the plate. I was looking at Trina. She'd showed up before I even got here, and she was currently eating at my table. Annoying the hell out of me.

When I got to Bora Bora, it was early morning. I had my first meeting on the plane, two hours before I landed, then I had my driver take me to my home there so I could get dressed. I found it in an uproar because Trina was at the gate trying to get into the compound. She was so loud I could hear her with the windows up on the car. When she saw me, she turned and put her hand on her hip and screamed my name as she walked to the car.

"Must you be ghetto?" I questioned as I rolled down the window.

"Yes! When the father of my child doesn't pick up the phone when I call. And blocks me from calling," she yelled irately.

"You say that like Tyanna is five, she's in her thirties, and

I blocked you because I wasn't paying for a trip to Paris. I don't owe you child support. Or any support at all."

"Robert, if you don't let me in this house so we can talk, I will make your life miserable."

"Trina, you already make my life miserable. I have a question; when was the last time you spoke to our daughter?"

She pulled open the door, and I had to slide over for her to get in the car. "Like I said, we can talk in the house, and I am hungry so you need to get on feeding me. I had a long flight, and I had to fly coach to get here, so I am in no mood."

I closed my eyes wishing I could kick my own ass. What on earth made me pick this woman? Oh yeah, she had a big ass and pretty eyes. Other than that, she brought nothing to the table.

"Trina, I have a meeting soon."

She rolled her eyes. "You own the company, tell them to wait."

That was Trina for you, thinking other people's time was not her concern as long as she got what she wanted.

So here I was sitting at a table with my child's mother, wondering if I should cancel my plans and find a nice cozy place to murder her, or just get off more money to get her out of my sight.

"You know I have given you more than ten million dollars over the years, and you still have come to me for more."

"I gave you a daughter, and you turned her into a boy. You owe me."

That pissed me right the fuck off. Tyanna was not a boy; she was a lesbian, not a boy.

"Tyanna is not a boy, and who she fucks isn't our business."

She rolled her eyes. "You made an absolutely beautiful girl a fucking dyke, and that's not my business? Oh okay."

My temper was flaring. "What was your excuse when she was three months old and you had nothing to do with her? Or five and didn't call for her birthday or send a gift to her for that matter?" She said nothing, just picked up her fork and ate her French toast. "Her sexual preference is the new excuse, but you don't have an issue with her paying for your house, or your car that you trade in every year."

"A small price to pay for the embarrassment she causes me," she said with irate eyes on me. Thunder was rising in my veins, and I could feel nothing.

"Bitch, are you for real? She is successful, and the only thing you ever gave her was beauty, and that's only on the outside. For years I have overlooked how you treated her. Hell, your mama wasn't a shining example of motherhood, and I thought that you would want better for you child, but all these years later, you are still looking for a payday for giving birth to her. You have done nothing to nurture her, not one damn thing. You don't agree with her lifestyle, fine! I don't agree with yours either; you lay down with powerful men to finance your life. Fooling them with pussy, and that's all you have to offer. You get one more thing from me—a trip off this fucking island and the knowledge that if you ever call me again for any reason, I will make your life a living hell. I would sick Jaxson on your ass, but you don't have a dime that is not connected to MY child. She can continue to support you, but this gravy train has reached the end of the line. Now get your shit and get out of my house."

"You know what, you think you can sit on your high horse; what if I told the world about all the things you like, baby? The things that you do behind closed doors. You don't think I know what your family does to rivals that get in your way? I will air out all your dirty laundry. You think I am scared of you? Lay a finger on me and that ten million will look like Monopoly money."

I got up from my chair and walked over to her. When I got to her, I placed my hand under her chin making her look me in the eyes. "Baby, the hold you have on me was over years ago. I feel sorry for you, that's why I do for you. Poor Trina, you never could keep a man's interest once you opened your mouth for anything other than to give a sub-par blow job. You think for a second if I let Tyanna know that you threatened me and her brothers, she wouldn't kick your ass out of that house and have you living on the street? You are letting yourself go, honey. Those wrinkles are showing your age. And you have fucked all the men with real power that would have you. That hood rat phase is going out of style. No one wants a woman that can't hold a conversation that doesn't require payment."

I slid my hands around her throat, squeezing gently. "You won't even be missed. Our daughter won't even notice you are gone, other than her bank account having more money. If you cross me," I smiled squeezing harder, the air coming out shallow, "I won't have an issue with hiding your ass where the sun don't shine. Use that brain of yours and think long and hard about what I am willing to do to keep what's mine. I was going to leave Tyanna out of this, but you have six months to get out of her pocket as well. Move out of her house, and go back to that project I found you in."

Her eyes were wide, but I wasn't finished. "I allowed you a grace because you had my child, but your fatal mistake was trying to use her. I should have stopped you years ago, that was my error." I smiled at her and she went pale. "Get off my island, get out of my house, and if you think I won't be watching who you talk to, you will be sadly mistaken." I let her go, and she placed her hand where mine was. I didn't back up though.

"Robert, I was just talking, I love our daughter.'

"Then prove it, stay out of my business and out of my child's pocket." She nodded, got up from the table grabbing her bag, and scurried past me. I didn't watch her go, but I heard the door open and then close.

"Linda," I bellowed, "can you clean the table?" I didn't want the reminder of Trina there. I called ahead and got her a plane ticket home. Then I got ready for my meeting; I was running late.

8

THERE ARE WORSE THINGS

Today was a hell of a day, and I was glad it was Friday. I was bombarded with calls from Davis, and after our last conversation, I finally cussed his ass out. The nerve of that son of a bitch calling me a bitch, before I acted like a bitch. He wanted to do business with Ty, I got that, but Ty had no interest in doing business with him. It got so heated, Ty came out of her office to listen, heard what he was saying, and took the phone. She listened for three seconds, her eyes turned a funny color brown, and she told his ass off. I don't even remember what she said; I just know when it was over, she told me to reschedule her day and we were going to get pedicures. My workday ended right fucking there.

After the pedicure, I had drinks with Sierra; she was running late, so I ordered and was halfway through my first one when she showed up. She wore a black pencil skirt and red blouse, she looked very stylish, but when I looked in her face, I knew something was wrong.

"Hey girl, what's wrong?" was my greeting. She put her bag down and hefted up on the bar stool.

"Nothing is wrong." She looked to the bar and waved her hand. "My boss is a jerk,"

She could say that again. Her boss was a demanding, lazy sack of shit.

She continued, "On a brighter side, I am seeing someone." She got a funny look in her eyes, not the "The sex is amazing look." Something close to worry.

"Okay, you are seeing someone; what's with the worried look?"

The waitress came and got her a drink; she ordered a margarita with an extra shot. When she did that, I asked the waitress for a shot; I knew this was going to be some bullshit.

"Okay, so I met this guy named Matt, he's a journalist for the local paper." I just looked at her listening for the foolery to start. "We have been seeing each other for the last six weeks and have been out to dinner three times."

The waitress came back with our drinks and shots and when she placed them on the table, I hit the shot fast. Sierra just sipped hers. "We slept together last night, and he asked me to have a threesome with one of his friends." She took another sip, eyes on me.

"Are you down with a threesome with his friend?" She shook her head no. "Well, don't do it." That was simple.

"He told me that if I didn't, he wouldn't see me again."

She looked heartbroken, and I could feel my blood pressure rising. Men like that shouldn't even be on her radar.

"Sierra, look, this is your body. You can allow whomever to share it, and you can tell a person no and not feel bad about it. You don't want to be his friend's plaything, say no, and whatever he says after that is on him. You just met the guy. Look around you, there are three guys to the left that have been checking us out. Men are easy to come by; your self-respect is harder. Say no and see who he really is."

There was something about telling a person no that brought out who they really were. Some people heard no and thought they could talk you around. They either gave you sweet and tried to change your mind, or they gave you shit and made you the bad guy. I wondered which one he would give.

Sierra pulled out her phone and sent a text; one I assumed was to Matt. She looked nervous.

"Honey, anything that is for you, you don't have to force. If this is the man for you, you will not have to change who you are fundamentally. You are the sweetest person I know, and I know you think that you have to do all this wild shit to keep a man—you don't."

"Lisa, you wouldn't think twice about a threesome."

I smiled and took a drink thinking of what Robert and I did with the masseuse the other day. "I wouldn't think twice about doing something I wanted to do. I wouldn't think twice about a threesome or orgy. I enjoy sex. I enjoy many aspects of it. I would think twice if my gut told me not to do it. If I thought for a second that my boundaries wouldn't be respected, I wouldn't do it. If I thought that I would be in anyway hurt, I wouldn't do it."

Her phone chimed letting her know she had a text; she took a deep breath and opened the message. I knew he'd said something hurtful by the look in her eyes.

"He said, he thought I was cool and wanted to have fun. He guesses I was a cock tease and he won't be seeing me again."

She took the last sip of her drink and put her eyes to the table.

"Sierra you are not what he called you. You had a

boundary and that is a good thing; he couldn't respect your boundaries and called you a name because of that boundary. None of that is okay. He was the jerk, better yet, he was the fuck boy, to let you go." She smiled at me and I continued, "The person that is for you is close, I can feel it."

I smiled at her. I know the person that was for her was Ty; she was going to fight me on it with Ty being a woman and all. But Ty was perfect for her. Ty was confident in who she was and who she loves. And if Sierra would just roll with it, she would be one happy person.

"You ever thought about dating a woman?"

Her eyes bugged out of her head.

I laughed. "You can't tell me you have never had a fantasy about a woman before."

"Lisa, are you asking me out on a date?" she asked with a low voice.

"Bitch, you would be lucky to have me. But no, I have never had a sexual thought about you. I would be interested in watching you have sex so I could critique it, of course." She rolled her eyes. "But no, I don't want your scrawny ass. I was thinking that it was time for a change. You know you keep dating these...men, and I use that term loosely. Maybe you should try the other side of things. A woman that knows who she is and what she wants in a partner would be a drastic change, but a good change nonetheless."

"I don't know about that, girl, I don't see myself eating pussy." I looked down at her shirt and saw her nipples peak. And she moved in her chair ever so slightly. She might not think so, but her body thought that way.

"Let me ask you something, if Matt had asked you to sleep with his home girl, instead of his homeboy, what would you have said?"

She didn't say anything, but she licked her lips and looked away.

"Don't answer that. I got all the answers I need."

She reached over, grabbed my drink, and took a long pull. I smiled at her.

"Sierra, no matter what you do, I want you to think on this. There is a person out there that is just for you, instantly you will be at ease with that person. You won't have to do or say anything to make them like or even love you, it will just happen. In the meantime, I can't wait for you to come to my company party at Club Drama next week. It's going to be lit. And who knows, the love of your life could very well be there."

"I doubt that I will meet the love of my life at some club, but I will be there."

"Good. I met someone."

She smiled at me. "You haven't mentioned meeting someone for a while, is it serious?"

I thought about it. "We aren't serious, we just met, but I like him. He is easy to talk to, he fucks like he's being paid, and he treats me like a lady. I like him. His name is Robert."

"Damn, girl, it's good to see this side of you. I can't wait to meet him."

I laughed. "It was only a weekend."

"Yeah, girl, but you remember his name. You don't mention just any man. It's been over five years since you said you met someone, and I know you have met plenty someones, and not once have you mentioned them. And last but certainly not least, your face got soft when you said his name."

I raised my hand calling for the waitress. I looked back at Sierra, and she had a look, and that look made me laugh. It felt good to laugh with my friend. I wanted the best for her, and whether she knew it or not, she was about to meet the best person I know.

Now I was home, my hair under a shower cap, seaweed mask on my face and fuzzy slippers on. I was going to relax. My phone dinged and it was Robert; that man sent text messages all week, and they were short and sweet. Sometimes he would send me pictures of flowers on the island he was on. Often just saying he was busy, but he was thinking of me. I liked that. I had dated plenty of guys, and usually got dick pics when they sent a picture, but not Robert. He showed me beautiful clear waters and asked my opinion once about fabrics for curtains. That ended with a FaceTime call so I could see the room, and him.

Now the text message read, **I'm back in town and want to see you.**

I wrote him back. **Currently sir, I am not in a visiting state, you don't want to see me right now. LOL.** If he saw me with my hair covered in goo and my face is the same way, he would run for the hills.

He wrote me back, **Baby I am too tired to do anything but talk, if you like, we can just talk on the phone, but I really want to hug you.**

That made my heart melt.

Fine. I will send you my address and know this, having it doesn't mean you can show up when you like.

I had only given a handful of men my address, and I hated when people just showed up at my house. I was always down to meet for dinner, or a show, but my house was my calm place.

I found the show that I wanted to watch and decided if the man was coming, the least I could do was feed him, so I started a meal. I'd pulled out salmon this morning, but it was a big piece and I hadn't really feel like cooking then. I figured Robert might be hungry and I could eat. I seasoned the meat and put on a pot of rice, adding scallions to it, and popped the salmon in the oven. I was about to rinse my face when the doorbell rang, and he was here. I opened the door and he had on a pair of jeans and red polo shirt. He hadn't shaved, and he looked so damn good.

He took one look at me with the goo on my face and smiled, then he did a head to toe look, laughed and pulled me into his arms. My arms went around him and felt his humor; I laid my head on his chest and smiled. When he let me go he said, "I like the shirt."

I looked down, my shirt said, "Amazing In Bed...I Could Sleep For Hours."

"Well thank you, sir. How was the flight?"

"Very long. Since you can't go out, and honestly when I drive home, I am going to crash, I was thinking we could do takeout."

That was sweet, and he was in for a surprise. "No need for takeout. I figured if you had to see me like this, I should at least cook for you."

I could smell the salmon cooking, and he sniffed the air and smelled it too. "Smells good. What's under the cap?"

Yeah, when we were together last week, I was curling a wig; he had never seen my natural hair. Honestly, I didn't wear it much and when I did it was in a bun. The one thing my mother gave me was my hair. I pulled the cap off and my hair came out. It was in small plats because I had detangled it and put it in twists. It wasn't stylish, it wasn't even pretty, but when I took the plats down, I could easily put it up in a ponytail.

"Why do you wear wigs again?" He asked as he touched one of the plats.

"I don't like dealing with my hair all week, and the wigs

stay in one place; this does what it wants." I shrugged and saw him taking in the living room and dining area. I looked at my room and was proud of it.

The walls were a soft grey trimmed in white. In the middle was a grey suede coach that sat under a gold light fixture. A glass coffee table held a gold vase containing orchids; there were grey armchairs, also with white and gold pillows. Underneath it was a rug that was also grey, white, and black, the colors making designs. The dining room had a table that sat eight with a long rectangular soft grey table and white chairs. There was also a side table that led to the hallway, with a mirror over it, holding books and candles.

My space was tranquil, not overcrowded, and I took time with every piece. "Your home is absolutely stunning."

I smiled back at him. "Thank you, if you like you can come with me or have a seat at the table. It won't take me long to fix our plates. I hope fish is okay?"

"Anything you fix is fine. I would go for a sandwich at this point."

Robert joined me in the kitchen, and I moved around the room, going in cabinets and making the sauce for the salmon. He was leaning against the sink watching me. After a few minutes, I looked at him as I stirred the pot for the sauce to keep it from sticking.

"What's on your mind, baby?" I said as I chopped scallions. I turned the heat off the sauce and pulled out the salmon, putting the sauce on top. After he didn't say anything, I looked over my shoulder, his gaze on me. I smiled at him.

"I'm trying to figure out how you are so damn sexy with goo on your face, your hair in plats, and a shapeless shirt on."

I smiled while pulling out two soft grey plates. "The silverware is in the drawer to the left of you, could you get it, and the drawer next to it has cloth napkins. Just pick two colors that match." I had four sets of napkins, white, grey, black, and gold. Depending on my mood I picked the colors according to my meals. They were a pain to keep clean, but I liked using them. I heard him opening drawers while I plated the food. I placed a salad that I was going to eat on the plate as well. I picked up the plates, and we walked to the dining room. I set the plates down, taking the silverware and napkins from Robert and gesturing for him to sit. He sat at the head of the table, and I smiled at him. It took quick work, but I set the table, lighting candles as I went.

"Give me one second, I need to wash this off my face."

He nodded his head and looked down at the plate. I walked to the hall, avoiding the mirrors. He'd said I was sexy, but I knew better. My bathroom was all white, with fluffy towels everywhere. I ran warm water and washed my face, drying it with a white towel. I put some Chapstick on my lips and walked out, going straight to the wine fridge. I pulled out two glasses and white wine.

Walking to the table, wine and glasses in hand, Robert spoke. "You know, for a woman that didn't plan this, you put together a fabulous dinner."

I beamed at him, and his face got a soft look that I liked. "I eat like this all the time alone; I don't mind my own company. I moved around a lot as a kid, and making friends just to lose them was hard. I found ways to entertain myself. I don't mind going to dinner alone and people watch. I like to make up stories about what their lives might be."

He picked up his fork. "I am rarely alone; even in the house, my housekeeper is there. She has worked for me so long she tells me what to do. When the kids were younger, there was always someone there, and then when they were teens, they had friends that came around. I miss the craziness of a house with children."

"Do you want more children?" I'd never imagined myself with kids. The way my mother treated me, I didn't think I wanted to bring kids in the world. His age was also something to consider.

"I don't mind children. I know if something happened to me that my kids would step up and give them what they needed, but I don't have to have more of them." He took a bite of his food and looked to me. "Damn, girl, you can cook."

I took a bite and had to admit it was good. "So you are building a resort, was it hard to get the permits for it?" I asked while sipping wine.

"The permits were relatively easy; we just had to deal with the environmental agency about preservation. We are in the final stages. How was your week?"

I swallowed and said, "Well, we had some contacts that went through. My boss is buying a plot of land in the boonies and building a subdivision."

His eyes came sharply to mine, but then he asked another question. "What type of subdivision?"

"It will be mixed use, a mall and some homes. I have to go into the office tomorrow afternoon to send the plans over for Monday. I would have done it today, but we left early for a pedicure."

"Your boss takes you to the nail shop?"

I smiled picking up my glass. "It's not like that. I had an exchange with a business associate of hers and it got heated. He called me a bitch, and I cussed his punk ass out. Then my boss got on the phone and called him a few names as well."

"Who the fuck called you a bitch?" His eyes were blazing, and his voice had risen slightly.

"Davis Popov, he is the supreme asshole of Denver. Don't worry, all of his calls will be hung up if he decides to call back. Anyway, you said you were frustrated earlier this week, what happened?"

He took a long sip of wine. Eyes closed and then he said, "My daughter's mother is a bitch. And she came to Bora Bora to ask for money."

"How old is your daughter?"

He smiled like just the thought of his daughter made him happy. "She's in her thirties."

"Then why are you still paying child support?" Was he behind on it? I mean with a child that old, why would you still owe support?

"First, I have never had child support. I raised all of my children. My sons because me and the mothers all decided that it was better if a man raised them. My daughter's mother wanted nothing to do with her. She did want a lot to do with my wallet. I have paid her to see her, paid her to spend time with her. And even after all these years, a phone call to my child for her birthday costs me. I am done with that shit. If Trina wants to be a horrible mother, who am I to stop her?"

I shook my head. "My mother is a crack addict. I have no idea where she is right now. She calls every few months and tells me what city she is in, but other than that she never calls. In third grade, she left me with my best friend's parents, and I didn't see her for three years. She refused to let them adopt me, but she did give them guardianship over me. She swings through town every once in a while, feeds me a lie about how she is getting clean, and then steals money and gets out of Dodge. It's funny, she can always find me. I have changed my number a few times, but Janice can always find me. I don't know who my father is, and I don't think my mother knows either. I lived with my grandma until I was five, and then she died. My mama took us from town to town, sometimes leaving in the middle of the night with nothing but a bag. I lived in hotels with drug users all around me until Sierra took me to her house. Her mama took one look at me and kept me. Best woman I know."

He was quiet for a while, and when he spoke his voice was low. "That was a lot, I don't see how you recovered from that." I was done with my food and placed the fork on the plate; I lifted my napkin to my face, wiping and then putting it on the table.

"You recover by moving on, you take the hits life gives you and you learn from them. I have some valuable lessons that I didn't pay for. My mother is always popping in and out, and I learned her sobriety had nothing to do with me. If she was clean, good for her, if she was a raving lunatic, just stay away from me while you do it. It sounds like your daughter can take care of herself. Believe me, there are worse things to happen to you than having a gold digger for a mother. Even if it's your gold mine she is digging in."

"You are wise."

I shook my head. "I had to be, I heard things at five that no child should know. Saw things that gives me nightmares to this day. But most of all I lived a life, I was never a shrinking violet. I knew what I wanted from the moment my mother put me in a by the hour hotel; I was never going to live like she did."

His look was perplexing, his eyes were soft, but he held on to that napkin like a vise grip.

"You are looking at me strange, don't tell me you were in a town called Longview in Texas."

"No, I don't even know where that is."

Well, that was something. "Never mind where it is, what's with the look?"

"I hate a sorry ass parent. I can't stand that shit! And to know that strangers took you in and took care of you makes me grateful. How hold was your mom when she had you?"

I didn't really know. "Honestly, I don't even know how old she is now. She never made a big deal about her birthday. She never made a difference about any day. She would get me a piece of candy for mine, but nothing major for hers. I was asked her birthday a while ago and couldn't remember it. I don't think about her often, just the story of your daughter's mother made me think of it."

I stood and started to clean the table. I reached for the plate in front of Robert and he took my hand gently; my eyes went to his and they were soft. He pulled me down to him, and I leaned over him; he reached in kissing me softly on the lips. It wasn't heated, it was sweet and gentle. It ended too soon. When he was done, he helped me clear the table. I could tell he was tired, so I did something that I never did.

"Stay tonight. I don't want to fuck. I just want to lay next to you."

I was standing at the dishwasher, too afraid to look at him. The words were out of my mouth before I could take them back, and I enjoyed his company. I didn't share my bed, I fucked there, but I only slept alone.

"I will get my bag out the car; I have one more outfit. I have to meet my daughter tomorrow for lunch, but I would love to lay next to you and rest."

I smiled at him, glad that he was going to stay, and even happier he wasn't going to make a big deal about staying. "That works. I have work tomorrow around eleven, and then my girl has to find a dress for a party my boss is throwing next week. So I won't be back home until late. Sierra and I are going home for dinner."

"You don't call her your sister?"

I thought about Sierra. In a lot of ways, she was my sister, and in a lot of ways, she wasn't.

"Sierra can go weeks without saying a word to me. And that doesn't bother me, she can be a little clueless. For example, she has no idea she is gay."

"Wait what?" he said laughing.

"You see, Sierra lives in a dream world. She doesn't stand up for herself, and when she does, she apologizes after. We are opposites in a lot of ways. She is dating men right now, but if the right stud walks by, she loses her train of thought. I have a plan; I won't put it in the universe yet, but I think I know the best person for her. Just wait, I have a perfect record, and this is going to be the best so far."

"You are a matchmaker?" he asked with a smile.

"Look, most millionaires have seven streams of income; if I can figure out how to monetize my skills in matchmaking, I would be rich by next year."

He laughed and then yawned. I felt bad for him; he looked tired.

"Baby, my bed is down the hall to the left; if you give me your keys, I will pull your carin to the garage and get your bag. My only request is that you take a shower before you get in my bed. Sorry, I only have soap that smells like a girl, but your skin will be soft."

He pulled me into his arms. "When I called I just wanted to hug you, maybe kiss you, I never thought that I would be sleeping next to you."

"I missed you too. Go to the shower before I change my mind; you got me throwing all my rules away. I don't usually cook for a man for a while, and I don't let a man stay the night ever. Get in the shower, Old Man. I will get you settled, then I am going to watch Scandal."

"Ok, baby," he said as he walked to the back of the house. I guess he found the bathroom, because when I got back from putting the car in garage, I heard the shower going. I thought about the car I drove twenty feet and smiled. It wasn't just any car; it was a Rolls Royce SUV. I had never seen anything like it. It was also white; I really should Google who he is. I found his bag in the back and grabbed it; then I walked through the house, taking his bags to him. I knocked and opened the bathroom door, and there he sat in my soaking tub asleep.

He was much too big for the tub, but he was very cute. I thought that I should wake him, but I had never seen him sleep, and he looked so peaceful. The water was still running and I saw that it was nearly full. I turned it off and he still didn't wake. I went through his bag and saw that he had dirty clothing inside, but I also saw a set of pajama bottoms and a shirt. I pulled them out. I walked over to the closet, got a clean towel out, and began to bathe him. Another first for me. I let the water drip down his body and really let my mind wander. When I looked to his face, I saw that he was watching me. I didn't stop what I was doing, I just took his hands and washed them, going up his arms to the rest of his body.

I pushed him forward and I washed his back. When I was done, I told him to sit back. I reached for his semi hard penis and cleaned that too. He grew in my hands and I smiled. "You are much too tired for that, sir; let's get you to bed before you drown in the tub."

He got up, and I handed him a towel as well as his pajamas; they were black pants and a white shirt, and I found it cute that we matched. "We match." He smiled at me and kissed my nose, before putting on his shirt.

We both got into bed and though I had wanted to watch Scandal, the soft bed and the full belly made me fall asleep quickly.

9

IN A DARK ROOM WITH A WOMAN

I woke to the feeling of my breast being massaged. I really didn't wake; I was woken by Robert's hands under my shirt. He was on my bare breast, but it didn't feel all that great.

"If you are trying to turn me on, let me tell you this type of squeezing is not it."

"I woke up with the thought of waking you while eating your pussy, but I was playing with your breast softly when I felt something."

That woke me up the rest of the way. "What do you mean you felt something?"

He squeezed down a little harder and I felt a small pain. "There, right here I feel something."

I took my own hands and felt where his hands were; I had never really checked, I mean I felt my boobs, it just wasn't for lumps. When I squeezed that part of my breast I felt it and then I looked at my nipples and noticed a white discharge. Robert sat us both up, his eyes intense on my breast. He squeezed the other one and nothing happened. Then he took both hands and searched for another lump. I

I Call Him Daddy Too

was stuck on the one in my right breast. My heart was beating wildly in my chest, and I couldn't feel exactly what he felt, but when I was about to stop, I felt it.

It felt like a Lima bean, hard yet moving through my fingers. It was deeper than I would have guessed and when I touched it, fluid came out of my breast. I knew I wasn't pregnant, I hadn't had unprotected sex in my life, and I was on birth control.

"Baby, you need to go get that looked at," Robert said, his voice very concerned.

"Why were you even on my breast like that?"

"I rubbed them, and when I came down to go to your stomach, I felt a lump in your breast. I thought I was losing it, so I searched again. Just when I thought it was a figment of my imagination, I felt it again, and that's when you woke up."

My mind was racing. *When did this lump get there, and why was discharge coming from my breast? I hadn't had a lover in a few weeks, could I be pregnant?* I threw the cover off the bed and ran to the bathroom. I went under the sink and pulled out a pregnancy test while pulling up my nightshirt and pulling down my panties. Robert was in the door, and I didn't care that he saw me peeing on a stick.

"Do you think you might be pregnant?"

I put the stick between my legs and started to pee as I answered him, "I don't know what is wrong, I just need to check everything before I call the doctor." Call my doctor, that's what I needed to do. "It's the weekend; I'll have to wait until Monday to talk to my doctor." I was in a panic, and I never panicked about anything.

"Okay, Alesia, just calm down. It will be fine, it's just a small lump. It's most likely nothing."

I looked back to the door as the stick was turning pink,

just one line. I'd left the box on the sink and couldn't remember what that meant. Robert calmly walked to the sink while I was getting off the toilet, looked down at the stick, and said, "Not pregnant, baby."

A rush of relief hit me, and then terror hit me. "The alternative to what it could be is..." I couldn't say the word.

I heard Robert speaking into the phone. *When did he get a phone?* "Dr. Lewis, I am so sorry to call you this early on a Saturday, but I have a small issue. My girlfriend found a lump this morning, and I was wondering if you would open the clinic for us. I would of course pay whoever shows up and you handsomely if we could get a better understanding of what this means."

He had a doctor on the phone—okay, I could breathe. I had questions, but all of those could wait.

"Great, we can be there in two hours, and if you could tell me how many staff members will be there, I would like to show my appreciation." He paused and then said, "You and three others, please tell them that I will make it worth their day off." He paused again, listening to the other end of the line. "I will have her bring those things. Again, thank you for taking my call."

He hung up the phone. "Get a shower, we need to be there in two hours, and I need to go to the bank. It's closer than my house. You have to be at work this afternoon, so wear something you can work in. Get in the shower and do your thing. I have something I can wear in my bag. It's a thirty minute drive. Do you think you can drive your car, or do I need to drive you?"

I didn't know what I could do, but if he was doing all of this, I could drive my car. "I can drive. How in the world do you have a Breast Cancer doctor's number in your phone?"

He stepped closer and pulled me into his arms. I laid my

head on his chest and heard his rapidly beating heart. He was so calm on the outside, but he was scared as well. I held him closer as he spoke. "My sister had breast cancer; all the money in the world couldn't save her life. After her death, I gave to clinics to help with cancer. At one of the banquets, I met this doctor. She helped low income women get breast cancer treatments. At the time, she needed new equipment, so I helped her with that. Sometimes she calls me when she has a patient that is running out of funds for treatment, and I pick up the bill. She was happy to help."

I laid in his arms and said, "I am sorry about your sister. I can't thank you enough for fixing this for me. I wouldn't know what to do with this. Thank you, baby." I lifted my head and kissed him on the lips, savoring the moment. When I broke the kiss, he patted my ass and told me to shower. I did what he said and got ready to go.

WE DROVE to a part of town I didn't go to often. The buildings were old and rundown, and I was really nervous for Robert in his Rolls. He pulled into a small parking lot, and I pulled in next to him. The clinic was dark on the outside, but when we got out of our cars, there was a smiling woman at the door. I walked to Robert and he held my hand as we walked in.

He greeted the woman who took my name and insurance information. "How is your morning going?" the woman asked as she handed me back my information along with some paperwork.

"My morning didn't start like I thought it would."

That was an understatement. I thought it would start with breakfast, and maybe a little head. I didn't think I would be in a clinic in the inner city. The woman gave me a sympathetic smile and told me to fill the medical questionnaire out and have a seat.

The seats were not the most comfortable, but I didn't complain. I filled out the information that I needed, and when I was done, another woman came out and called my name. Robert got up with me and walked to the back. He placed his hand on the small of my back, and I felt his strength. The woman took me to a room where she drew my blood. Her named was Tasha and she talked to me the whole time, taking my mind off of the blood draw. I was looking around the room and saw a small girl sitting in the corner. She was watching me and Robert with interest. I smiled at her, and she smiled back shyly.

Tasha started to speak, "I didn't have a babysitter. I had to bring her. I promised if she was really quiet that I would take her to the bookstore."

Robert smiled at the little girl, and she smiled back. Then he asked her what types of books she liked, and she started to list off all sorts of books. As we were finishing with the blood draw, Robert asked her name and she told him Annissa. We walked out of the room and he waved goodbye to her. We walked to another room; it had small lockers that could use an upgrade. I was told to take off my shirt and bra and put on a gown. I did as I was told and didn't have to wait at all. I was taken to a room that Robert couldn't come in, but at the door he kissed me and told me, "You got this." I smiled at him and walked into the room.

The room was very white, very clean, and very cold. There was a huge machine there and it took up most of the space.

"My name is Kiara, and I will be doing your images. I will have to touch your breast, is that okay?"

"Baby, a stranger touching my breast is the only thing that I am used to in this situation. I don't mind strange women touching my boob. In fact, I encourage it."

She laughed and placed my breast on a glass shelf. "Now I am going to lower this down, and it will be uncomfortable, but I can be quick."

It was quick, then she came back and did the same to the other breast. I was then ushered out of that room. Back in the hall was Robert, he was talking to a beautiful black woman, her hair in a pixie cut and she had on a lab coat. When she heard the door open, she smiled at me. "Good morning," she said with a cheerful smile. "I am Doctor Linda Lewis, I'm so happy to have you here this morning. I am going to do one more thing and then I will call you later and give you the results." I smiled at her and nodded.

Robert took my hand as we walked down the hall. We were led to a dark room, with a bed. Dr. Lewis told me to lay back and open my gown. I did as she asked and then warm gel was placed on my breast and she turned on the machine. I've seen this machine in movies but had never used one. Usually pregnant women used an ultrasound. I didn't know they were used for cancer scares. I closed my eyes and spoke.

"I swear when I thought we would be in a dark room with a woman seeing my breast it would go differently."

Robert and the doctor both erupted in laughter. "We can work on that, honey, as soon as we find out what's going on."

"For the first time in my life, I don't think sex will fix this feeling. I mean good sex could fix some things; I just don't think it will fix this."

The doctor was busy with buttons and pushing into my breast. I didn't know what she saw, but I was hoping that little Lima bean sized lump was nothing. It had to be nothing. And I promised myself after this I would check my breasts often.

I closed my eyes and tried to block her out, remembering the night before. It was perfect, and this morning showed that he was perfect. He didn't have to show me where he found that lump, he could have kept going until we were having sex, but he'd stopped his own pleasure to make sure I was fine. I had no idea how much this was costing him. He didn't even let me go into the bank when he got the money to pay for today.

"All done," she said with a soft voice. "I will call you soon and give you the results."

She was going to call me, which meant it couldn't be that bad, right? She led me back into the locker room, and I got dressed.

I took a moment with my hand on the knob of the door. I closed my eyes and asked God to make this okay no matter what. I opened the door and immediately heard Robert's voice.

"I would like to thank you all for taking care of Alesia in such a beautiful way. You didn't have to come in on your day off, but you did, and I wanted to make it worth your while. In each envelope there is five thousand dollars in cash."

Everyone screamed and then the little girl, Annissa, jumped up and down. Robert looked at her and he handed her a card. "Princess, this is my number, you can call me anytime, but I want you to make a list of books that you want and call me with the list. You were so good while your mother worked, and I want to help you find all the books that you love."

The little girl jumped up into his arms and gave him a kiss on the cheek. The rest of the women smiled as they looked on.

"As for the clinic, I would like to remodel the space, completely. If you don't mind, I will send my designer in to make sure that the space is up-to-date as well as comfortable, and this won't affect the donation that I give quarterly."

Dr. Lewis gasped, holding her hand over her face; the other women were wiping away tears. When they saw me, they all gave me hugs and told me that everything would be okay and that they were happy to help me. Robert and I walked out of the clinic with the women waving to us. When he got to the car, he spoke.

"I have to meet my daughter in a few minutes; I want you promise to call me when you get the results."

I put my arms around him, laying my head on his chest, and his arms went around me. "I promise to call you as soon as she calls me. I'm positive it's nothing. I think she would have told me while I was here."

He grunted and squeezed me. I squeezed him back and let go. Turning to my car, he walked behind me and opened my door. I slid in smiling up at him. He closed the door, and I watched him walk to his car, get in, and drive off.

10

DEATH

I had to get in the office, but I was hungry, so I swung into a fast food restaurant and got something quick. I needed to go to the store later and felt that a little retail therapy would be good for me today as well.

I got to the office and all of the other offices in the suite were dark. The office that I shared with Ty was at the back of a massive office suite. It was always bustling with people and laughter. I loved working here because Ty was really good at assembling a team of capable people. The office was in three sections: Building, Restoration, and Real Estate. All departments worked independently of each other, but they also worked together. Ty could build anywhere, and it was always a challenge to find the perfect place. Each department had a department chair, and many times before they could talk to Ty, they had to talk to me. I had my finger on the pulse of the entire operation.

My office lights were on, which meant that Ty was there.

"Hey, girl," I said from the entrance of our office.

She stuck her head out the door and said, "We should have done this before we left; I need to send out three long emails in time to meet my family for golf. My dad is in town and wants us to go for a round."

I hadn't met Ty's father, but I had met her brothers. They were all very handsome, but off limits. I loved Ty, and we were closer than most boss and employee.

"Girl, you are going golfing, when did you start that?"

"My father is convinced we make more money when we go golfing, so that is where we are going. Honestly, I suck, but not as bad as Jaxson, so I get to make fun of his swing."

I smiled at her. "Well, what I need to do will take a few minutes. I can help with the emails that you need to send. We can have them done in no time."

I opened my laptop on the desk and printed out the papers that I needed to have signed for Monday.

We were almost done when I heard the elevator ding, and out came five men: four I knew and one that I knew intimately. My heart dropped when I saw Robert. He wore a pair of khakis and a white Nike polo shirt. His eyes were on me in a different way, assessing me.

"Hey, Papa Smurf," Ty said from behind me. I stood stock-still, I couldn't move or breath. Robert took his eyes off me and engulfed his daughter with a hug. The other men had eyes on me and their father as well; I had to pull it together. I took a deep breath and focused on breathing while moving.

How could this be? He wasn't surprised to see me, so that meant that he had to know that it was a possibility that I worked for his daughter. And how many Howards were there in Denver?

It's official, I had horrible luck. I knew what my boss's father looked like naked.

All of that went through my mind as I put a fake smile on my face and proceeded to act like I had no idea what the man tasted like.

"It's nice to meet you, Mr. Howard, good to see you guys."

I have met all of Ty's brothers, and not one of them looks like their father; Ty didn't look like that man at all, and I had a hard time wrapping my mind around the fact that he was her father.

I extended my hand and he shook it—well, it was more like a caress than a shake. I took my hands away and started to turn to my desk; I needed to get out of here.

I didn't know what to do, but I needed to escape. "Well, you guys have fun with golf, and I will get everything shut down here.

Ty smiled at me. "What would I do without you, Lisa?"

If she knew I was sleeping with her father, she would most likely fire my ass. I didn't say that, I just smiled at her. "I would never quit; what other boss would take care of me like you do?" She reached out an arm and I hugged her. I really did love Ty, and the thought of hurting her, God, that destroyed me.

I needed to end this; no matter how good the last few weeks were, I had to end this. I could find another man. I couldn't find another Ty. She wasn't just my boss, she was my person. We talked about everything, she never judged, and she always—and I mean always—had my back.

Ty looked me deep in the eyes, searching mine, and I had to pull it together.

"You okay, girl?" Ty asked me in a hushed voice.

I plastered a fake smile on my face and said, "Girl, yes, I was just thinking of what I was going to do today."

"If you don't like your plans for today, why don't you come golfing with us? There are always men on the green looking for a date. And since they flirt with me with absolutely no shot at me, you would fare well."

I smiled at her and heard the chuckles of the men in the room. "I'm going shopping with Sierra for the party Friday night. I will call you tomorrow, maybe we should have lunch. I want to tell you more about Sierra."

"You already have my attention about Sierra, but if you come to the house, I will cook and we can have a movie night."

"That sounds great." And it did sound wonderful, but my stomach felt funny. *Should I tell her I slept with her father? Would she look at me differently? Could our friendship handle this?*

Ty and her family started to walk to the door, and her father was hanging back. I watched them leave, thinking I would never be a part of that family. Robert turned around and caught my eyes, and he stopped for just a moment mouthing to me, "We will talk."

I knew for a fact that we wouldn't. From this moment on, Robert Howard was off limits. And the part of me that believed in finding *the one* died.

RETAIL THERAPY and Dangerous Men

I closed down the office soon after they left, deciding that I need to pull myself together. I could do this. I could end things with Robert, and Ty would never know. Robert was what I was looking for in a man, I could say that even having gone days without seeing him; he was still ever present in my life. He didn't just call and talk about sex, he talked to me about my day. About my plans, and even my side business. And just this morning, he took care of the biggest scare of my life. I hadn't gotten a call and it was the afternoon, so I assumed all is well.

I didn't feel like shopping; I wanted to crawl in my bed

and forget today. It was shit. But, I'd made a promise to find Sierra a dress, and I could do with a few hours with my mind occupied.

Sierra had texted me five minutes ago saying that she was inside DSW for shoes and I could find her there. I pulled the car into valet and walked into the mall. I saw the entrance to DSW, when my named was called and I turned and saw Davis Popov walking with a small child and a teenage boy. Before I could ignore him, he spoke.

"I would like to say I am sorry that I got out of line. Please forgive me."

"I'm not on the clock, so this conversation is free; you will never get to Ty if it has to come through me, and let's be clear, all roads to Ty come through me. You can keep that weak ass apology. You meant what you said, and the fact that you saw me in public and decided to utter a word to me is beyond me."

His eyes hardened and he looked me up and down. I began to turn when he grabbed me by the arm. "You won't live to regret that."

The hair on my arms stood up. "Bitch, you don't scare me. You hide behind threats, and I don't take threats kindly. Denver is a big place, but one word from Ty and you won't be able to find a patch of land to shit on. And you will live to regret it. Now take your punk ass hands off me before your son sees you on your knees like the bitch you are."

He removed his hands, and I turned and walked into the store. I found Sierra, and she smiled when she saw me and then saw the expression on my face.

"What the hell is wrong with you?"

I closed my eyes exhaling a long breath. "Girl, this is a fucked up day, and it seems to get worse with every hour.

But I am here for you, so I am happy. You found something?"

She scrunched up her nose, shook her head, and taking my arm, she led me out of the store. I didn't see Davis, didn't really look for him. What I didn't know was that he saw me. And Sierra.

"So you are telling me that Robert is your boss's father?"

I had just told Sierra about the Robert/Ty situation. I told her this over a rack in a small dress shop in the mall. I told her after my phone rang and it was Robert. I didn't take the call, sending him to voicemail, but then he called me right back. I didn't take that call either. I would deal with him later tonight to end this shitty day, and hopefully tomorrow would be better.

"Yes, and no matter how much I like him, I love Ty and I won't betray that friendship."

"Look, you said Ty is cool. I don't think he would mind you dating his father."

I didn't correct her when she called Ty a man; I needed her to have an open mind when she met her. I had no doubt that Ty would make Sierra feel like a princess, and she wouldn't give a damn that she has a vagina.

"Would you be cool if I dated your father? What would I say, 'Hey Ty, you know I call him Daddy too.' Yeah that wouldn't work."

She rolled her eyes. "First, my dad is your dad." I couldn't argue that. "Lastly, whoever his Dad dates isn't his business. If you make him happy for a night or a lifetime, what does that have to do with your friendship?"

I stopped pretending to look at dresses and looked at her. "Sierra, what if it all goes wrong? What if we have a bad breakup?"

She looked me dead in the eyes. "And what if it all goes

right? What if he is the man that was meant for you? You are forcing yourself to give him up, and like you said, anything you have to force you shouldn't do."

I closed my eyes seeing Robert, his warm smile when I had goop all over my face, my hair in plats, and he still called me beautiful, saying it like he meant it.

I opened my eyes, looking at my girl, her words playing in my mind. I looked down at the rack seeing a coral dress, it was off the shoulders with a knee length hem. I pulled it out and showed it to her. "This would look good on you."

She took the dress out of my hand and let her fingers run down the fabric. She then looked at me, smiling. "One thing about you, you can always find the best dresses."

I smiled at her as we walked to the register. "I heard every word you said, and I will think hard before I make any decisions."

We had to leave the mall and get to Mama and Daddy's, so she went to the parking lot and I went to valet. While I waited on my car, the phone rang; it was a number I didn't know, but it was out of Denver. I answered it.

"Hey, baby girl." It was Janice; I must have talked her up last night, I hadn't heard from her in months.

"I'm good, Janice, where you been?" I saw my car pull up and walked to the driver's side handing the man his tip.

"You won't believe this, I was in jail." I could believe this, she was mostly in jail for public intoxication, but I wondered what the charge was this time.

"Sorry to hear that. What were you in jail for?" My car connected to my phone, and I started down the road.

"This fuck boy tried to stiff me on my score, and I stabbed his ass. You know I ain't letting no one steal from me."

Oh Father. "When did you get out of jail, and when did this happen?"

"Girl, that was five months ago; anyway, I told my probation officer that I was going to live with you. I will be there in a few hours from Portland."

I damn near wrecked my car. "Janice, what the hell? You can't live with me!"

"Girl, in that big ass house you got, you won't even know I am there."

I doubted that seriously. "The answer is no."

"Fine, you work for a real estate agent, why don't you find me a nice little house you can afford and I will move there?"

"I don't work for a real estate agent. I work for a housing development and commercial development company. We don't rent shit; we sell houses, Janice."

"Fine, buy me a damn house!"

"Have you lost your goddamn mind? I am not buying you a damn house, and you are not living with me. Call your parole officer and tell him you don't have a place to live." The fuck.

"Like I said, Alesia, I will be there some time tonight, have my room ready."

Then she hangs up the phone. I close my eyes for a brief second and wonder if I can pack up and move before she could get to my house in a few hours. After an impending visit from my mother, I didn't want to see anyone, but Sierra's parents weren't just anyone. Sam Brooks could turn a bad day into a great one in just one hour.

11

WE WILL WIN

"So you are seeing an older man, and you find out not only is he your boss's daddy, he is a billionaire?"

"How do you know he is a billionaire, Daddy?" That was Sierra, but how did he know that?

Mama took one look at me and told me that she made cookies, and to tell her what was wrong with me. I took the cookies and told Mama and Daddy about my issue with Robert. Daddy walked out the room for just a moment and then he came back with that question.

"How don't you know he is a billionaire? I went to the Googler and found him in two minutes. He has five children —all grown, all successful. The man has resorts all over this damn globe. I keep telling you girls to use the Googler; it will weed out some issues. You can pay a small fee and find out his criminal history. He doesn't have one, by the way."

I rolled my eyes, and Sierra just shook her head. "Daddy, I hate I told you about Google."

"Lisa, I don't see the issue here. Look, you date the man, he falls madly in love with you, and I have five grown successful grandchildren. And I can show them off and Jake Hamilton doesn't have the upper hand on grandchildren anymore. Then when all of those children have children, I will be the first one with great grandchildren. I like this plan."

All Daddy's plans included us having grandchildren. After Jake Hamilton had grandchildren and started telling Daddy how his life is so much better, all Daddy has been talking about is Sierra and I getting pregnant. "Daddy, it's been two weeks, why are we talking about grandchildren?"

"Look, you dated that boy Lewis for six months, let me meet him and everything, had my hopes up, and then you left his ass a voicemail saying it wasn't going to work, blocked the boy's number, and I had to talk to him. You have been seeing this man two weeks and look like I kicked your puppy every time you mention breaking things off with him. A father knows his children, and child, you got deep emotions for this man."

"I don't have deep emotions for him, Dad," I told him this lie.

"You told him about your mama yet?"

Shit. I didn't answer. "You dated that boy Lewis and he didn't even know I wasn't your real daddy. That boy knew nothing about you! He didn't even know your address to send you flowers."

"He has a point, Lisa." That was Sierra; Mama was stirring a pot of sauce for her spaghetti and didn't say a word, she just looked at me with that knowing mother look.

"Look girl, you and your boss are friends, he knows you are a good person, and he will be happy for you both I think you can take this slow and see where this is going. Don't tell him now, give it some time, but don't break up with the man; he could be good for you."

I nodded my head. "Now tell Daddy what else is in that head of yours."

I wouldn't tell him about the cancer scare. I wasn't ready to talk about how that scared the shit out of me, and I wasn't ready for Daddy to know how Robert stepped up. "My mother called and informed me that she was just getting out of jail, and she was moving in with me."

Daddy did a low whistle, Mama shook her head, and Sierra said, "When did that happen?"

I took a bigger bite of cookie; I loved mama's philosophy of eating dessert first when you had a problem. With a mouth full of cookie I said, "While waiting for my car at the mall."

"Damn, you are having a shitty day." Sierra could say that again; I hadn't even told her that I was still waiting on my test results. I looked at my watch and saw that it was after four, and still no call.

Daddy spoke, "They have a new apartment complex for drug users to get on their feet. I saw it in the paper; we can see if they have space. The good thing is they help them find a job as well as education. This could be a good thing. If she had months without drugs in her system, it might be easier to get her off them for good."

Mama said, "All things work for the good for those who love the Lord. Baby, this could be a good thing. Her staying with you could make your relationship better."

"Or she could rob me blind, sell my stuff to a crack house, and disappear. You know the things that she does."

No one said anything, because I was right. Mama set dinner in front of us, and we began to eat. There is nothing like Mama's spaghetti it; could solve world peace.

I LEFT Mama and Daddy's house an hour later, needing to get home so I could get to Target. I didn't buy a thing at the mall, and I wanted a some stuff for the bathroom. My phone rang as I was pulling into the parking lot. I didn't recognize the number, but it was a Denver number.

"Hello," I said as I found a parking spot.

"Hey, Alesia, this is Dr. Lewis; can you talk?"

My stomach was doing cartwheels, and I was glad I had parked the car. "Yes, I figured you didn't find anything, thought that you would call me soon after to tell me that."

"I'm sorry, Alesia."

"It's cool you didn't call me earlier."

"No, I am sorry because you have breast cancer." I don't know what she said after that; my ears rang so loud I couldn't hear her. The words *breast cancer* rang so deep inside of me, I felt my stomach turn. I barely got the door open before the contents of my stomach came out.

No cookie was going to fix this. No amount of retail therapy was going to fix this either. Before I knew it, a scream came from inside of me that rattled the windows. That didn't fix it either. I vaguely heard Dr. Lewis say Robert's name, and I thought to myself that he couldn't fix this either. I cried, disgusted with the tears flowing down my face, dropping to the breasts that were trying to kill me.

My phone rang. I don't remember answering, but I heard Roberts voice. "Baby, just tell me where you are, and I am on my way to get you."

"I'm at Target, fuckin' Target. I found out I was dying at fucking Target, Robert."

"You are not fucking dying!" he roared through the speakers.

"Your sister died, and you said yourself no amount of money could save her," I choked out on a sob to him. "I don't even have that kind of money. What the fuck am I going to do?"

"You are going to tell me where you are, and I will handle the rest."

I didn't know where I was, I couldn't think of street names, all I could think of was **breast cancer.**

I heard a voice, a woman's voice. "Are you okay?"

There was a woman standing at the back of my car, her basket pushed behind the car, looking at me.

"No, I have breast cancer." I said this and broke down again. I felt arms go around me, and I was in her arms. She held me in her arms, taking off my seat belt so she could hold me tighter.

Robert spoke again, "Alesia, tell me where you are."

The woman spoke, "She is in her car at the Target on California. I will stay with her until you get here."

"Thank you, I'm on my way." I heard the phone hang up, but I didn't hear silence. The woman told me she would stay with me, she told me that I was going to be alright, and when I told her I was afraid I was going to die, she held me tighter and started to pray. Telling the God she served to let me have life, to give me a long life; I cried as she spoke, but she kept praying and holding me. I heard a car screeching to a stop and didn't have the strength to look up, but I heard Robert's voice.

I heard vaguely that her shoes were ruined from standing in my vomit. I looked down at her shoes and saw that he was right. She told Robert she didn't care, she just needed my number so she could check on me. Robert carefully pulled me out the car and picked me up in his arms. The door was opened and I saw that Marcus was there. I couldn't process this; all I could do was sit in his car and try to hold myself together.

I didn't look around, I just looked through the windshield thinking I was dying. A piece of me that was giving me pleasure was killing me. I felt Robert's hands cup my face, and I looked at him. His warm eyes were red with unshed tears. "I am going to take you to my house."

I shook my head. "I want to go home."

"Then I will take you home, and I won't hear about me leaving. I am staying with you."

I didn't want to be alone. I knew all the reasons I should tell him to leave, but I couldn't leave him like this. I didn't have it in me at that moment to push him away. I would worry about Ty tomorrow, but today I needed him.

We pulled into my driveway, and I saw that Marcus had driven my car. I didn't know what Robert told him, didn't have it in me to worry too much about it. My door was opened and Robert pulled me out, carrying me inside. Marcus had the door opened when we got there. Robert walked me to the bedroom and then into the bathroom. Marcus followed behind. He sat me on the side of the tub and said, "Let me walk Marcus out, he won't say anything to Ty until you are ready. He and all of my boys can be trusted with our relationship until you are ready, okay, baby?"

I took a deep breath, my eyes going to the floor. I didn't watch Marcus and Robert leave. I just sat there, my hands going to cup my breasts. They were a traitor; how could something so beautiful kill me?

I heard the shower turn on, and then felt his hands on the hem of my shirt. He pulled it up over my head pulled me up to my feet, and undressed me. I stood before him completely nude, and for the first time, I felt ashamed of my body. Robert stood before me and undressed. I watched him, and when he was done, he pulled me into his arms and held me with my breasts pressing against him. When I felt them on his body, I pulled away. Turned away to the shower.

When the water got hot, I got under it, feeling it run down my body. I heard the door close and felt Robert behind me. He pulled my back to his front. "I hate my breasts, Robert."

"I can see that." He rubbed up my arms.

"I want them off me now," I said, and my voice cracked.

He held me tighter. "We can have that happen. What did the doctor say?"

"I don't remember a word she said after she told me it was cancer."

He kissed the side of my head. "I will call her after we are out of the shower. We have to fight this with everything we've got. This is *our* fight, Alesia. You are not alone."

"I can't ask that of you, it's only been a few days."

"It could have been weeks, or months, or years. Time doesn't matter. I know what I have in my arms, and I won't lose it. Not even to cancer."

I shook my head, the words too sweet to handle, and silent tears ran down my face. "I will never be able to feed my babies from my body."

He held me tighter. "When this is over, if you want babies, we will have them. You might not be able can feed them, but you can love them. This isn't the end of you; I don't ever want to hear you say you will die of this. That is admitting defeat, and defeat is not what we will have."

"Okay, baby, I won't let this defeat me."

He reached over to the soap and started to bathe me. "This is the fight of our life, baby, we have to be united. This won't win, we will."

12

TODAY IS THE DAY FOR SHOPPING

Robert and I were sitting on the couch, watching Scandal. He had never seen the show, and I had to introduce him to Olivia Pope. We'd started from the beginning, and he was hooked. We were now on the tenth episode, when there was suddenly someone at the door. I knew who that someone was, and I didn't have it in me to fight. Robert was up before I was; he was wearing pajama bottoms and a black tee. Marcus had gone to his house and packed him a bag, then brought it back a few hours ago. It was well after midnight, and being snuggled up to Robert while watching my favorite show made me happy. The person on the other side of the door, however, didn't make me happy.

Robert opened the door and was face-to-face with my mother. Her clothing was simple but clean. She wore a pair of jeans and flip-flops with a shirt that said, *Made of sage and hood and wish a motherfucker would.* Her hair hung long, and it looked like she was clean. Really clean.

Even on crack my mother was pretty, but off of it she was stunning. Seeing Robert made her take a step back.

I got up. "Hey, Janice."

"You didn't tell me that we were going to have company," she said and batted her long eyelashes at Robert. He looked her and then to me. My mother was tall and built. Drugs didn't take that ass away, and honestly, I was happy to see that she looked good.

"I told you not to come."

She leaned down, picked up a duffle bag, and walked in, pushing me and Robert to the side.

I took a deep breath, too damn tired to fight, and watched as she put her bags next to the sofa. "What y'all watch'n?"

I didn't feel like this, I didn't feel like shit. "Mother, I've had the day from hell. I won't go into all of it, but today I found out I have breast cancer. I don't have time for you. I don't have time for your lies. How about I go to my room, and in the morning, I will see what you took and sold for your next fix. I will take inventory of what's left so I can sell the rest to pay for whatever treatment I am having."

The room was utterly silent. I took that as consent that she would take what she wanted and be gone in a few hours.

I WOKE to the smell of bacon and thought today was already turning out better than yesterday. I felt arms around me and looked behind me.

"Good morning, baby." His voice was gravelly from sleep, and I felt that in my clit. I smiled at him, leaning up to kiss him.

"You cooking?"

He smiled at me. "No, that would be your mother."

I sat straight up. "My mother is cooking in my kitchen?"

"Yep," he said while sitting up, his chest bare as he did.

"My mother hasn't cooked anything but crack in over twenty years."

"Well, she is cooking bacon this morning. I went out to see what she was up to at sunrise. She was writing in a journal; when she saw me, she asked if you were able to sleep. She also asked me who I was and gave me a very stern talking to about hurting you."

My mother was up journaling, instead of robbing me blind, and then she gave him a stern talking to... "I don't know how to deal with this."

He pulled me into his arms. "Honey, I talked to a woman last night that saw the error of her ways in one foul moment. She knows that she isn't someone you can depend on; she knows that you don't trust her. And she also wants to prove that she can be trustworthy."

"Robert, I have heard all of that before. She comes in, says she has changed, and I get let down, and then I am at the store replacing the things that she stole. I don't buy it; maybe she will stick around until the parole officer shows up and sees I don't live in a trap house, and then leave to live her life." That sounded more like what my mother was about. Herself.

He kissed the side of my face. "I think that your mother will prove you wrong, and if she doesn't, I will be here to make sure that it's okay."

"You sure are planning for the long haul. I mean, my mother will be here a week tops, but you sure are thinking about being here at least until the cancer is gone.

He smiled at me. "Well, you cooked me a meal that I still remember, and it doesn't hurt that you have a body like a goddess."

When he mentioned my body, my face fell and his eyes went guarded. "I have no idea what cancer is going to do to my body. But on the bright side, twenty years of crack, and my mother still looks good. Maybe chemo won't be that bad."

He laughed a little. "Look, I didn't want to say anything, but your mama does not look like a crackhead. I plan to be here; I missed you when I was gone, and I missed you on the golf course too. Trisha Morrison tried to make me look under her skirt three times. She is recently divorced and looking for husband number three. He won't be me."

I smiled at him. "You are a catch; do me a favor and don't tell my mother your last name. I told my daddy your name, and in two minutes he was already planning out our wedding so he can have grandchildren." His eyes got big. "Don't worry, he wants the grown ones. He is in competition with his friend who has grandchildren. Apparently his friend has four grandchildren, and Daddy thinks that if he gets five, he will beat him. And once your kids have kids he will be a great grandfather before his friend is. He has it all planned out."

"Well, I hope he knows what he is asking for; those boys can give me the blues. But that girl of mine has a special place in my heart."

With the mention of Ty, my heart sank. "I don't like lying to her, but I don't think we should tell her either. She knows a lot about me, and there are things she accepts about me because I am her friend. I don't think she would accept those things if she knew we were a couple."

"Things like what?"

I looked in his eyes and remembered that if he was for me, nothing about my past would stop him from caring about me. "She knows about my clients, has even referred people to me. She also knows that I am sexually fluid. I have been in a relationship with both women and men, sometimes at the same time. I like sex, Ty knows I am a member of a sex club, she has even gone with me a few times. And I have seen her in a sexual situation before."

I looked at him, and he laughed. "I know that this is going to sound weird, but none of that would make her not like you for me. I have things I don't share with any of my children, and who and what I do in bed is one of them. I am not surprised Tyanna was in a sex club; she *is* my child. I have memberships all over the world. When you are ready to tell her, I will talk to her. It will be fine. As for now, we focus on our fight. We have cancer to worry about."

Before I could say anything, there was a knock on the door. I took a deep breath and said, "Come in."

"I know y'all hear me in there cooking, and if you didn't, you smelled it. Get dressed and come eat." After she said that Janice walked out of the room. Robert started to move, but I was stuck for a moment. She'd actually stayed the night. Robert called my name when he got to the door, and I looked up at him. My mind was telling me to move. I got to the door and took my robe off the back. I closed it as I walked out of my room.

The table was set, there were pancakes in the middle with bacon and sausage, and there was a platter with eggs and juice as well. It was set really nice.

"The table is beautiful, Ma."

She gave me a shy smile and pulled out a seat. "Come on and sit down, don't want the eggs cold."

Robert pulled out my chair, and she watched him closely. I sat down, and he took the head of the table. Something about that made my heart warm inside. He reached for a plate, handing one to my mother and fixing mine. I smiled at him and he winked.

"How are you this morning, baby?"

I didn't know how I was. "Honestly, I don't know. Yesterday was a shock. I think today I am going to process. Look over my insurance policy and see what they will offer. I have lunch with my boss today, so I will let her know what is going on. Robert called the doctor last night, and I have an appointment with one of her colleagues on Tuesday. They have a plan, and we will hope that it works."

I tasted the food, and it was really good. Janice had never cooked for me as a child; she always fed me something, but she never cooked. Honestly, we never had a kitchen really. "This is real good, Ma."

She smiled at me. "My baby needs her strength. Now about what you said last night."

I cut my pancake, waiting for the bullshit to flow so I could nip it in the bud. If she thought that one breakfast was going to solve all the bull she had put me through, she was mistaken.

"They made me do anger management while I was in jail; I thought it was bullshit. But I had drugs in my system, and I didn't care about the class. For the first week my body was detoxing. That was no fun, and I never want to do it again."

I'd heard that before, she had been in and out of rehab all my life. She would get clean, and then be home a few days and be back on that shit. I didn't say that, I just listened.

"I know I have said it before, but I had never laid in my own sick. I never was so sick I couldn't hold my own... Never mind. During all of this I was in a cell alone, no one checked on me. I could have been dead. Honestly, I thought I was going to die. Then I heard you; you weren't a woman, you were a little girl. Couldn't be more than five, and you laid down next to me. Asked me not to leave you again. I know it wasn't real, it just felt that way."

Her eyes held mine, and I could feel the emotion rolling off of her.

"You came to me again some time later, you were a teenager, you sat in a chair looking at me on the floor. Told me every way I'd disappointed you, and everything you said was the truth. Told me if I died, you wouldn't have anything to miss but a headache."

Now she had tears in her eyes. I looked at Robert, he wasn't eating, he was watching this play out. I looked back to my mother, my heart racing in my chest.

"The judge offered me probation, but I asked to stay in jail and serve my time. I knew that I wasn't strong enough not to get out and be back in a trap house. He offered to let me out three times; I declined each and every one of them. I went to therapy, took a hospitality course, and learned to use a computer. I lied to you; I don't have a probation officer. I do have a job though, I start Monday."

Wow, my mother had a job. She'd worked here and there but nothing solid. And she'd stayed in jail to get clean—not because she had to, because she wanted to.

"I'm proud of you." When the words came out, she closed her eyes and a single tear ran down her cheek. My eyes got misty too.

"I know I don't deserve your trust. I *know* this. But I am asking you to give me a shot. I won't say that the first thought I had when I got out wasn't to get a hit. It was, but my next thought was that I had a job to get to, a daughter to be there for. Last night when you said you had cancer, and you expected me to steal from you and walk away, it cut me to my soul. I deserved every ounce of that pain. I know what kind of mother I have been. One that doesn't even deserve to be called Mama. I might have messed that up, but I hope we can be friends. I hope to prove to you that you can trust me with your pain. I promised myself the last day I was in counseling that if I failed you this time, I would never come back."

No matter how much time passed, she always came back. Always told me she missed me, no matter if she stole my money weeks later or not. Something about this time made me believe her. Maybe the steadiness of her hands and eyes. The fact that she wasn't sweating, needing her next hit.

She continued, "You need me now like you have never needed me before, and I will die before I let you down again. I will hold your hand; I will hold you up even if I am on my knees. I will not fail you." She said that last part emphatically.

I waited a moment, letting my eyes search hers. "Do you have what you need for work?"

She looked down at her plate. "I have a pair of black pants and a white shirt. Got it from a program in jail."

"What hotel will you be working at?"

She looked back at me. "AC Hotels by Marriott."

That was a nice hotel. When I'd dated Lewis that's where we'd gone; Daddy was right—I never went to his place, and he had never been to mine.

"I have a question. When you called me earlier, why didn't you say all of this? I would have been happier to see you if you'd led with this."

She smiled. "Being an asshole is something I can't shake. I wanted to surprise you, with the new me. But honestly, baby girl, I am always going to be Janice, just a sober Janice."

"Nice to meet you, sober Janice, and I don't mind you

being an asshole. I can be one as well. I guess we have that in common."

She bit off a piece of bacon and smiled at me.

"Ma, you need more than one outfit to work in that job. It's a nice place, and the front desk people always look stylish. You are more than welcome to look in my closet, but I wasn't blessed with all that ass, so we might have to go shopping today. I am really good at finding statement pieces."

"You need all of your money, baby," she said in a hush.

"Take it as a loan, you can pay me back a little at a time with the money you make."

"I want to help with rent. This place has to be expensive, and I can help with that. If you tell me how much it is a month, I can go half with you."

My house was paid for, but I didn't tell her that. "We can talk about rent after your first check. Let's eat and hit the streets. I need an outfit or two that doesn't show cleavage since most likely I won't have any."

I meant for it to be a joke, but my heart wasn't in it. My mother's eyes filled with tears, and she looked down at her plate.

"Ma, yesterday was the day for crying; today is the day for shopping."

"Okay, baby girl, today is the day to shop."

13

IN MY HEART

Robert told me he was coming with me; he said he was going to make sure that if I had a breakdown, he was there. He said it in a way that made me feel warm and fuzzy, so I let him go. We were all dressed, and I was trying to figure out how he was going to fit in my car along with my mother, when there was a knock on the door. A tall, very dark, bald man was at my door when Robert opened it. His name was Clyde, and he was Robert's personal driver. My mother gave me a look, but I didn't say anything. There was a black Escalade on the curb.

My mother was oohhing and ahhing at the car, and when Clyde opened the door for her, she smiled brightly at him. I rolled my eyes at her; I could smell that she had washed her outfit from last night. Come to think of it, that duffel was pretty small. She would need more than work clothes. Clyde let us out in front of the mall and told Robert that he would call and ask where we were when he found a place to park. I spotted White House Black Market and took Janice there. It was my go-to place for business clothing. After a brief argument about how much it cost, she tried on an outfit. It fit like a glove and she looked outstanding.

My mother was on her phone trying to find coupons when Robert walked up to us, grabbed the clothing, and went to the register. He pulled out his card and paid for it. The card he pulled out was the Amex Black, and my mother snatched it out of his hand and looked at, turning it over in her hand. Robert didn't seem to mind; he pulled out his phone and called Clyde. My mother handed him back his card and pulled out her phone.

I knew the instant she found him, as she walked over to me. "Sam told me about the guy you broke up with over voicemail. If you do that to him, I will kill you myself."

I rolled my eyes at her, and we walked out of the store.

The breakdown happened in Macy's. My mother needed bras for work, along with panties. I had forgotten about the cancer at that point. I was really enjoying myself with my mother when I saw a sexy teddy; the bra had red sequins on it. I thought I would look great in it, bringing attention to my breasts was one of my power moves. Then I thought about my breasts killing me and I burst into tears. My mother dropped everything she was holding on the floor and pulled me into her arms. She whispered in my ear, "Let it out, baby. Give it to Mama and I will make it all better."

I did like she asked and when I was done, Robert had all of her things in a bag already paid for. "That's enough shopping for today; let's get you home, and we can all watch Scandal together."

I gave him a weak smile, and we walked out the store; a few people stared at me as we went. My mother held my hand on the car the ride home. Clyde brought her bags in, and she went straight to the kitchen. She came back with some tea and told me to sip it slowly. I thanked her and did as she asked. Mom gave Robert a look then walked into the guest room.

I didn't ask what the look meant, I just saw Robert bend down and take my shoes off one at a time. He took the shoes to my room then came back.

"You need to make a few phone calls, honey."

He was right; I needed to tell the people that meant something to me what was going on. My first call was to Mama and Daddy. When they picked up, they told me Sierra was at the house as well and that made me only have one more phone call to make. I asked them to put me on speaker and they did that.

"Yesterday I found a lump in my breast." There was a collective gasp. "Robert had a friend that specializes in that, and she saw me the same day. I have breast cancer; Dr. Lewis told Robert it was stage three, but it's an aggressive form. I will have a plan on how we deal with it later this week."

"Baby doll, sit down." That was Daddy, he called Mama baby doll. I could hear Mama in the background crying. I knew that woman loved me; for us it was love at first sight.

"My baby. Lord, not my baby," I heard Mama say. I looked up at Robert, but his eyes were on the hall door. I looked that way and saw my mother standing there. Her eyes bright with tears. I didn't have children, but I could imagine listening to the woman that raised your only child and hearing her grief along with the love she had for her.

"I can come over; we can watch a movie or just sit and talk if you want."

I smiled at the phone. "I have company. Robert hasn't left my side, and neither has Janice. I am in good hands. I promise. But Mama, if you could make me some cookies, that would not go to waste."

"Baby, I will bring you all the cookies you want! Whenever you need me, you call. I want an update about doctor's appointments, and I will sit with you through chemo. You are not alone, Alesia. I let you do your thing because that is who you are, but I want you to know you are my baby. I won't let you fight this alone. As soon as we get off the phone I will be getting on the prayer line and adding your name."

I smiled at the phone. "Thanks for that. I have another phone call to make. I want you to know that I love you. All of you."

Daddy's voice choked when he said he loved me. Sierra and Mama were both openly crying. I pulled myself together and thought about the people who'd made my life so much better as a child.

Janice had walked back down the hall. I looked at Robert, picked up the phone, and called Ty; it rang three times and she answered, "Hey girl, everything alright?"

"Not really." I heard some giggling in the background, and Ty told someone to give her a second. I heard a door open and close and imagined her leaving the room to find somewhere quiet.

"Okay, girly, what's up?"

I took a deep breath and said, "I found a lump in my breast, it's cancer. I found out last night when the doctor called me to let me know."

She was quiet for a long moment. Then she spoke in the quietest voice. "I can come over now, or you can come here. Is this why you canceled earlier?"

"Partly. Some of it was that my mother showed up. She is clean, and I mean squeaky clean. She has a job at a local hotel, and she starts tomorrow. We talked, well, mostly she did the talking, but I liked all that she said. The other part is that she met my boyfriend, and she likes him." I looked up at Robert and he gave me a smile.

"I didn't know you were seeing someone."

"It's new, and I didn't think he would step up the way that he did, but he has been wonderful. We can talk about him later. The main thing is that I need Tuesday morning off; I have an appointment with the doctor, but I have to make sure that all is well at the office. Monday I will set things up for Tuesday."

"I am not worried about work. I need you to take care of yourself. I can manage."

"Do you remember how your office was before I got there?" Before I started working for Ty, she had never had an office assistant, and the office was a mess. Ty was always dealing with trivial drama, and she got half of what she needed done.

"Lisa, you make my life easy, and I do my part in making sure that you are okay as well, but right now, I need you to focus on beating this. Your pay will not change; I will pay you whether you are there or not. I want you to heal, and this disease…"

She let that hang, and then I heard her break down, her tears causing tears of my own.

"This disease can't win because a contract needs to go out. I need you around to help me find the love of my life. I need you to tell me wild and crazy stories, and I need you to make me a better person. You are the person I lean on, I know you are a little younger than me, but you are my person. I don't want you to worry about the bills or work. I want you to go in there and kick cancer's ass."

I smiled through my tears. "I plan to kick cancer's ass. It won't know what hit it. I won't lose; I don't know how to admit defeat, and I know this will be hard, but I can do this.

I Call Him Daddy Too

And I will work for as long as I can; we both are going to retire soon. I want a hot cabana boy sucking these toes in Mexico."

She laughed. "That's the Lisa I love. We can do this. I have your back, and the offer is still open for me to come over."

"Girl, go enjoy your night; I have a hot man here, and I feel like playing."

"Don't hurt him, girl, and I will see you in the morning."

I ended the call and looked at Robert. "She has my back in any way I need her. She is not going to stop my pay, and I just got a raise, so the money will be right on time."

"Is money an issue for you?"

"No. I mean I am not some millionaire, but I have over 600K in the bank; my goal is a million. Depending on how cancer does, I won't be able to do my side jobs. While you took that call earlier, I looked up my insurance, and it will cover a lot. I also have supplemental insurance and a cancer rider on it. So I should be good for a while. I know cancer can be expensive, so I will call Alexander and have him look over my finances."

"My Alexander?"

"Yes, your Alexander. I started using him a few months after working for Ty. I told him my goal, and he has helped me get to it. I don't know what my stocks look like, but he can tell me. My house is paid for, and my real overhead is shopping, which I could stop for a while. You don't have to worry about me; I can handle this."

"Good. Are you ready for bed?"

I sat up, putting the phone down, and getting closer to him. "I'm ready to be put to sleep." My voice was husky, and I let my eyes travel the length of his body. I leaned in licking his lips, and he took the invitation, pulling me to him while kissing me passionately. My hands went up his shirt and I felt the planes of his abs. His hands went to my ass, holding me close to him so I could feel his erection. He broke the kiss and I pouted.

"I'm all for letting people watch, I just don't want your mother to walk in."

Eww. My face made him laugh, and we got off the couch, turning off lights as we went into my bedroom. Robert closed the door and then he was on me. Taking my clothes off while I undressed him. Before long, he was inside of me, his powerful body making mine moan. He held me in place with my leg over his shoulder. Dropping straight dick. I climaxed within minutes.

Robert turned me over without leaving my body and slowly grinding inside, taking his free hand to massage my clit. I could barely breathe as he slowly brought me to climax again.

"I want to taste you, baby." And when I did, he was divine. Our essences mixed was heavenly.

"Damn, we taste good."

He pulled my face to his. "Let me taste."

His mouth touched mine, and then his tongue swept in giving me another note of his flavor. I moaned kissing him back. His body pressed mine into the bed. His body joined mine, and he moved slowly taking me higher in the slowest way possible. I couldn't teach this, no matter how hard I tried.

He broke the kiss, looking me in the eyes when he spoke softly, "You don't know this, Alesia, but you are mine. I don't care how long it takes for you to realize you belong to me, but one day you will know." And when he said, "know," he pushed in so deep I screamed his name. "I know what I want, Alesia; I know I want you, and not just for now, but for the rest of my life."

He kissed me when my mouth formed a question. I didn't even remember what it was when he was done.

"I've had all types of women in my bed. I haven't had one that got into my heart."

I was in his heart; how did this happen? I was going to ask, but he moved his hips and the only thing that came out was, "Oh my God."

"Let me get on my job and put you to sleep; I've got work in the morning."

And boy did he fuck me—hard, fast, and ruthless. I lost count of the positions he put me in. But when he was done with me, I slept like a baby.

14

RUN AS FAST AS YOU CAN

It was Friday, and this week had been emotional to say the least. I went to the office Monday; Ty had gotten me roses in every color, each with a handwritten note telling me all the ways that I make her life better. Also in each note was a gift card: some for dinners, some for wigs, and some for augmented bras. Something that I never knew existed.

It seemed that overnight she'd done some research on things that breast cancer survivors needed. She even got me a maid to clean my house once a week. There was lunch for the office where she explained that I would be in the office on a limited basis. I got hugs and love from everyone. At the end of the day when I got home, my mother had a dinner ready for me. She'd had a half day on her first day and said that Robert had sent Clyde to pick her up. She had gone to the grocery and made fried chicken, cabbage and rice, with hot water cornbread. We sat up and talked well into the night; I only went to bed when Robert showed up later that night.

Tuesday was the appointment and it lasted all day. I had

blood drawn, all types of images taken, and at the end of the day, met a team of doctors. The cancer had spread to my left lymph node and needed to be removed. It would be better that I removed both breasts, and chemo would go on for three months, once every week. They would fight this aggressively since it was very close to the next stage. They talked about possible hospital stays and in the end, told me that things would move very fast in the next few days. I would have to inform my employer and family that I would need extra support.

The main thing that I had to be ready for is that I would lose my breasts and most likely my hair in the next few days. My first chemo session was set for the following Tuesday. I was told to get rest, which I did on Wednesday. Okay, I laid in bed, ate cookies, and cried all day. My mother and Robert were at work, and I hid the evidence when I knew they would be home. Thursday I did the same, except Mama called and said she was on the way. After faking it for all of five minutes, she and I crawled into my bed, cried together, and watched *How To Get Away With Murder*.

So tonight, I won't be crying. I will be hooking my girl up with the love of her life, and maybe finding someone to bring home to Robert. The club was a block from the Marriott and, I'd already booked a room. I texted Robert and told him to meet me there after eleven. I wore a bandage dress with cut-outs to show all the skin that was legal to walk down the street in. Sky high black heels with peekaboo toes. My dress did not say cancer patient, it said here to fuck, and that's what I was going to do. After hooking up Ty and Sierra.

Ty let everyone off early, but she stayed behind to finish up the deal; she wouldn't arrive there until the party was in full swing. That gave me time to get everyone in a party mood and to get enough liquor in Sierra for her to not think too much.

Drama was lit, and the DJ was on fire; he played all the ass-shaking music that a person could want. I watched the door, hoping that Sierra actually showed so I could get this relationship off the ground. I was getting a drink when I looked toward the door and Sierra walked in. That copper dress fit her like a second skin, her makeup was innocent, but that dress definitely said, "Fuck the shit out of me." I couldn't have asked for better. I met Sierra on the dance floor and handed her my drink, hoping to get her a little tipsy before Ty arrived.

"Girl, you look amazing!" she said when she took the drink. She had to speak loud to be heard over the music.

I smiled at her. "Thank you, and you look fuckable. Let's get to our section."

I made sure Ty had a private section. I was going to introduce Sierra and when Ty pulled out the "Ty Magic," I was going to leave them and let nature take its course. I looked around the club and saw a man that I had never seen before. He was tall, dark, and oh so handsome. Not as handsome as Robert, but he would do. I wondered how Robert felt about guy on guy. I thought it was hot, but he could have some reservations.

"Hello there." He looked me up and down, smiling like he was going to get lucky. I hated men like that.

"Hey." I started up the stairs, but he stepped in front of me.

"You are so pretty, wanna dance?"

I smiled stepping forward. "Not at all."

I stepped to the left and walked away from him. Sierra was looking behind me and smiling. I was on the stairs leading up to the private room when she spoke. "He was cute."

"He was arrogant with a little dick. I will pass. Honestly, I am in the mood for the female persuasion." I sat down and looked around, hoping Ty wasn't here yet, but as my eyes scanned the room, there was a beautiful blonde. Short red dress and she was smiling at me. Yeah, she was more like it. She walked through the crowd and I watched her hips sway to the music. I licked my lips, and her eyes heated.

"So, I finally get to meet the infamous Ty."

Oh yeah, she was going to meet the infamous Ty, but more importantly, she was going to meet the woman that would change her life. "Yes, and she finally gets to meet you."

Her face was priceless. She had a doubt on what I said, and I was about to burst that little bubble; she thought she was here to meet the man of her dreams, but she was going to meet a woman, and I was interested in how she would handle it. I was going to make her really think. "You thought a man would have daycare in the building and have it set up where his employees could have lunch with their children daily? Yeah, no."

I took a sip of my vodka and looked over to the blonde. I thought of what fun Robert and I would have with her. Just as I was about to speak, Ty walked in, commanding the room. I loved that about her; she didn't have to say one word to show she was in control, she just was. Now that I think about it, her father did the same thing.

"Look, Ty is a lot of things, and one happens to be a woman. As a matter of fact, she's the woman who's walking up right now."

Sierra turned and I watched; she didn't say a word, but her body spoke volumes. Her lungs seized and when I looked closer, every hair stood up on her arm. I smiled. I looked over at the blonde and noticed she was watching me as well. I winked at her.

When Ty walked up the steps, she didn't give Sierra a complete once-over; if she did, she would have tripped. "Thanks for the bonus, Ty."

She gave me that million dollar smile and said, "Did you spend it all already?"

I watched Sierra. Ty might have not said a word to her, but everything that was Ty was speaking to a place deep inside of Sierra. Yeah, girl, get all of that Ty goodness.

"Ty, I think buying that company will be good for your bottom line. It's growing fast. Hell, I am glad you let me in on the deal."

Ty had bought a small start-up company, and the reports said it would do a pretty turnover. I figured since my side business was going to go on hiatus, I needed to diversify.

"Good, I see good things happening with that company. Ty, meet my bestie Sierra Brooks. Sierra, this is Ty Howard." The moment Ty's eyes hit Sierra, she was in a trance. I was liking this.

"Nice to meet you, Sierra." I watched their hands touch, and Sierra's eyes dilated. I saw her body react. I saw her mouth open and nothing come out. Then she stood and ran. I mean track star quality running. People stopped dancing and drinking, just to watch her go. I had a million ideas about what would happen when they met, but her running was not one of them.

"You've got to be fucking kidding me," I said under my breath. Ty looked away from the running Sierra, who obviously ran into the bathroom. "Let's give this little bird some time to think." I took a sip of my drink, thinking Sierra was going to make this a late night. I was supposed to be resting;

I planned to fuck the blonde girl until I fell asleep, and hopefully, after I was done, Robert could have a fun night. Looks like that was going on ice. I should text Robert and tell him I was planning to bring home a treat. I thought better of it though, wanting to see his eyes when the blonde walked in.

"So what did you think of Flo Joe, also known as Sierra?"

Ty laughed. "She's beautiful. And when I touched her, I swear an electric shock went through my body. If we can get her out of the bathroom, I think I would like to get to know her."

Good, but I needed to let her in on a secret. "I might have told her a lot about you, but I never mentioned you were a woman."

She gaped at me. "Are you telling me that woman is straight?"

I rolled my eyes. "Look, she just doesn't know she is gay. I figured you could solve that problem. You like a challenge, right?"

Ty rolled her eyes. "Can we get her out of the bathroom first, and then I guess I will help her with her sexuality."

Great, I have to get her out of the bathroom. I have to make sure she doesn't lose her fucking mind and run away from the best thing that could happen to her. My damn job is never done.

"Come on, let's get her out the bathroom." We walked through the crowd to the bathroom. When I passed by the blonde, I whispered in her ear.

"Later tonight, let's have some fun."

She smiled a sexy smile and said, "I would love that."

Ty was waiting by the bathroom door, rolling her eyes. I walked to her. "What, I'm trying to get you some, why would I deny myself?"

Ty chuckled. "Let's get in there." She walked into the bathroom ahead of me.

We walked in as two women were walking out; the last stall was the only one occupied. I stood in front of it, and so did Ty. Before we could say anything, we heard Sierra. "I'm an idiot."

"You aren't an idiot." That was Ty, so damn sweet.

I was about to burst the bubble. "Nope, she's right. She's an idiot."

Ty took a deep breath. "Lisa, the objective is to get Sierra out of the stall, not make her stay in there forever." She was right, I had a man to get to. I also had a blonde that I planned to spank, so I needed to get her out of the damn bathroom.

"You can't be in here." Jesus, this girl is losing her damn mind. Ty was a woman; I mean tonight she was dressed as a man, but I have seen her in a dress and I would fuck her.

Speaking of women I should fuck, I hope ol' girl isn't finding someone new. It would be hard to find a new girl, one that I think Robert and I would both enjoy.

"Technically, the sign on the door said I could be. I assume you're talking about me, so I can. Lisa has explained that you thought I was a man." I rolled my eyes. "I came in to see if you were okay, but if you would like for me to leave, I can."

Damn, Ty was good; she even got her purse. Hell, I forgot that. Then Ty did the best move I had ever seen. "Outside, there's a car and a driver waiting to take you wherever you would like to be. I'm sorry I made you uncomfortable."

Well, I'll be damned, she was going to walk away. Make her come to her. Damn, I never knew she was this good.

Sierra spoke, "Miss Howard, you didn't make me uncomfortable."

But Ty wasn't finished. "I hope you stay. Your dress is beautiful, and I would hate that you wasted all that effort in getting ready just to go home so soon after getting here. If you decide to stay, I will keep my distance."

With a tip of Ty's head, she walked out the door.

"Girl, if you don't get your narrow ass out the stall, I am going to rip your head off."

Sierra didn't open the door, but she did speak, and her voice made me sad. "I don't know what I felt, it just... I don't know. Then I looked like an idiot, and hurt her feelings. Now I don't even know if she's mad or thinks I am some homophobic nut job."

"Look, if you want her to think you are a sane person, come out of the stall and come dancing with me. Don't get in that car without her, girl, you can do this."

The door opened and she walked out, still looking beautiful. "You know whatever you are feeling is okay; we can discuss all of this...after we dance."

We walked out and got on the floor. I spotted Ty at the bar, sitting there drinking alone, in all her power and grace. She was in solitude. A lioness among her pack, but still alone. I looked at Sierra, and her eyes were on her as well.

"She's beautiful isn't she?" I asked her.

She never took her eyes off the girl. "Too beautiful for words, so beautiful she scares me."

"Best friend of mine, remember we don't force nothing, but when life hands you beauty, you take it."

"I can't... Not yet." I looked over to Ty again, she had the bottle in front of her; I looked back at Sierra.

"Then let's dance, maybe if you sway those hips, she will come your way."

She gave me a shy smile, and then she caught the beat. The DJ was playing "Make You Proud." She started to swing her hips to the music. A couple of minutes later the blonde walked up and we danced together. I put my ass all on her pussy, grinding on her.

"Damn, girl, put it on her." We all laughed.

I whispered in the blonde's ear, "What's your name, baby?"

She said, "Evanka." Her eyes were the clearest blue I had ever seen.

I smiled at her, telling her, "I'm Lisa. Who did you come with?"

She whispered in my ear, and my arms went around her. "My friend works here, she invited me to come."

I nodded, then close to her ear I asked, "How would you feel about a threesome tonight?"

She looked over her shoulder to Sierra, who was swaying her hips to the music. I pulled Evanka closer. "Not her, with my man. He's at a hotel around the corner; we can meet him there and have fun tonight."

"How do I know I am going to like him, if I don't know what he looks like?"

She had a good point, but I had an answer for that. "Baby, if he is not your thing, that's cool, it can be just you and I. Tonight you get to explore the best of both worlds."

I licked the spot right under her ear, and she shivered. And I liked that. I looked over at the bar, and Ty was gone. I stopped moving, looked around the room, and she was nowhere to be found.

"Damn it." My harsh words stopped Sierra from dancing.

"What, girl?"

"I think Ty left." Sierra's body stopped moving and looked behind her.

Devastation was written all over her face. "I think I am

going to go." Her voice was small, and I could barely hear it over the music.

"You sure, girl?"

"Yeah, I am sure. I will call you later. Dinner Sunday, right?"

"Yeah, Sunday sounds good." She leaned over and kissed me, then walked away.

Evanka watched the entire exchange, and I noticed the man in the suit was also watching us. I turned my head away from the retreating Sierra and focused on the woman in front of me. "Have you eaten?"

She shook her head, and I led us to the buffet. There wasn't a long wait and she grabbed some finger food. I texted Robert.

"Be there within the hour. Be ready."

A moment later I feel a vibration.

"Ready and waiting, honey."

I smiled down at the phone then looked up at Evanka. "Eat up, baby, there is a long night ahead of you."

Davis...

"What do you mean, she went home with some woman?" Jamison was the man I hired to set my plan in motion for Lisa, I hated incomitance.

It was after midnight, I had to get out of bed with my wife to take this call, and it was pissing me off.

"Sir, I approached her, was about to ask her out, and she said no before I could get two words out. She wasn't interested. I watched her; she was sitting with the friend, the one from the picture."

After Lisa's blatant disrespect, I followed her around the mall, snapping pictures of her and the woman she was with

—the same woman who was on the pictures I received tonight. This country with its woman empowerment, made that bitch think she could tell me no. Then disrespect me in front of my children; she would pay for that. My plan for tonight was to teach her some manners. Not that she would get to use them after tonight, but she didn't take the bait. It seemed the little whore enjoyed pussy. I should have sent a woman as well; I know better for next time.

"Since you failed, go home. I will come up with something myself."

I looked at the photo of the woman she was with...pretty thing. I wouldn't mind playing with her for a while. A plan formed in my mind.

15

EVANKA

Evanka and I left Drama soon after Sierra went home. I told her where we were going so she could tell her friends; I wanted her to have confidence that she would be safe with me. When we got in the cab, she kissed me, and I kissed her back, my hands traveling up her legs finding she wore no panties. "Damn, baby, you are so wet for me."

I pushed inside, and she was wet and tight. Evanka moaned when I touched her G spot. I looked over at the cab driver and saw he was watching in the mirror. I decided to give him a show. Her legs stretched as far as they could with the dress being so tight and the limited space we had. Her pussy gushed with excitement, and I pulled away, hearing her protest. With my eyes to the mirror, I placed my fingers in my mouth. I heard her inhale swiftly, and I heard the driver groan. I felt her hands at my face, and she pulled me in, tasting herself on my tongue.

When we arrived at the hotel, she fixed her dress as I handed over the fare. The cab driver's eyes were blazing. I smiled at him and got out of the car. We walked into the hotel, and I remembered the last hotel I was in, all the luxury. I vaguely wondered if Robert was going to have hives from staying somewhere that didn't have two thousand thread count bed sheets. I smiled to myself as we got in the elevator traveled to the third floor. I'd booked the hotel room earlier that day and had it stocked with everything a night of wild sex should have. I was careful with my drinking; I wanted to be able to think clearly. My mind was on pleasing two people when Evanka walked up to me, putting her mouth on mine.

"What's he like?" she asked as she went down my neck.

"He is tall, dark, and handsome, and knows how to use his dick."

That's all she needed to know about Robert, all she needed to get through tonight. The elevator opened, and we walked out. I quickly pulled the key out of my purse and let us in. There was soft music playing when we walked in. There was only a bed, nightstand, and dresser with a TV on the wall.

Robert was standing in front of the TV, a game on silent when we walked in. His eyes came to the door, and I watched him looking at her. I know what he saw: long blond hair, beautiful breasts, and a slim waist.

"I brought you a present, baby. All she is missing is a bow."

Evanka laughed softly, and Robert's burning eyes came to mine. I took her hand and we walked to him; he wore sleeping pants and nothing else, his defined body on display.

"Robert, meet Evanka. Evanka, Robert.'"

She lifted her hand to meet his, and when they did, he lifted her hand and kissed it softly.

"I only have one rule." Both of their eyes came to me. "No kissing each other on the mouth."

I don't know why I said that, I'd never had that rule before, but his mouth was mine. The way he kissed was more intimate than sex.

They both nodded.

"Any rules, Evanka?"

She looked shy for a moment, so I kissed her cheek. "No need to be shy, baby, whatever your rules are, we will abide by them." I could see her relax.

"No ass play."

"That's fair. Robert, do you have any rules?"

His voice was so filled with lust when he spoke, my pussy got instantly wet. "I just want to watch you fuck her first." His eyes moved to the dresser.

Evanka's breath got stuck; I'd brought my strap on and had it laid on the dresser.

"Have you ever had sex with a strap?" I said while walking over, undressing as I went.

I looked over my shoulder and both of them were standing there watching me as I went. Earlier that morning, I'd picked one that was average size, not knowing who I would be with tonight.

Robert walked behind Evanka and kissed her neck, her eyes fluttering closed. Then his hands drifted down her sides until he reached the hem of her dress, lifting it over her head. She stood before us completely naked as I buckled the strap around my waist.

I walked over to her, my heels clicking on the floor as I went. I touched her softly on the stomach before walking around her, my hand following my movements. Robert stood back allowing me to walk completely around her. Her body was beautiful, not a flaw on it. She couldn't have been over twenty-five, and I wondered if she would remember this night for the rest of her life.

"My goal tonight is for you to remember every feeling you have tonight. I don't want you to forget one second."

When I was face-to-face with her, I noticed that the room had one more thing: a chair, and Robert was sitting in it. His pants now gone, his hard shaft in his hand being stroked. I leaned in and kissed her, making it a show for him, all tongues licking and sucking. I fucked her mouth like I planned to fuck her pussy. Her hands went around my neck, pulling me deeper into her, kissing me so good my eyes closed.

I ended the kiss. "On the bed, little mama." Her hips swayed as she walked the short distance to the bed, and I watched her get there. Her knees going on the bed, I added, "Stay just like that." She stopped moving, her ass in the air, her legs wide and her glistening pussy on display. I squatted behind her, placing my mouth on her clit, moving my tongue around her clit. Hearing her gasp at the sudden attack, I sucked her clit hard, and she moaned. I licked her slit to catch the juices that flowed. I ate her with wild abandonment, my face wet with her arousal. It didn't take long for her to come, screaming her release. I sucked a little longer making sure that she had all she needed. When her body relaxed, I stopped. I looked over to Robert, his face in ecstasy, his shaft hard as he pumped his dick in his hands.

"You better not come," I said to him.

"Wouldn't dream of it, baby," he said while smiling.

I looked back to Evanka; her eyes were on Robert and his hard shaft. With my dick in hand, I quickly guided it inside of her, slamming in. She screamed, and I fucked her ruthlessly. Holding her down by the neck, my shoes giving me the height I needed, I asked, "You like that, don't you?"

She answered screaming, "Yes." Honestly, I was talking to Robert, but I was glad to hear that she was happy as well. She didn't have to tell me she was, the sounds her pussy was making let me know she was about to come again. Sweat trailed down her spine. I saw Robert get up from the corner of my eye. Evanka was screaming, her body began to shake with her climax close. I couldn't deny that mine was close as well. I lifted one leg off the floor, placing my foot on the edge of the bed, going deeper, and that's when her orgasm hit. I rode her hard making sure that I milked every scream from her. Her poor body didn't know what to do. She continued shaking, her screams echoing around the room. When the screams died down, Robert was standing next us.

"That was fucking sexy."

I pulled out of her, dropped in deep squat, and pulled his dick in my mouth. Sucking him, loving his taste. He pumped in my mouth making me deep throat, and I swallowed him making moans come from his mouth. I bounced up and down making sure not to lose his dick in my mouth, deep throating him. I could taste the pre-cum. With my fingers, I unbuckled the strap on, making sure not to drop it on the floor.

I stood knowing he was close, not wanting him to come. "My turn." I walked to the bed, laid on my back, and spread my legs, looking at Evanka wondering if she would take the hint. She did, and soon her mouth was between my legs, sucking on my clit. She wasn't a pro, but the sounds she was making turned me on. "Lick my slit." She did as she was told diving her tongue deep inside. Bobbing up and down, tongue fucking me. I heard the crinkle of the condom wrapper and opened my eyes to see Robert place the condom on his erection.

"My turn, baby girl," he said in a low voice, placing the

head of his dick in her opening. When he pushed into her pussy, Evanka's mouth left my clit and she moaned.

"Don't stop what you are doing to me, no matter what he does to you," I admonished.

Robert's thrusts gave her a nice rhythm, and I held her head to me as he had his way with her.

"Yeah, baby, please us both."

She moaned into me; the vibrations on my clit did amazing things to me.

"You feel that power, baby. Pleasing two people at the same time. You are a goddess, did you know that?"

She shook her head all while sucking my clit, and I moaned. The sound made Robert move faster. I rubbed my pussy in her face feeling my orgasm coming closer. My eyes were on Robert, his were on me. I was so turned on that I came just as she did. Both of us screaming his name.

16

OKAY WILL TAKE A WHILE

I was sitting in the chair at the hospital, headphones in my ears, trying to think of anything but the poison that was dripping into my body. It was Monday and my first treatment of chemo. I thought about last night, Robert had come over after my family left. Janice had Mama and Daddy over, Sierra as well. Mama and Janice cooked together, we looked over old photos of me and Sierra and laughed. Janice hadn't seen most of the photos, and she looked over years of my life with a melancholy.

When they left, Janice was in her room; I walked in after watching her at the door, she didn't even notice me there.

"Hey. You okay?"

She took a deep breath. "I was thinking of all the moments crack stole from you. I should have pictures of you smiling and happy. I don't even have a baby picture of you."

I sat on her bed patting the seat next to me; she came and sat there. I put my hands around her pulling her close. "You know having you here right now is the best thing. I didn't know how much I needed you until you got here. We don't have the past, Ma, but we do have the future. No matter what happens in the next few months, I feel I can depend on you to be there for me."

"I won't let anything keep me away from you. I will be here for you. No matter what."

"Then we have time to fill a photo book with new memories."

She smiled a sad smile and nodded. "Baby girl, I made a hospital bag just in case you need it for tomorrow, and when you get home tomorrow, I will have the room ready for you to go straight to bed if you need to. I also went to the store and got what we would need to make you feel better. I have done some research and found some lollipops to help with nausea. I got as many as I could find."

"Ma, you see, those are things that make this easier. You thinking ahead, you doing sweet things like lollipops makes me know that you love me. I had doubts for years, but I know now that you love me. And I want you to know that I love you."

She pulled me into a hug, and I laid my head on her shoulder taking her strength.

The nurse touched my hand, and I opened my eyes looking at her. "You okay?"

"Sorry, I was just thinking. I'm okay."

"You have someone that wants to sit with you, a Tyanna Howard. You mind if she comes back?"

"I don't mind."

The nurse walked away, and then I saw Ty in all white. She wore a pair of ripped jeans that hung low on her hips and a plain white tee shirt. Her hair hung around her face. I looked around the room and saw eyes on her, but she only had eyes for me.

"Hey, girl, how's it going?"

"Well, you know, just letting a little poison in my body, nothing major."

She gave me a sad smile, and I looked away. I knew that pity was something I would start getting. I hadn't had pity in a long time, and I'd always hated it.

"It's going to be okay. You know that right?"

"Yep. Did you even go into the office?"

I didn't want to talk about things being okay. Okay was a long way away, and I wasn't sure that I would get that far. I didn't want to think how long okay would take. I knew in a few days that I would lose my breasts, most likely my hair, and God knows what else. So I didn't want to think about okay yet.

"I went in early, got some emails out, and made sure that the office was open. You do a lot before I get there. Did you know that?"

"I am well aware of all that I do to make your life easy. I got up this morning and cleared out some of your emails; I couldn't get through them all, but I saved you about an hour."

I usually got to the office at seven in the morning. The office didn't open until nine, but I had coffee brewing and emails sent. Lights on and computers waiting to be used. This was the first time in years on a Monday that I wasn't in the office.

"You have all of these people spoiled. I had ten emails about passwords; people don't even know how to log in to get the computers up and running."

I smiled at her. "I will come in this week and do a quick tutorial on getting ready for the morning. Maybe make a schedule so everyone can have a day." That would give me something to do. I had no idea how chemo was going to do, but I knew sitting down all day wasn't it.

"You don't have to do that. People will figure it out," Ty said while placing her hand on mine.

"Ty, you are paying me a full salary, I know you want to help, but as long as I can work, I will work. Case closed."

She searched my face, then changed subjects. "How was the party after I left?"

"It was fine, I didn't really stay long; I had a threesome with my boyfriend with a girl from the party, it was fun."

She smiled at me. "Damn, girl, most people would be crying two days before chemo, you go and have a threesome."

I'd cried all last week, I was done with the tears. "Hell, I might as well get an orgasm out before I can't."

"You have a point. How was Sierra?"

"Embarrassed. But she was okay, sad that you left. Don't worry, I will come up with a plan."

I took a deep breath; I was getting nauseous. I closed my eyes trying to control the feeling.

"Nurse," I heard Ty saying.

"I'm okay, she gave me a bag. I can use it if I need it. You should get back to the office." My head was starting to spin, and I could feel my stomach doing crazy moves.

"Are you sure you want me to leave?"

I nodded, not wanting her or anyone to see me sick. With understanding she kissed me on the forehead and told me she would call me later.

I didn't watch her leave. I was concentrating on not losing the contents of my stomach.

"Put this under your tongue," the nurse said, and I did as she asked. My head was still swimming, but I didn't feel like I would throw up anymore. I heard someone sit in the chair and opened my eyes, shocked to see Robert.

"Don't worry, Tyanna left. I saw her sitting with you and

waited in the waiting room until I saw her leaving. I waited a while and saw she wasn't coming back, so I came in. Now sit back and relax, I don't want you worried."

I didn't have time to worry because the contents of my stomach were coming up my throat. I grabbed for the little blue bag and purged my morning breakfast. The nurse came and told me that she was adding more nausea medication to my bag.

When the treatment was over, I was sent home with nausea meds. They didn't work; I threw up all night, too weak to even leave the bathroom floor. Robert went out to the drug store and got supplies. In those supplies was a bed pan, and I cried silently when I saw it. Knowing deep down I would need it.

Deep down I knew this cancer wasn't going to go away easily. I was going to have to fight with all I had, I just hoped it was enough.

17

GYM SOCK

Alesia has been the hospital for over two weeks; every time they fix one thing, something else goes wrong, and I was a mess. I haven't slept in days and have to force myself to take a shower. I am beyond worried; we are only two chemo treatments in, and this is not going as planned. I knew it would be hard, I knew that there would be hard days, I just didn't think they would come this fast. Yesterday she had her breasts removed. She went in like a soldier; she broke down after the surgery. She asked me to leave, so I left, and she screamed so loudly when I was gone that it took all I had not to go back in there and hold her. She had to deal with that loss alone. I think because we are together, she will see herself differently.

I just want her, we can buy breasts later; I will do whatever she needs, even if it means breaking my own heart. It was in that moment I stopped walking and realized that I loved her. I loved every piece of her, especially the broken pieces. I needed to sign contracts and make a few calls in order to get back to her.

I walked into my home office. I didn't want to talk to

anyone, didn't give a damn about the money that I was missing. I just wanted to get back to my baby. I knew this morning was another day of chemo, and she would be sick. Last night before I left the hospital, she was doing better. She was able to walk a little and was in the bathroom. She seemed to be there a while and I wanted to make sure she was okay. When I knocked on the door and walked in, she was standing at the vanity staring in the mirror, running her hands through her hair, and it was coming out in clumps.

I walked in and watched her shed silent tears as the hair was piled in the sink. She only had a small patch in the back, and it seemed if she touched that it would fall as well. "Baby," I said softly, my sadness for what she was going through rang through the air.

"I knew it would happen, I thought I was prepared, but I wasn't. Today was a good day, I kept down jello. I thought it was turning around, maybe my body was getting use to the poison." She put her hand at the back of her head and the last patch began to fall. "I guess not."

I pulled her to me, turning her into my arms. She came willingly, her body smaller each time I held her. She spoke in my ear, "I want to ask you something."

"You can ask me anything."

She pulled away and looked me in my eyes. 'While everyone went to the cafeteria, the hospital counselor came in and asked me about my power of attorney, if I was ever unable to make my medical decisions. I put your name down. I should have talked to you first, I know I should have, but I made the decision." She placed her hands on the side of my face. Looking deep into my eyes, she added, "I don't want my family to fight after."

"There won't be an after of anything, you are going to

beat this." My heart was beating so fast with the thought of losing her.

"All good strategies have room for if something goes wrong. This is mine. If something happens, if the treatment doesn't work, I want you to give me a few days to come back, but after a few days, let me go. They won't let me go, but I know if I ask this of you, you will let me go, even if it hurts because you will do anything for me."

I couldn't hold back the single tear that ran down my face, splashing on her hands. She leaned in kissing my face. "Before all of this, I got my affairs in order; I made you executor of my estate."

"I don't want to talk about you leaving me, I want to talk about you fighting to stay with me, to stay with us all."

"I plan to stay, this is just my contingency plan. I know this is a lot to ask, and I know we just met, but I trust you with everything."

I held her eyes, loving the fact that she trusted me, and hating the fact that I would make those decisions. I hope it never comes to that, but if it came to that I would do what was best for her.

"I will do what's best, my baby. Just know you can't leave me no matter what. I like having you around."

"I plan to be around." She kissed me softly, and I savored the moment.

I was sitting behind my desk thinking about last night. When the phone rang, I looked down at the phone and saw it was my Vice President.

"Good morning," was my greeting. I liked John, he was good at his job, and when I asked him to step up and take some of my workload, he was all over it.

"Morning, I have hit a snag in the contracts with Preston Morgan."

I didn't like Preston at all, he was a judgmental prick. "What's the snag?"

"He claims that he was reluctant to do business with a man with several..." He paused and it was a long pause.

"Spit it out, John."

"He doesn't want to do business with a man with several bastard children."

Did he just call my children bastards? I could feel my temper rising.

"He also said he talked to your daughter's mother and she told him some of your perversions in a private setting."

Trina was playing with me, and I was about to lose business because she was in my business. Fine, I could show her better than I could tell her.

"End the contract with Preston, don't worry about it; I know several investors that would like the opportunity. I will reach out to them. As far as my daughter's mother, I will handle that now."

"I would appreciate that. How is your girlfriend? I put her on the prayer list at my church."

"That was kind of you; she is doing okay. Chemo is no joke."

"I can imagine, well, I will ring off. Thanks for the opportunity to show you all that I can do."

"You are doing a good job; have a good day."

I ended the call and called Johnathan, the phone rang twice, and he picked up.

"What's up, Pop?"

"How long was the non-disclosure agreement for Trina and I?"

I heard him take a deep breath in. "What has she done now?"

"She has been discussing what I do in my private time,

that's all that I know, and I only know of one person she has told, but once he found out, he ended a contract. I can't have that, I will figure out what to do silence him, but I have to deal with Trina first."

"The paperwork for the non-disclosure is for fifty years after the date, it also says that she has to pay you a million dollars within thirty days and that's per incident. She doesn't personally have that much money, and what she does have, more than likely my sister gave to her."

"I'm adding Jaxson to the call, give me a second." I clicked over and called Jaxson.

I could hear the sleep in his voice. "Damn, it's early, Dad."

"I have Johnathan on the line, we have a Trina issue that needs to be addressed."

I heard Jaxson move and Johnathan on the computer. Jaxson said, "I have the live feed to her house, and her personal accounts. What am I looking for?"

That was my boy, he could find what I needed in a second. "I need to know if she has been talking to any associates of mine. I need to know what she has told them, and how much damage control I need to do. I would also like dirt on everyone that she has spoken to. I need leverage, I also need her broke, destitute; I don't want her to be able to buy a piece of gum without me knowing." Jaxson and Johnathan were silent. "Am I understood?"

In unison they said, "Understood."

I hung up the phone. I had other things to worry about, I was not losing money because Trina decided to run her mouth. She thought she could ruin me, but I would destroy her. I needed to find an investor, and then I thought about it; I could do it myself. I would reap the benefits alone. I was going through my emails when the phone rang with Trina.

That didn't take long; Jaxson was efficient.

"What do you want?"

"Put the money back," she said with a hatred.

I opened an email from Jaxson with seven names on it. All men that I had done business with, along with a considerable amount of dirt on them. I opened the file about Preston. Good ol' Preston might not like that I had baby mamas, but he didn't have an issue with underage girls. He liked to frequent a club in Japan that served up girls as young as twelve.

"Years ago, you signed a non-disclosure agreement. It is still in effect, my dear, so that's my money." I looked in my account and there was only three million. "And it looks like you still owe me."

"You put me in this position," she yelled.

"You put yourself here, not being able to accept our child put you here as well. You don't get to fuck me unless I let you. You should know that. When I am done with you, you won't be able to have shit. I told you if you crossed me, I would put you back where I found your ass. I meant what I said." She was breathing hard, and I could imagine the look on her face. "There won't be a rock for you to hide under. I know all the men that you have talked to about me, I know the money that you charged for information, and they will pay as well. No one will listen to a word you have to say when I am done."

"Robert, what will Ty think about what you are doing to me?"

"I have no issue telling her about what you have done to me. She won't give a damn."

"But she will care that you are fucking that little cancer patient."

How did she know about that?

"You never learn, Trina, not once in all the time that I have known you have you learned a damn thing. There are men out there that don't mind having my leftovers, and I have let them. The issue is they see you are nothing too and cast your ass aside. You will never be Alesia. I would have been done with you years ago if it wasn't for our daughter. You say one word about my relationship and they won't find you ever."

Her breaths were shallow. "You won't kill me," she said.

"Baby, I won't even pay someone; I will do it myself. I will look you in the eye and squeeze the fucking life out of you. Cross Alesia and you will be shit under my feet."

"Robert, I have nothing, you wouldn't leave me with nothing; you loved me at one time."

"Bitch, I never loved you. I have never bared my soul to you, have never even told you about my damn day. I fucked you. I think of you no different than a gym sock I used as a teenager. I gave you time to get your shit together, and in that time you found it necessary to try and fuck me. I don't feel sorry for your ass, but if you cross me, you won't live past that."

I hung up the phone, pissed off, and called Jaxson. When he picked up the phone, I said, "Destroy her, leave her nowhere to run, and everyone that she talks to, make sure that they learn a lesson in crossing me that they never forget."

"With pleasure." And then he hung up.

I closed down my office, seeing that I was there longer than I'd needed to be, thinking I wish I would have told Tyanna weeks ago about Alesia and me, but now wasn't the time. We had to get through cancer first, and then I could give Alesia the life she deserved.

18

NINE MONTHS, TWO DAYS, AND THREE HOURS LATER

I stood in the mirror looking at myself, something that I had avoided for the last few months. I saw the changes on the outside: my hair was gone, and the forty pounds that I had lost was evident in every part of my body. I didn't have breasts, just a long wide scar where they used to be. But I could stand and I could breathe, and I didn't care one bit that I had lost so much coming into this fight. I had my life and just this morning, I rang the bell saying cancer was over.

Now it was time to pick up the pieces. I didn't get to go back into the office; my body had a horrible reaction to the chemo, and I nearly died once. Through it all, my family stood by my side. Janice was taking each day with me, all while working. I didn't know when she slept, because she was either with me or behind the desk at the hotel. She had lost some weight as well, not from drugs, but from worry. She and Robert spent many nights at my bedside taking care of me.

I touched the scars where my breasts had been, missing them, but knowing that if they stayed, I would have died. I didn't have a lot of energy in the last few months, so I didn't have time to grieve losing so much, but I stood there and finally let my emotions come forward. There was a time I saw myself as beautiful, now I wasn't so sure. I was a warrior, no doubt the doctors had given up once because I was in a coma and they didn't think I would wake, but I did, all of my parents at my side. I couldn't die; no, I wouldn't die.

I thought I was dreaming when I saw my grandmother come to me, asking me to come with her. I refused and she stayed with me for hours. I know now it was days, days of uncertainty for the people that loved me. When I woke, I fought harder, not willing to leave this earth until I had to. My mother needed that photo book, and she wasn't going to only have memories of me sick.

I looked down at my clothes on the floor; in the pile was a rubber bra, the breasts inside the same color as I was. I heard the bedroom door close and I looked to the man that had stood with me through it all. Robert.

"You feel okay?" In the last few months, I'd hid my body from him, having my mother help me bathe even though he said he would do it. I couldn't bear him seeing me like this. I leaned against the vanity, allowing him to see me in full. My body was on display, and he looked at me lingering on where my breasts used to be.

"Nope, I'm not okay. I was thinking of the battle, the scars, the loss. I want to say something to you. I know you stood by me, held me up when I couldn't stand, but I am free. If you want to leave me, you can. This body isn't what you signed up for."

He jerked his head back when I spoke about my body. "You think so little of me?" he whispered. I went to speak, but he cut me off. "For many days I sat beside you, listening for your breathing, not knowing if it would be the last moments I would have you. I told you, you were mine. We haven't had time to discuss the future because we didn't know if you would even have one. I don't give a damn about the scars; if it bothers you, I will find a plastic surgeon. The weight will come back. Hell, you wore wigs when you didn't have to before cancer. I don't give a damn if you walk out the house bald, because you are walking. Damn it, Alesia, I love you. Not for your body, because of your soul. You couldn't pay me to walk away now, and I won't let you push me away."

Tears flowed down my face. "I don't know how to do this, how to be who I used to be. I was beautiful before I know I've survived, but a part of me didn't."

He walked to me and placed his hands on my face. "Alesia, you are beautiful." He said this fiercely. "Baby, all the parts that matter, all the things I loved before, survived. I don't need breasts, I need you."

I laid in his arms holding him tight. "I wanted to give you a way out," I said into his chest.

"Baby, I am searching for a way in. Let me love you. Let yourself be loved. I know this is hard. I know your mom left before, but I won't leave. She and I talked a lot in those hospital walls. She has a lot of regrets, baby, and she wants to make it right. I know that the trauma of losing her makes it hard for you to accept that a person won't leave. I have never asked a woman to marry me, but I want to ask you. First, we have to be truthful with Tyanna.

In all these months, I hadn't had it in me to tell her about me and her dad. At first out of fear she would be upset with me, and then I was worried about losing a friend when I could have been losing my life. The business of living was the most important thing for me. Now I had to tell her. I just didn't know how.

"You want to get married? I have never wanted to do that."

He looked down at me. "You never wanted to be married, not even to a billionaire?"

"Nope, but I wanted to be a millionaire. I was close. I have to start over now, work a little longer."

"Have you checked your account?" I shook my head. I called Alexander often to ask how the hospital bills were effecting my account. He just told me insurance was doing its job. So I left it at that. I pulled out of his arms and walked into my bedroom. Finding my phone charging on the nightstand, I picked it up, opened my bank account—something I haven't done in months—

and had to sit down.

My account held three million nine hundred thousand dollars and change.

"What the hell did you do?"

He walked over to me, took my phone out of my hands, and a put it back on the nightstand.

"I asked Alexander how much you brought in a month, doubled it, and told him to send you an allowance to pay the hospital bills. I found out yesterday at the Bell party that Tyanna paid all of your hospital bills herself. Alex is writing it off on her taxes in some type of loophole so it works out for her."

I reached for my phone, found Ty's number, and called her. When she answered, I tried to sound angry, but my voice cracked. "Did you pay all of my hospital bills?"

"Nope, Howard Charity did, and I didn't want you to know about it. Let's never speak of it again, and I will see you back at work in a month."

She then hung up the phone. I looked down at it, thinking, "Holy hell, I can't believe she did that." I couldn't believe

Robert either. I looked at him. I was about to speak when Robert beat me to it.

"You mean the world to my daughter, you mean more to me. I can live without marrying you if you want. I can't live without you. I faced that possibility and it didn't feel all that great. I lost more nights' sleep than I care to count, just hoping you would pull through. You don't want to be married, fine, will you be my partner in life is the question?"

His partner in life, I liked the sound of that, but I still had reservations. "Let me wait on my answer until we talk to Ty. Then I will give you my answer."

"Fine, I will wait. Do you know how many women would love to be my wife?"

"I can guess about five, maybe six if you count the chick at the country club."

He chuckled when I said chick. "You know you make a man feel ten feet tall," he said sarcastically.

"Your ego will be fine."

"Oh, my dear, you have no idea how you wound my ego."

I smiled at him. "You know if I wasn't this woman, you wouldn't want me. If you just wanted a wife in all these years, you could have had any woman you wanted. You didn't want an easy woman, you wanted one that would make you work for it."

He nodded his agreement. "I need my head examined. You are going to make me sweat, aren't you?"

"Not at all, I don't want to be married. I don't see anything that marrying you offers me that I don't already have."

He smirked. "Baby, if you think what I do for you now is a big deal, you should see what I would do for my wife."

I rolled my eyes. "Unless you are taking the three million

out of my account, I am good for life. I don't see what more money would do for me that I can't do for myself."

He crawled to the end of the bed; when he got there, he put my foot in his lap and started to massage it. "My wife would have access to all of my money, she would have access to all my resorts, she would have access to me at all times."

"Do I not have that now? Can I not tell you where I want to be and you would make that happen? We have covered that I don't need your money, and news flash my darling, here you are in front of me. I have all the access that I need, sir. A ring won't make that more."

"Fine, Alesia, we don't have to get married."

"I mean you would be the lucky one if you married me."

"Oh would I now, and how do you figure that?"

"You could brag to all your friends that you found a woman that loves sex so much that she invites others in. And I only deal in high end clients, and many of them know that I am the best in bed in all of Denver. You would look like a stud at the ripe old age of fifty-six."

"You don't say," he said with a laugh, and then he squeezed the instep of my foot, and my eyes rolled back it felt so good.

"Plus"

"Oh, so there is more?"

"There's a long list, I could go on for hours, but I will leave you with this. Until your dying day, you would never know what or whom will be in our bed. You won't have to worry about ever getting bored with me."

He pushed my legs apart, I still laid nude, and as he came up to me, his eyes heated. The last time he and I had made love was eight months ago; it didn't go well. The motion made an okay day really bad at the end. I couldn't deny that I was a little nervous, but I had a question.

"When was the last time you were intimate with anyone?"

"Alesia, when in the hell did I have time to fuck someone? I was either working, and a lot of that was done in hospital waiting rooms, or I was with you. Honestly, I don't even remember the last time I jacked off to relieve some pressure."

"I was just asking; I don't want you to think I am upset or would be unhappy that you did. I had intentions of calling in a favor to take care of you when I couldn't."

"I don't want anyone but you."

I rolled my eyes.

"Alesia." His fingers were suddenly under my chin. "Look at me." I turned my eyes to his. "I don't want any other woman but you. The nights that I got to lay beside you were better than any sexual encounter I have ever had. Because there were times when I thought that would never happen again. I don't want another woman. Yes, threesomes are fun, and watching you while we play is sexy as hell. But, baby, lying next to you, hearing you breathe easy, watching your body relax next to mine—that is better than anything that sex could bring me."

His voice was so sincere that I couldn't hold back the tears. I leaned in and kissed him ever so sweetly. I wanted to breathe him in, wanted all of his essence inside of me. I pulled him closer, taking his pants down with my hands; he helped me.

"We don't have to make love, baby," he said with his mouth still on mine.

"Yeah we do, I think I can do this. I want you so bad. I have for a long time." There were times when I wanted him so bad I would ache, but I didn't have the strength to do it. I wasn't up to full strength by any stretch of the imagination, but I could do this not only for him, but for me.

When he slid into me, I moaned from missing the feel of him. He took his time, his eyes never leaving mine.

"You were so good to me, baby," I told him. "I couldn't leave this world and leave you in it." His stroke went deeper inside of me as my back arched. "I'm afraid of forever, baby. Forevers have never turned out that way."

His mouth hovered over mine. "We can take this day by day as long as you are by my side."

He kissed me, and I kissed him back holding him to my body with my arms and legs. "I can be at your side for a lifetime." And I could, I could hold him close like this forever.

"Say it again, say that you will be by my side for a lifetime."

He went faster, my orgasm coming to me, a feeling I hadn't had in such a long time. "A lifetime, baby. Just you and me."

"You and me, baby. I'm close, I think you are too. Come for me, baby. Let me have what I have been missing."

At his words I grind against him and find my release, He then rode me hard and found his own. I was tired, but I was sated. After a moment, he got up and went to the bathroom. He came back with a warm wash cloth and washed his arousal away from me. I wanted to keep him close, he was gone for only a moment, but it felt like a lifetime. He came back and got under the covers with me.

"No more life-threatening scares, baby."

I snuggled into him. "No more scares, baby. Just you and me."

He kissed the side of my head and sleep came to me. I welcomed it, lying in the arms of the man I loved.

19

HAPPINESS

I woke to Robert on the phone. "Yes, we can be there at nine in the morning. No issue with that. And the procedure could be done the same day as long as I have the okay from her doctor?"

What the hell was he talking about? I sat up to the sound of his voice.

"Great, I will have her doctors send you the okay in a moment. Thank you for seeing her in such short notice." He paused. "Thank you, see you soon."

He hung up the phone. "Good morning."

"Yeah, all of that. What was that call about?"

He leaned in and kissed me. He was up early; I looked at the clock and saw that it was after eleven in the day. Okay, maybe he wasn't up early; I was just up late.

"I was thinking about last night." Oh yeah, last night was great. "You are not happy with your body right now. The weight will come back, your mama's cooking will do that, but I can fix your confidence with your breasts." Without thinking, my hands went to cover my scars. "See, it's that you are mine, and I don't give a damn about your breasts being gone, but you do."

I mean I did. "So you have a solution for that?"

He came and sat on my side of the bed. "I would like you to see my plastic surgeon."

"You have a plastic surgeon?"

He looked up at the ceiling. "Okay, look, full disclosure. I have dated women that needed work done, and I paid for them to have it done. I liked this doctor, and we went into business. I turned one of his clinics into a resort, like the rest of my hotels. It's smaller, of course, but everything is top of the line. It's a good living."

"So you called them this morning?"

"Yes. And we have an appointment tomorrow. Since you just had labs done, he will take those labs and do the procedure tomorrow afternoon. You will have breasts by the time you go back to work."

"No more plastic titties?"

"Nope, all we have to do is get on the plane."

I jumped out of bed, ran to my closet to pack, and saw there was a bag already ready.

"Your mother packed for you. All you need is a shower."

I ran to him, swiftly kissed him on the lips, and took my shower.

DR. SHARI WAS AMAZING; he took one look at me and told me he would fix it all. I was a little skeptical about it, but I went with it. After the surgery I was wrapped like a burrito, but even through the wrap I could see I had breasts. It hurt like a bitch, but I burst into tears. Robert pulled back the curtain, took one look at me, and called for a nurse.

"Happy tears, baby, happy tears," I said through a sob.

He looked at me and gave me a small smile. "Good, but the nurse wanted me to call her when you woke."

The nurse came in and asked me about my pain. Since I'd just experienced cancer, it was minimal, but she still gave me pain meds. I was drowsy but happy.

"Baby, I can't wait to bounce these titties in your face!" I yelled to Robert, and he laughed.

"Keep your voice down, crazy girl."

"I don't have nipples, but who gives a fuck, I GOT TITTIES!"

The nurse came in. "I see she is feeling better."

"I feel great, and the best thing is, I GOT TITTIES. BIG TITTIES AND NO FAKE TITTIE BRA FOR ME."

She smiled at me. "After all you have been through, I am glad you are happy, but you need to rest, honey."

"I need to go to go the club, I need a tube top and heels. Take these babies on a test drive."

Robert burst out laughing and the nurse smiled at me. "Maybe next week, but this week you need to rest."

"K, I will rest, but I want a tube top, Robert, a bright one with shoes. Ma'am, do you know when the last time was that I bought shoes? It should be criminal."

Robert rubbed my legs. "We can buy shoes as soon as the doctor says you can go out."

"Oh great, I need shoes, and a tube top, and new bras. I burned the old ones."

I did, in a fit of rage I threw all my bras in the fireplace; it was soon after my breasts were taken off.

The nurse gave me a sympathetic look. "No sympathy, girl, I got my life, and I got titties, so life is good."

She smiled at me. "Yeah life is good. We can move you to the suite if you'd like."

"Why the hell not." I was happy. I was alive and if she wanted me to go to a suite, damn it, I would go to the suite.

20

WATCH ME WORK

I was three weeks past post op with the breast implants, and I was finally going out. Robert was taking me to this club; he didn't tell me which one and I didn't give a damn. I hadn't been out since Drama Club, and I was ready to dance. I wore a red and black corset dress, and I was sexy. My new breasts were amazing, I even had tattooed nipples. I was in Robert's house, it was my first time being there, and baby, let me tell you, it was something to behold.

It sat at the foot of the mountains, and it was huge. It made Ty's house look like a baby mansion. And she was on a half an acre. Robert's house was on four acres. I'd asked him. It had twenty-two bedrooms, and when we walked in, the foyer was so big there was an echo when I said, "Wow." That wasn't all—the kitchen was as big as half of my house.

I was greeted by servants, I mean real ones in black and white dresses and suits, and they were all working around the house. It was surreal. Ty had a housekeeper, seeing this made me wonder what I was thinking when I'd said no.

We were standing in the foyer when I looked up at him.

"You should have brought me here when you asked me to marry you; this would have been a very good incentive."

"You're right, but in my defense, I thought my money didn't move you."

I looked at him. "Baby, this house is impressive. I want a tour."

He took me on a tour: there was a library, a study, movie theater, and bowling alley. The gardens were awe inspiring, and I just stood there with my mouth open. "Should have asked right here. Right in this garden with lights twinkling, and I would have said yes. I would have regretted it the next day, but I wouldn't have left you at the altar."

He laughed. "I have places way more beautiful than this; I could really impress you."

I shook my head. "I don't need to really understand how rich you are, I need to live in denial, I need to focus. We are going out tonight. I need to get ready. Where are my bags?"

"I'm sure one of the staff took it to my room; we can go get it, and I can show you the rest of the house."

And the rest of the house was more than I could ever think about having. My dream was to stay in my own home until the day I die, but I could get used to staying in a home like this. I could stay in a tent if I got to sleep next to Robert, but I wasn't going to tell him that.

When he walked me into his bedroom, it had two large doors; he opened both doors, and the room was elegant and sexy. Royal blue and silver were the main colors, and the bed was by far the largest bed I had ever seen. We could have five, maybe six people in that bed. "Why is your bed so big?"

"When the kids were younger, we would all pile in bed and watch a show; they still come by and get in my bed. I upgrade the bed, every few years, but I keep the size."

There was no TV in sight. "Where is the TV?"

He walked into the room ahead of me and went to what I assumed was his side of the bed, opened a drawer, and hit a button or two. A large screen came out of the ceiling, and I watched it move. "Well, I'll be damned."

He pushed the button, and the TV went back up and you couldn't see it. I looked around the room and saw there was another door, one that was closed to the left, and another door to the right of the bed that was open. I walked to it and saw it was the bathroom. Not just a bathroom, but a luxury bathroom. Extra-large claw foot tub and walk-in shower that could hold seven people; behind door number one was a closet, and it held suits and casual clothing. Then there was another closet that had clothing inside. Women's clothing. Shoes of all kinds, purses, and in the middle was an island. I walked to the island and pulled out a drawer and there were jewels, rubies and diamonds. Sapphire necklaces and earrings. "Lift the top." His voice caused me to jump; I looked at him watching me and did as he told me.

There were ten rings, one more beautiful than the next. Some even yellow diamonds. My legs felt weak. "This is your closet, there is everything you could need in here to be ready so I can show you off. More importantly, those rings are engagement rings—pick one, or pick them all, I don't care—but when you are ready to commit to me, put one on. I hand-picked each one of them. One for every month you should have been my wife. I can give you the world, my love, I just want you to give me you; I will handle you with so much care."

As he spoke tears streamed down my face. I looked around the closet and took in the beauty of it all. Hermès bags and Louis Vuitton: all sizes and colors, some classic, some eccentric, all beautiful.

"There was so little hope when you were in the hospital, so I dreamed for us both. I dreamed of you wearing those clothes, those bags, my ring on your finger. Sometimes when you were asleep, I would shop. In shops all over the world finding beautiful things just for you. I dreamed of your wearing them, I wanted you to come home to beauty. I dreamed of you coming home to me."

"Stop talking." He did as I asked. Watching me.

I walked around the closet, looking through his dreams of us. It was beautiful.

"When I was a little girl, I had dreams of coming home to beauty. I have long forgotten those dreams. My mother left me with Mama and Daddy, leaving me nothing but a box with my belongings. Not really much. She didn't even say goodbye. For years I was afraid to come home and find that I would have to leave. I dreamed of having a home, one that was all mine. I even dreamed of the man that would love me in it. Years of the wrong men made me forget that dream. As you were talking, I remembered."

I turned to look at him. "I remembered wanting a man that thought of me, that saw all of my flaws and loved me anyway. One that didn't see my past and run. One that didn't know my mother and assume I would be just like her. I dreamed of you. I didn't know your name, or what you would look like, but I knew there was a man in this world just for me. I don't care about the house, or the jewels. I care about you. We could live in a shack on the side of the road, and I would happy as long as I was with you." He came to me, wrapped his arms around me. "I want to put on that ring, I want this dream to be real, but I have to tell Ty. I have to let her know that this is real. Then she has to give her blessing."

He looked me in the eyes. "Then we need to tell her, so

both of our dreams will come true." I nodded, and he kissed me. "Get ready, baby, I want you to see the club." He walked to the door and looked back to me with a smile on his face. "And, baby, I would do a lot of things to keep us out of a shack on the side of the road," he said with a smile, and I laughed pushing him out of the closet.

He walked out then, leaving me to find something to wear. I had fun looking through it all, even the bright colored tube tops that made me laugh. I picked the corset dress; it was tight, it was short, and it made my breasts look amazing.

You would think I wouldn't care about breasts, but honestly, I had a newfound appreciation for them after losing them. Robert came out of the bathroom in all black. Black suit, black shirt and tie. "Damn, you look good." He got closer, and I could smell his cologne; he smelled like money.

"The car should be out front; are you ready?"

I was ready. Ready to say fuck the club and bounce on my man's dick.

"I know that look, hold it 'til later, I really want to take you out tonight."

I grabbed a small Gucci clutch and walked to the door. "You know if we ever got stuck in the house, you could run it as exercise."

"Or we could go to the gym in the basement."

He just took all the fun out of it. I stuck my tongue out at him.

"You crazy girl," Robert teased.

I walked down the stairs and made sure to put an extra swing in my hips. There was a man passing at the end of the stairs, and he stopped his journey and opened the door for us. "Have a good night, sir and ma'am."

"Thank you, Alfred."

The door closed behind us, and I turned to him.

"That is not his name." Robert smiled and looked at me. "You hired him just because his name was Alfred, didn't you?"

"No, I hired him because he does good work, not for his name."

"I would have hired him for his name."

He chuckled as we got in the car.

"So where are we going?"

His phone vibrated, and he pulled it out of his jacket pocket. He spoke as he sent a message. "It's a private club, a friend owns it. There are different sections, places to dance or eat. I think you will enjoy it."

He was hitting buttons and I left him to it, enjoying the ride. My mind drifted to Sierra. I hadn't heard from her since the ringing of the bell. She hadn't been to the house in a long while. In fact, since the day before my first chemo session. I pulled my phone out of my purse and went to our last text messages; it had been weeks. I had tried to call her, but only got voicemail. In the last few months, I had been so concerned about cancer, I'd let Sierra fall through the cracks. But that didn't explain why I hadn't seen or heard from her.

I turned to Robert. "Did Sierra come to the hospital while I was sick? Maybe when I don't remember?"

"She came once while you were unconscious; she called Janice a few times, but I really didn't see her often."

I could have been angry, but cancer was intense, maybe it was too much for her. I didn't say that out loud, I just sent her a text message.

. . .

Hey girl, I am doing much better, and we will discuss what is wrong with you very soon. So get ready to talk.

I hit send and put the phone back in my purse. "As of Monday, I am back on my Ty/Sierra matchmaking I am a little rusty, so I will give myself a week. With work and getting back in the swing of things, I will need to pace myself. Can't drain myself. Got to come home and do my man and all."

He gave me a wicked smile.

"But I think I have a plan, one that by this time next week, Sierra and Ty will be on the road to getting together. Then I can tell her. She will be so in love with Sierra, she will want that for us as well."

"I'm glad you have a plan, baby. We are almost at the club."

We were almost nowhere; I had traveled this road to get to Aspen, and there wasn't much to see out here. I had never seen a club. "Did he build it while I was sick?"

Robert took his eyes off the screen and said to me, "No, it's been there for years."

"Is it invisible, because I have been out here a lot and have never seen it."

He smiled at me. "It's not meant to be seen, but it's there, don't worry."

A club that is not meant to be seen, what the hell did that mean?

I heard the blinker of the car and saw there was a road, one that I had assumed went to some ranch. We turned and drove about a mile from the main road, and I saw a house of all stone, the lights around it looked like torches, and there were cars everywhere. We pulled to the front of the home, and our door was opened. Robert got out and reached a hand back to help me out. The first thing my feet touched was a stone walkway. I was worried about tripping in my heels, but Robert held my hand and guided us inside. Two men were in the very inside and asked that we leave our phones in a lockbox. Robert pulled his phone from his pocket, and I followed him, finding my phone in my purse.

When the phones were away and a small key was given to Robert, the man asked, "Would you like to dine first, sir?"

Robert turned to me and asked, "Are you hungry?"

I didn't know what I was other than nervous, but I nodded. Robert and I were led to two huge double doors, two large men flanking both sides. I could hear faint music in the background, but then the doors opened and it took a moment to process what I was seeing.

Naked women were doing acrobatics from the ceiling. Three of them in loops that reminded me of hula hoops, and they were hanging upside down going in circles. There were several other women hanging from what looked like very long bedsheets, naked as well, dancing, climbing up, and falling down gracefully.

Robert leaned into me. "Welcome to the Circus, baby."

As we walked further into the room, I noticed it was dark; the only lights were from the candles on the tables and red lights along the wall, giving the room a forbidden ambience. A woman led us to a table, and I noticed that I was overdressed; most of the people there were almost nude, some were very naked. As we made it to the center of the room, I noticed TV screens and on them were people, all naked, some performing sexual acts. I almost ran into our hostess just looking at the screen.

Robert helped me to my seat, and we were handed two menus. I put mine on the table and looked again at the screen. On the bottom there were words; I looked closer and saw on the video it said "The Lion's Den." On the screen there were several people having sex, one woman had three men at once, and I couldn't take my eyes away.

Out of nowhere, I heard a voice and looked up to a beautiful woman with curly black hair, only wearing a pair of panties. "My name is Jenna, I will be your server." She placed two glasses of water in front of us. I took my glass as soon as it was set down and took a very unladylike swig.

She looked down at me, smiled, and said, "First time here?"

I nodded.

"I would recommend the chef's special tonight. Braised lamb, herb rice, and sweet potato purée."

That sounded great, a naked woman was giving me recommendations on dinner while I watched the screens with essentially orgies playing.

Robert spoke, "We will have that. Along with red wine."

She quickly picked up our menus and sashayed away.

I finally spoke directly to Robert, "You know I have done all types of things, I have been watching people have sex for years, but I have never seen anything like this."

He leaned in. "Would you like to leave?"

"Hell no, I want to know what porn channel that's on so I can watch at home."

He laughed softly. "Those are live feeds from inside of each room; those are the things that are happening now."

My eyes whipped back to the screens and I saw a new couple fucking doggie style. I looked back to Robert. "Are we going in those rooms? I thought we were dancing tonight?"

He pointed to a screen I hadn't seen mostly because it was darker than the rest. It looked to be a club; I could see a

DJ with headphones on spinning, and people with and without clothing dancing.

Robert picked up his glass as I looked back to him, and he spoke to me, "We can just dance if you like, or we can walk the rooms and watch." He took a sip of water, then added, "Or we can participate."

I was too overwhelmed before to acknowledge I was turned on but the way he said, "participate" made my clit jump. I took another sip of water.

Robert gave me a wicked grin and then turned to the screen.

"Alesia." He said my name and I turned to him. "I love you very much. We can do whatever you are comfortable with. I don't mind you fucking another man as long as I am there. But no names, no identity of who you are. This is fun, this is a safe place to play. If you are not feeling something, just say no and walk away. I won't leave you for any reason."

When he was done, our wines were delivered, and we sat watching the screens.

OUR DINNER WAS HEAVENLY, and we were now heading to the Lion's Den. We walked down a hall and there were several doors and several people walking in all stages of dress. Some completely naked, others in suits like Robert. The Lion's Den was almost at the end of the long hall, and when we opened the door, there was soft music as well as moans and screams of the occupants.

We walked around the room, but I stopped because my eyes were fixed on a woman pleasing two men with her mouth. Both men had large dicks and she was having no problem pleasing them. Robert pulled me into his front and leaned down into my ear. "Is that what you want, baby, to suck me and another man off?" I squeezed my thighs and shook my head no.

"I want to suck you off while everyone watches. I want you to know you are getting the best head in the room."

I could feel his dick against my ass, and I pushed up against him. "Are you taking your clothes off, or do you want just your skirt up?" I wasn't ready to show my body off yet. I was still underweight, and I liked the new titties, but I wasn't ready to show them off just yet.

"Skirt up. I don't have any panties on." I was hoping after a night of dancing, I would ride him on the way home, so I'd ditched the panties.

"Get on your knees, baby." A thrill shot through me and I did as I was told, unbuckling his pants and finding he too didn't have on boxers. He was rock hard, and a bead of pre-cum was weeping from his penis. I licked it and felt his body shudder. I then began to suck him in earnest, my eyes on him as I did. I deep throated him and he put his hands on top of my head. Moving my head to the rhythm he wanted. I could feel eyes on me and that turned me on so damn much. My hand was wet from pumping his dick, but I had to touch myself. With one hand I pumped his dick as I sucked, with the other I played in my pussy. Vaguely I noticed feet around us, that only pushed me further, making me suck harder, move faster.

Suddenly I was up, turned around with face against the wall, my skirt pulled up, and then Robert filled me to the hilt with his dick. I screamed with each brutal trusting of his body into mine. I opened my eyes and saw we had a crowd of people watching; some men had their dicks out jacking them. I was close when a man walked up to us; looking to Robert, he lifted his hands and said, "May I?" Robert must have given his consent because the man placed his fingers on my clit and I went soaring through the air. My orgasm so hard I bucked against Robert's dick and the man's very capable hands.

I heard Robert say, "Condom?" It seemed to be a question because I heard the wrapper crinkle. Robert kissed the side of my head, then whispered, "He's next, baby."

Robert pulled out of me, and I sagged for a second against the wall. Then I was turned around, my head against the wall, and the man with the capable hands was lifting me up and slid me on his dick. I screamed out, still sensitive from my orgasm. His dick was thicker then Robert's but not as long, and he could fuck. I bounced up and down on his dick, my eyes trained to Robert who was getting a blow job from a man. But Robert's eyes were on me. He only closed them when the man deep throated him; I had never been so turned on in my life.

My partner's thrusts began to get erratic, and I knew he was about to come. I could see the strain on Robert's face as well, trying to hold back his climax, and I yelled to him, "Come down his throat, baby, I want to see." With my command he came, and not just a little, a lot. I could also feel my own orgasm rush through me. It took all I had to keep my eyes on Robert as I came, but I did, and he watched me.

My feet were on the ground, and the man patted me lightly on the ass as he pulled away. I didn't watch him leave. I watched the man with Robert; he was worshiping the last dripping of Robert's cum. The man stood and turned to me, his eyes blazing, and I watched him come to me, his mouth full of Robert's cum. He stared me in the eyes, and I thought he is going to kiss me, then he dropped to his knees. With a gentle hand to my middle, he pushed me back against the wall. Taking my foot in his hands, he lifted my leg around his shoulder and then his tongue found my slit. It was a surprise; it was more than I could bear knowing this man had just given my man an orgasm and then he gave the evidence of it to me, inside of me. He licked me hard, grazing my G-spot as he licked. I came quickly and as I did, he sucked my clit with wild abandon. Luckily Robert was there to hold me up when my legs went weak. The man licked and sucked my clit until the tremors left my body. He stood up and said, "You both taste amazing." Then he smiled and walked away.

Robert picked me up, and we left the room; there was a sitting area outside, it looked like a little cave, and he sat with me in his arms. It took me a moment to contain myself, and when I did have focus of what was going on around me, I looked to him and saw he was looking down at me. Contentment was written on his face.

"I think my legs won't work anymore."

"That's okay, I don't mind carrying you."

I snuggled into him. "I really want to go dancing, but I don't think I have it in me."

He kissed the side of my head. "We have got to build up your stamina. Maybe I should have had you take a nap before coming here."

"You didn't tell me it was an erotic club. Do you have to be a member to be here?"

"There is a membership, and you have to be vetted to get in. There is a quarterly health exam, and rules. Did you enjoy yourself?"

"It's beautiful and mysterious; I really enjoyed it after the initial shock."

Even this little cave we were in was nice; I could see in the corners there was a mini fridge, and the couch where my feet were was comfy. A woman wearing an apron and nothing else walked past us. Robert stopped her. "Can you bring a fruit and cheese pack for us?"

She smiled at us and said, "Right away." Then she turned and walked back in the direction she was going. Mere moments later, she returned with the tray. Grapes, cheese, and strawberries along with two flutes of champagne. I took a sip and the bubbles tickled my nose.

"I love you, Robert." I didn't know where that came from, but I knew I had to say it at some point. I had never told a man that I loved him, but I had heard the word thrown my way many times. The strawberry was stuck in the space between Robert and I, as he was about to feed it to me. "I know that I have never said it, but I hope that I show it."

"You show it, baby."

"Good, I am not a lovey-dovey person, I won't say this often, but I love you."

He looked down to me. "What made you say it now, and why here?"

I thought about why now, and then it came to me. "You and I work; tonight shows that. The closet, here in this club. Don't get me started on all the things you did when I had cancer. Holding me when all my hair fell out, making sure I was not only physically okay, but you took care of my mental health as well. I love you for all you did and still do for me."

"It is my absolute pleasure to take care of you. You are the kind of woman that doesn't need anyone to take care of you, but I love doing it. I love seeing your face go soft, your eyes smile at me, and I have many things, but having you is the best thing I have ever had."

"Wow, you have had a lot of women."

He chuckled. "I have had a lot of women, but not one like you."

"Have you had a lot of men?"

His eyes went wicked, and I was a little turned on. "I have had men in the past. I have never dated a man, never wined and dined one. I don't generally find men attractive, but the ones that I do, I show my interest; the man tonight followed us from dinner. I thought he wanted you, but it turns out he wanted both of us. When you were with Josh."

"Wait, you know his name?"

"Yes, and you know him as well. He is a lawyer all over the TV for insurance."

Huh, I didn't notice. I mean I was in another world, but I should have noticed him.

"Wait, do you know all of the people here?"

He shook his head. "No, I know some of the people here. I have business with some of them. We don't let the two mix and if anyone says anything about this place, or what goes on, there is a hefty fine. They are also put out and put on a list for other clubs where they can't join."

"Wow, that's comforting. I don't really care if people know what I do in my spare time, but I could see why you would care."

He took a deep breath. "Tyanna's mother tried to out me. While you were sick, I had to sue her; she and all of my children's mothers have a non-disclosure agreement. She broke it, so she owes me twenty million that she doesn't have."

"Does Ty know?"

"No, she has no idea, but the money that Tyanna has set aside for her mother is now being rerouted back into Tyanna's account. If I could figure out how to get her out of Tyanna's house, I would."

I could see that. "We can work on that together. You are

not the only one with mysterious ways. I can be a Petty Betty if I need to."

I was feeling much better, the fruit was kicking in, and I was ready to party some more.

"You know, I'm ready to shake my ass for you; let's go dancing," I said while standing. "Give me a few days. I can get Ty's mom out the picture. Don't you worry."

He stood, took my hand, and we walked out of the alcove. "Okay, baby, you come up with a plan, and I will sit back and watch."

"I like when you watch, baby."

He pulled my hand up to his mouth and kissed it. Then we walked toward the sound of music blasting.

21

BABY MAKING

Lisa has just told me the good news about Tyanna and Sierra; it seems just a few hours in each other's presence, and they are falling fast and hard. I am happy for them. I want Alesia beside me, but she said she needed to concentrate on getting them together so when we finally tell Tyanna, she will understand the attraction because she experienced it. Honestly, I want to tell Tyanna to mind her damn business and stay out of my personal life. I know that is not the answer, I know that I have be patient, but I am ready to move my baby into the house and for us to start our life.

All of the boys love her; through the cancer they all spent time with her, and during the time when we thought we were going to lose her, they all silently had my back. Marcus even sat with me as I cried about her condition. He wanted me to tell Tyanna about our relationship so they could all support us openly. But no matter what, I wouldn't put Alesia in that position. I wanted her to be sure about us, sure enough to tell Tyanna proudly that we are together.

Alesia just left the family gathering. I had already told my mother about her, but I haven't told my sisters yet because they can't keep their mouths closed and I was afraid it would get back to Tyanna. I am so sick of hiding, it's unreal. I am a grown man, I can see who the hell I want, but Alesia wants Tyanna to accept us out the gate. I was ready to leave, ready to go to her. We had plans to sleep in the same bed tonight; last night she stayed at Tyanna's to make Sierra comfortable, but we stayed on the phone all night—well, most of the night—until she got the call that Sierra's apartment was bombed.

Davis Popov wanted our attention, and now he has it. I plan to buy everything that he could possibly want. I want to make sure that he isn't breathing when I am done. During Alesia's illness, she sat through some of our meetings, and we worked together to solve problems. If you were a problem, we quickly solved it by neutralizing you.

I hated neutralizing Tyanna's mother; for years I'd overlooked the things that she did to Tyanna and to me. She never saw the value in my baby, and when she came out, not that she was ever in the closet, her mother treated her like trash.

I sat in the room listening to my family talk about baby making, and how they would choose one of my sons to help Tyanna have a baby. I thought we should be discussing Alesia and me; whose sperm we were using was not on the top of my list. The news broke into the Broncos' game. There was an accident on the highway to Alesia's house. I was about to look away when they said a red Mini Cooper was involved. My stomach dropped and I stood to get a better look at the screen, and that's when I saw it—the license plate.

All I could hear was a loud ringing. I thought for a second that I would faint, and then I got control of myself and stormed out of the house. I needed to get to her, and she needed to know leaving me wasn't an option.

22

ON A BEACH

I woke sitting on a beach; I could feel the sand under my hands, and I looked out over the ocean. It was like no water I had ever seen. In the distance was a city, tall buildings glimmered in the light. They looked like jewels in the sky. I looked around me and saw that I wasn't alone; there were others there and none of us were dressed for the beach. I looked back over the water and saw people, they were walking on the water. I stood in wonder at what I saw.

I looked at all the faces as they approached the shore, and I recognized one of the people—my grandmother. She didn't exactly look like herself; she looked younger than I remembered. The worry lines in her face were gone, and her smile reached her eyes like I had never seen before. Months ago, I remember her coming to me, asking me to leave with her. I'd refused then. I looked down at myself and my outfit had changed, I was wearing a white dress, one very similar to the one that my grandmother wore.

"You have to come with me now, honey." I looked in her eyes as she reached her hand out to me. I looked around the beach and saw that the people standing with me were also wearing white now. Many had taken the hands of what I assume were their loved ones. I didn't take her hand.

"I won't accept that this is over; I have more to do, more life to live. And I can't leave Robert. I made a promise to him that I wouldn't leave him."

She looked at me with sympathy. "He will be fine, and one day you will have the pleasure of coming to get him from this very beach. Heaven is on the other side, all you have to do is take my hand. It won't hurt at all."

I couldn't do that, I wouldn't do that. I turned away from her, walking away from the city over the ocean. Weaving through people trying to find my way out. People were disappearing around me, but I couldn't leave.

"Baby girl, it's your time. Your body couldn't handle the accident."

Then I remembered it, my car going over that freeway, how it all happened in slow motion. The painful impact, and then I was here. Wherever here was.

"Where am I?" I said while walking away, searching for a way out.

"You are in the in between, a place you wait until you can come to the other side. You are ready for the other side, my baby."

"Says who? No one asked me if I was ready, and I have a life, one that I want to live. I will not leave my life!" I could feel the tears on my face as I searched for the exit. "How do I get out of here!" I yelled at the top of my lungs.

"There is no out, you can only move forward. I know you loved your Robert, but you must leave him behind."

"I won't leave him behind, I won't leave my family behind, and I can't leave Janice now that she has it all together. She can't lose me now. She has worked hard to gain my trust; I won't leave her now."

My grandmother gave me a sad look. I didn't look at her long, I kept walking away from the shore, and that's when I heard him, his voice somewhere close.

"Baby, you can't leave me."

I started to run to his voice.

"Lisa, you can't go back," my grandmother screamed behind me. But I didn't listen, the further I got away from the shore, the closer I could hear his sobs, the wailing of his sorrow.

"I'm coming back to you, I will find a way." I ran until there was no more sand, and only darkness.

My grandmother's voice echoing for me to slow down, but this was my way to him, I could feel his love the farther I ran from that beach. Could hear his screams, and I ran faster. I could see a cliff in front of me and I ran to it, my grandmother yelling for me to stop, but I ran and jumped into the darkness. His screams were my only guide. I felt heaviness, and then pain like I had never imagined. But then I heard it, the beep of a machine.

Beep. Beep. Beep.

"I think she's back."

You can bet your ass I was back. I wasn't leaving just when I could have it all.

I was tired, and sleep was near, so I let it come.

SOMEONE WAS HOLDING my hand and talking gently to me. "It's been a while, baby, and I know your body has been through the wringer, but it is time to wake up." That was Janice. I willed my eyes to open, but they wouldn't. "You've got this handsome man here, he hasn't left your side; those doctors are saying you might not ever wake up, saying you might be brain dead. I don't believe that; you have got to pull out of this. We have a photo album to make."

I tried with all my might to squeeze her hand. "She squeezed my hand, Robert," my mother said, and I heard movement.

"Baby, look at me. Open those pretty eyes for me; it's been days since I saw you. Just open them for a few seconds and let me see you."

I fought my way to get to him; I wanted to see him too. Bright light crashed into the darkness, and I felt pain. "That's it, baby, try one more time."

I tried again, and my eyes locked to his. He was crying and then he laid his head on my shoulder. Weeping.

My mother ran out the door screaming that I was awake. I looked to the door, and people were coming in. Robert was moved away, and they flashed lights in my eyes and asked me questions.

I could understand them, but I couldn't get the words to come out like they should.

"It's okay, don't stress yourself. We are just happy to see you awake. Are you in pain?"

I looked to Robert, who was on his phone, and tried to see if I felt any pain. I couldn't speak, but I could shake my head.

"That's great, I called the doctor and he will be here soon. I want you to rest if you feel tired. Your brain went through a lot from that crash, and it needs time to reboot. You had your family scared for a while, but I think we are out of the woods now." She smiled at me, and I smiled back. Happy to be alive.

I WOKE to Ty sitting at my bed, my hand in hers. And she was speaking softly.

"I want you both happy. I want you to be okay."

In a soft voice I said, "I am okay. I love you, Ty."

Her beautiful green eyes were on me, and they had unshed tears in them.

"I didn't want to lie to you; I was afraid to tell you about Robert and me. I didn't think you would approve, but every time I was going to give him up, he showed me all the ways he could love me. I have never had that before. I wanted to tell you so many times. I was just scared you wouldn't like him for me. You know so much about me."

She moved her head to the side, as if she was perplexed with my statement. My words were wonky so maybe she didn't understand me.

"Lisa, you are one of the best people I know. You are kind, and smart, and a damn go-getter. I love all of this about you. My father is lucky to have you. I won't lie and say that I wasn't upset, but I have watched him while you were sleeping, and that man loves you. I have never seen him love a woman likes he loves you."

I smiled at her; I could feel his love right now, and he wasn't even in the room. She kept talking.

"You were already my family. None of us want to lose you. My brothers love you as well. I always found it funny that they were at the hospital when you had cancer. I later found out it was so Dad could leave for a while and take care of business. I should have noticed that he was in love with you, but I couldn't bring myself to believe that he could actually love any woman."

I thought about Robert, before I spoke. "I think he has unlimited capacity to love, I think he just didn't find what he was looking for, he was searching just like I was. I want our life to be beautiful, I want long days just him and me, I want family dinners, and our family growing with more children. I want at the end of life, when I stand on that beach again, to have fulfilled all of my dreams."

"What do you mean you stood on a beach?"

I thought hard about what I had seen. "I think I was dying. I stood on a beach in all white; my grandmother wanted me to take her hand and move over to a city that was so beautiful I can't put it into words, but I couldn't leave him. So I ran away, and then I could hear Robert, feel his pain, and I jumped into nothingness because I heard his voice was on the other side of it. I couldn't leave him."

As I spoke, tears were streaming down Ty's face. "I was outside of the door looking in; nurses were giving you CPR. My father was screaming for you. He was beyond grief, I have never seen anything like it. They had stopped pumping your chest, and the nurse was about to get off you when the monitor started to beep. Dad's knees buckled."

It was crazy that it was all real, but somewhere deep down I knew it was.

"I couldn't leave him, and deep down I couldn't leave you either. You are my person. The thought of hurting you is more than I could bear. I love you. Please forgive me for not telling you."

She kissed my hand. "You have nothing to be forgiven for; I just want to know the story of how you met the love of your life. Just leave out all the sex parts."

I laughed her, and more tears came tumbling.

The door opened, and Robert and all of his boys came walking in. Brent looked at us and then turned hard eyes on Ty. "If you are making her cry about her and Dad's relationship, I will shoot you."

I looked at the men in the room and said, "She was

asking me about the greatest love story ever told, minus the sex. These are happy tears, nothing worth prison time."

I could see Robert relax, and the rest of the boys smiled at us.

"You can tell that story later; right now you need to decide on moving in the house with me, and what you are going to do with your house."

I looked to Ty, then back to Robert. "I know I just had a traumatic brain injury, but are you asking me to move in or telling me?" I sat up further in the bed, hoping he would see he was irritating me.

"I am asking in any way where the answer would be you are moving in with me."

I rolled my eyes and heard chuckles.

"You know how many women would jump at the chance to move in with me?"

"You keep saying that, honey. I will move in with you only because of the garden, and the servants, and maybe that closet you showed me," I said teasing him.

"Long as you are moving in. Now you need your rest, and I need to have a meeting with my children. All of my children."

"I'm not sleepy, I want to be in on the secret meeting." I knew what these meetings looked like and I wanted all the parts of this.

"It's about Davis Popov; he was killed the day of your accident."

I looked around the room. "Did any of you do it?" The room was quiet, and I waited.

"None of us killed him, but I found the men that carried out the accident that you were in; there were texts that he sent to them saying he didn't have the money to pay them. I took all of his money out of every account," Brent said this with little remorse. "So, no, we didn't kill him, but our actions led to his death."

I tried to muster up sympathy, but I couldn't. The things he did to Sierra and the accident that almost cost me my life wouldn't allow me to feel too bad for him. "I don't think we should ever discuss this again. We should try to help some of the people that he screwed over, but we should let things work themselves out."

Robert spoke, "Is there a way to get back at the men that did this to Alesia?"

I spoke up then, "We could enter into an endless circle of getting back at people. I am alive, the people that did this to me were doing a job, let it go. Davis can't hurt any of us again. Let this go, and let's all move forward. We have too much life to live to get stuck in revenge."

Robert walked to me, kissed my lips, and said, "Too much life indeed. We are done with Davis, let's move forward."

23

ANYTHING TOGETHER

Alesia was getting out the hospital today. Tyanna has been watching us like a hawk; she told me in the hospital that she was happy Alesia and I were together, even said she wished she had of come up with the idea, but she still had some reservations, I could tell. Alesia has had some brain swelling, so she is a little slower in comprehension; the doctors say this will pass with rest and time.

I was walking into the hospital, when my phone rang, and it was Tyanna.

"Hey, Pop, are you picking Lisa up?"

"Yeah, I just got to the hospital."

"Good, I talked to Alfred and he said all was ready in the house."

I had three nurses brought in for twenty-four hour help. I also had therapy coming in daily. "Yeah, it's all set up."

There was a long pause, then, "Daddy."

The way she said it made me stop in my tracks, and the people walking behind me had to go around me. "Yes, Sweetheart?"

"I have been watching you with her, and I have never seen this man before. To see you love her is a thing of beauty. I am proud of you." I smiled into the phone and started walking again. "The other thing I wanted to say was my mother called me."

Oh shit, this is not what I wanted to talk about.

"She said that her utilities were off and she had no money. I tried to send money to her but the money was returned into another account."

Yeah, that would be right. I made sure that she had no money at all.

Tyanna's voice got quiet. "I asked her what she had done, and she said crossed you."

I looked to the elevator, but couldn't get on in fear that the call would drop.

"She also told me she'd threatened to tell me about who you were dating; I assume that it was about Lisa."

"That's a correct assumption." I took a deep breath, trying to reason some of the things that no daughter should know about her father. "She also told some business associates about what I did behind closed doors. It cost me money."

It also cost Preston jail time. Jaxson tracked his next visit and contacted Interpol about the illegal, underage girls in that club he went to. He was caught there, and his company went bankrupt in a matter of hours with all his shareholders jumping ship. I bought all that was left and was rebuilding it as we spoke.

"I don't like the fact that she tried to hurt you. I told her I wouldn't talk you out of it, that I would stay completely out of it; it's not my business."

I laughed softly. "Seems your brothers taught you a valuable lesson, my dear."

"Yes, they did. I know you need to get the Lisa, and I will let you go, I just wanted you to know that I have your back, even if having your back means silently watching."

"I love you, sweet baby, and for you I will leave your mother whatever peace she can find. But she won't get a penny from you ever again."

She drew in a deep breath. "I understand that. I tried to buy her love, now I know that love is the best free gift you can have. Sierra's parents love me, and not because I bought their love, because they are just loving people. I have all that I need, and since I never had Trina to start with, I won't miss her."

That made me sad, but it was true, she had never had Trina.

"Baby girl, I love you, and I will see you soon."

"Bye, Daddy." And she hung up.

I GOT to Alesia's room and paused at the door; she was standing in window, looking to the skyline. She looked healthy for the first time in a while. Wearing white jeans that showed off her ass, the weight was coming back, this accident had slowed it for a while, but she still looked good. She didn't have a wig on and her hair was coming in nicely, a short Afro. I remembered the first time I'd seen her hair in those very cute plats. I smiled at the memory.

"You ready to go, beautiful?" She turned to me, and I could still see some swelling, but she was here and that was all that mattered.

"The nurse just had me sign my papers; I have to wait for a wheelchair."

I was walking to her as she spoke. Her words slower than usual. I didn't want to show my worry, mostly because I didn't want her to worry.

"I'm willing to wait; I'm glad you are coming home to me."

When she first woke, she didn't remember me; it took a day or so, and then she remembered us, and Tyanna not knowing. She panicked and then Tyanna told her she was happy for us, and Alesia was also happy. I wanted her that happy for the rest of her life.

"You didn't give me much choice, but I don't mind. The therapist here said I should try yoga, and your garden is the most beautiful place."

I would show her beauty soon; I had a plan. "Good, your mom is coming to the house to see you after you get home."

I was letting everyone come over, we were going to eat a late lunch, and then I was sending them home, mostly because Alesia needed to rest, and some of it was that I wanted us to be alone.

"I was looking out the window and I remembered something."

I wrapped her in my arms. "What did you remember?"

"My grandmother came to see me while I was asleep, she asked me to come with her, and I told her I couldn't. I'd promised you that I would fight to live for you. We sat on a park bench, and I told her about you. I remember waking up to you."

As she spoke, my heart squeezed, thinking how close she came to dying twice. It was more than I could bear.

"I loved my grandmother, Robert, but I love you more. I won't leave you, and I want you to stay with me. No matter what life throws at us, together we can get through it all."

I kissed her forehead. "Anything together."

A man knocked on the door with a wheelchair, and we gathered all that she had and were on our way home.

24

YELLOW DIAMONDS

We arrived at Robert's house, and there were a lot of cars; I didn't boggle my mind trying to figure out who all was there. If something didn't come to me right away, I got a headache, and if I really thought about it, dizzy spells came along with it. I learned really fast to let the memory come on its own.

We pulled up to the door and Clyde was there, to open my door. He was in street clothes, and he wore a huge smile when he saw me.

"Hi, Clyde."

"I am so happy to see you, Lisa; how are you feeling?"

"I'm better; has the old man been giving you a hard time?"

He smiled looking over at Robert. I looked in his direction and saw he was giving me a look. I smiled at him. Clyde said, "He has been bearable, kind of."

I looked over at Robert. "Robert Howard, you be nice or I will spank you."

He smiled a wicked smile. "There goes my baby."

I rolled my eyes. Liking the fact that I could spank him.

My brain was constantly on sleep, remembering, and sex. You would think other things would cross it, but they really didn't.

Robert took my hands as we walked up the steps, and Alfred opened the door.

"Alfred! It's so good to see you." I don't know why I wanted to hug him, but I did.

He was shocked for a second, and then he pulled me into his arms. "Been praying you would pull though, I am so happy you are here. Don't scare us like that again, child."

I hugged him tighter then let go, and before I could say a word, Robert spoke, "I hired her a driver; she won't be driving a damn thing ever again."

I looked at Robert, pulled away from Alfred, and put my hands on my hips. "I'll be damned if you know where I am at all times. You act like I pushed me off that bridge. I will be buying me a new car as soon as I can remember where my wallet is." I said this with anger, then he looked at me with amusement.

"We will see."

"Yes, *you* will see!" I snapped. He outright laughed, and my temper flared. I walked in the house and again was taken aback by the beauty of it. I felt eyes on me and looked around and saw my family there, even Ty and Sierra. They were leaned into each other, and I loved the beauty of it.

"You two look good together," I said as I looked to them; they just smiled, and Sierra had a tear coming from her eye.

"No tears needed, I lived. You guys pulled your heads out of your asses, and now we can all move forward."

Daddy Sam spoke, "Yep, and thanks to you, I got successful grandchildren. Told all my friends about it."

Daddy and his grandchildren. I smiled at him and felt Robert come up behind me. He pulled me into his arms.

"You know, the sooner you let me have my way, the better life would be," I told Robert, and all the men rolled their eyes, but Ty smiled.

"She's right, Pop, happy wife, happy life."

He didn't say anything out loud, but he squeezed me, and I laid back in his arms. Janice came out of the back hall. "The food is ready. I kicked your cook out, by the way," she said to Robert. "Ain't nobody cooking for my family but me when I am home."

Everyone made their way to the dining room, but I excused myself to go up the bedroom. I needed to get something. I went into the closet and opened the case that held my rings, the ones that Robert gave me. All ten of them in a beautiful row. I picked up the yellow diamond and placed it on my finger. I closed the case and walked back out of the room, hoping Robert wouldn't catch me.

I walked into the dining room, and everyone was passing plates around. Janice had made food that I'd loved my grandmother to cook. I sat down next to Robert and took the bowl of purple hull peas that Sierra passed. The table was long, and everyone had a seat; when I reached for the bowl, Sierra gasped. She took the serving dish out of my hand and almost pulled my left arm off to get a better look at my ring.

"Is that what I think it is?"

I looked to Robert who had adoring eyes on me. "It's one of my engagement rings. Robert told me to put it on when I was ready to get married."

In unison, all of Robert's kids said, "He asked you to marry him?"

I smiled, placing my hand on his. He lifted it up and kissed it gently.

"Yeah, he asked me a few weeks ago. I wasn't ready to say yes, but now I am."

The room erupted in applause and congratulations, and I beamed. Robert held my hand the entire time I ate, and I could feel his love. And all the love filling the room.

EPILOGUE

We stood on the beach in Bora Bora watching the sun fall into the sea. Robert holding me, and I was just happy in the moment. I'd had my dream wedding; all my family and friends were there. Even the doctors and nurses that treated me were there. When the doors opened in the church, and I saw Robert standing at the end of the aisle, his eyes so full of love, I kissed Daddy on the cheek and ran to him, jumping into his arms. He caught me and the crowd laughed and cheered.

For a wedding to be planned a full year in advance, it went by very quickly. It wasn't long before I was lifted off my feet and ushered into a waiting car to the airport. Robert checked off another one of my bucket list items, and we joined the mile high club in a spectacular fashion.

The hotel was owned by Robert, and we had a private villa to enjoy, with a private beach and pool. It was amazing. We have been here two weeks, and tonight is our last night. I hadn't found the right time to tell him my secret, we were so busy having fun, but I did tell the staff.

While we were here, Robert didn't notice that I hadn't

had one sip of alcohol. He also didn't notice that the temperature of the hot tub was lowered, but the staff was discreet about all of it. Some of them even coming up to me when Robert was away doing business wondering if I had told him yet.

"You know, next year when we come back, the baby will be with us," I said as I turned around in his arms.

"I am all for being a doting grandfather, but I am not bringing a newborn to this island unless it's mine."

"I was talking about yours." I smiled brightly at the expression on his face, wonder and love, and so much more.

"Are you saying you're pregnant?" he said on a whisper.

"Yep, the doctor confirmed it at my checkup before the wedding." Yes, a week before the wedding I found out that I was three months pregnant. "You haven't mentioned the weight I put on; I didn't know how to tell you."

He pulled me in his arms. "Baby, the way your mama cooks, I just thought it was from that. Are you happy?"

"I am over the moon. Are you happy?"

He picked me up and turned us around. "Happy isn't the word." Then he leaned his head back and screamed, "I am going to be a daddy!"

From the villa we heard hoots and howls as well. And I laughed.

I wish I would have trusted myself with loving Robert sooner. I wish that I would have told Ty, so she could have been on this journey with us, but all of that led to this moment. To the life that our love created. I couldn't have asked for more. I had time to live and love this man, and this baby, and I couldn't wish for more.

THE END

ABOUT THE AUTHOR

What was a stay at home mom to do while her family slept? Write. Write about dirty talking alpha males who had a thing for spankings and handcuffs.

Now her alter ego Mariah Kingsley writes about love, life, murder, and toe curling sex. The concept of what happens after "Happily Ever After" changed her life.

Now a blushing mom who never imagined she would run across her work on her mothers kindle loves the life. The author, blogger and avid reader now has several books for your enjoyment.

Made in the USA
Middletown, DE
18 February 2023

24365009R00110

FINDING HIS
Forever

DOMS OF THE COVENANT BOOK 4

SAMANTHA COLE

Finding His Forever

Copyright © 2024 Samantha A. Cole
All Rights Reserved.
Suspenseful Seduction, Inc.

Finding His Forever is a work of fiction. Names, characters, businesses, organizations, places, events, and incidents either are the product of the author's imagination or are used fictitiously. Any resemblance to actual persons, living or dead, events, or locales is entirely coincidental.

Cover designed by Cover Me Darlings
Proofread by Cutting Edge Editing

No part of this book may be reproduced, scanned, or distributed in any printed or electronic form without permission. Please do not participate in or encourage piracy of copyrighted materials in violation of the author's rights. Purchase only authorized editions.

Chapter One

Matthew Behan thanked his lucky stars he could do his job at the front desk of The Covenant with his eyes closed because he was utterly exhausted. Between working full-time as an EMT, going to school to become a paramedic, all the studying and clinical rotations that went with it, and working part-time at the BDSM club he belonged to, sleeping was a luxury lately. His EMS schedule rotated—twenty-four hours on, followed by forty-eight hours off, and sometimes, he'd pick up a half or "split" shift for overtime. As a result, his club shifts, which helped offset his annual membership fee, and his nights off when he could play, also rotated. The latter wasn't often recently. Hell, he couldn't even remember the last time he played with anyone except for an occasional scene with one of the Whip Masters.

He had no clue how or why, but somehow, his almost disgustingly sweet parents had raised a masochist. Controlled pain for pleasure was something he craved—he was just wired that way. Unfortunately, at twenty-six, he'd yet to find a sadist he was attracted to who was single, interested in an exclusive D/s relationship, and looking for a submissive to beat regularly. Oh, and who didn't turn out to be a douche bucket after a few weeks.

Out of all those factors, at least one or two was missing in every gay Dom he'd met over the last few years. So, as of late, when he had time, he scened with one of the club's Whip Masters—Dominants skilled with the bullwhip, who took turns servicing needy, masochistic submissives on nights when the club was open.

If Matthew wasn't so tired, he might've checked to see if Mistress China could fit him into her schedule tonight. *Maybe Sunday night*, he thought, since that would be his only free time between now and his final exams. When he wasn't working or sleeping for the next six days, he'd be studying his ass off.

It was three weeks before Christmas, and hopefully, by the new year, he'd finally be a certified paramedic in Florida with the pay raise that went with it. He would keep his fingers crossed and pray to St. Michael, the patron saint of police officers, firefighters, and EMTs/paramedics, for two or three weeks until he found out if he passed his final written and practical exams. As the testing dates grew near, his anxiety spiked higher and higher. He didn't know what he'd do if all his hard work for the past two years was for naught.

A couple stepped up to the desk in the lobby on the club's second floor. Matthew immediately recognized the handsome Dom, who'd been a full-time member for about two years, but not the pretty submissive with him. "Good evening, Master Renzo. How can I help you tonight?"

"Hello, Matthew," the Dom said with a pleasant smile. "This is my guest, Katie. Here's her paperwork, including the signed NDA."

He handed over several pieces of paper, and Matthew quickly scanned them, especially the non-disclosure agreement, to ensure the woman had initialed and signed all the appropriate spots. A separate page confirmed she passed her background check. Finding everything in order, he opened a drawer beside his hip and pulled out a yellow band. "Welcome to The Covenant, Katie. I just need to put this around your wrist."

When the brunette held out her hand, he attached the band in place, ensuring it wasn't too tight or loose. "This indicates you're a guest and not cleared to play on the premises. You'll need to remain with Master Renzo at all times unless, of course, you need to use the restroom. If you have any problems or lose track of Master Renzo, just look for a dungeon monitor wearing a gold vest or one of the security guards in the red polo shirts, and they'll help you." After working there for almost four years, he could probably recite all that in his sleep.

She gave him a shy but grateful smile. "Thank you."

"You're very welcome. Have a good evening. You too, Sir."

Master Renzo nodded as he put a possessive hand at the small of Katie's back. "Thank you, Matthew."

"My pleasure, Sir."

As the couple headed for the heavy wooden double doors that opened into the main club and the big bouncer guarding them, Matthew grabbed a red pen and a new manila folder from a nearby stack. He wrote Katie's full name on the tab, tucked her paperwork into the folder, and filed it in the cabinet behind him. A yawn broke loose, and he used his hand to cover his gaping mouth. If only he could close his eyes for a few minutes, but if that happened, he knew he wouldn't wake up for hours.

Glancing at the clock under the desktop, he groaned. Ninety minutes before his shift ended. Then he could go home, collapse on his bed, and sleep until after noon if he wanted. He didn't have to be at work until six tomorrow evening for an overtime shift he split with another EMT. Still, like most metropolitan areas, Saturday nights were usually the busiest of the week for Tampa Fire Rescue, which covered the emergency medical services for the city. He and his partner would probably run their asses off unless, by some small miracle, they caught a rare break.

Matthew loved his job, though, whether it was busy

or slow. During career day in his junior year of high school, a paramedic/EMT team gave a passionate presentation about their chosen profession. Right then, he knew he wanted to join their ranks as soon as possible. Okay, so he may have also been influenced by the fact that the paramedic had been hot as freaking Hades, and Matthew nearly drooled all over his desk as the man talked. Regardless, his decision of what he wanted to do with his life was etched in stone that day.

The door to the parking lot swung open, and several men strode in, including Masters Devon and Ian. The two of the three Sawyer brothers and their cousin, Master Mitch, owned The Covenant. They'd been incredibly supportive of Matthew's career path over the past year, constantly reminding him they could move his club schedule around to accommodate his classes and fieldwork. Manning the front desk a few times a week was the only way he could afford the membership fees to one of the most elite and private BDSM clubs on the Gulf Coast. He'd also become close to several of the club's submissives, including the owners' significant others, so he planned to keep the position even if he got promoted to paramedic.

While Devon and several others headed for the double doors, Master Ian stepped over to the desk, speaking over his shoulder to someone behind him. When the other man came into view and stopped next to the owner, Matthew almost fainted. Master Delmar Sutton briefly toured the club a few weeks ago, and Matthew had been caught by several of his submissive friends salivating over the yummy Dom. They'd teased him relentlessly for a few hours. Unfortunately, he was recovering from a whip session with Master Carl that night and still felt the drugging effects of subspace. Otherwise, he would've sashayed across the room and made sure the visiting Dom noticed him before he left.

From the little he'd been able to find out over the following few days, Master Delmar was gay—*yay!*—and had just recently moved to Tampa from the small city of Morrison, Ohio. He was also interested in joining a local lifestyle club. Since he was there again tonight, hopefully, it meant he decided to become a member of The Covenant.

In his late thirties or early forties, the man stood about six feet tall, definitely worked out, but not to the point his muscles bulged, and had thick chestnut hair. Since he was now close enough to see them, Matthew noted that the Dom's eyes were a wicked hazel—brown, green, and amber swirled together. He was dressed in rich mahogany leathers, which molded to his slim hips and long legs, and a white button-down shirt, with the top few buttons undone and the sleeves rolled up to his elbows. His five o'clock shadow just made him look more delicious, and Matthew longed to have that scruff scrape across his entire body.

He straightened, put on his most professional yet flirtatious smile, and thanked the Goddess of Twink submissives everywhere that he'd decided to wear one of his favorite outfits tonight. The crimson satin boy shorts showed off both his front and rear assets. A black leather harness crisscrossed over his slender but toned shoulders, waxed chest, and back. Because he was currently working, he also had on a gold bowtie. Simple yet seductive and hopefully enticing. He quietly cleared his throat and prayed his voice wouldn't crack like a prepubescent boy when he greeted them. "Good evening, Sirs."

Master Ian nodded. "Good evening to you, too, Matthew. This is Master Del. You should have his new membership card back there."

When Master Del smiled at him, Matthew almost wilted into a heap of desperate and aching flesh and bones. The man had dimples. Freaking dimples! *Sigh*.

Remembering he had a job to do, he removed the lanyard from around his neck and quickly found the key to the locked cabinet beneath the desk. "Um, welcome to The Covenant, Master Del."

"Thank you—Matthew, was it?"

He blushed as the Dom's gaze raked over his body with evident appreciation. His heart pounded as goosebumps skittered across his skin, and a shiver went down his spine. "Y-yes, Matthew. I mean, yes, *Sir*, my name is Matthew, which—which is my name."

Ugh, can you get any more flustered? Goddess, help me!

Master Ian arched an eyebrow at the submissive, then smirked and shook his head. It was rare for Matthew to be so out of sorts around a handsome man. Usually, his flirtatious brat emerged when he was attracted to someone, and the head Dom knew that.

Locating the new key card, he held it out to Master

Del with a trembling hand. Expecting the man just to take it, Matthew gasped, his heart skipping a beat when the Dom gently grasped his wrist. "I'd ask if you were interested in playing tonight, pup, but you appear dead on your feet. Master Ian, I hope this doesn't indicate that you push your employees too hard."

The club owner's eyes narrowed as he studied Matthew, who squirmed under the scrutiny.

Uh-oh.

Master Ian's mouth turned down into a fierce frown. "When was the last time you slept, Matthew? You're pale and have dark circles under your eyes."

Damn it. He'd hoped the little bit of concealer and black eyeliner he put on earlier would've helped hide his fatigue. Sighing inwardly, he knew better than to lie to one of the most dominant and astute men he ever met. "I slept about five hours last night, Sir. It's been a busy week, finishing my clinical rotations and preparing for my finals."

"And on top of that, you're working here along with your EMS shifts, right? When you started the paramedic program, I thought we agreed that you'd let me or Masters Mitch or Devon know if you were overloaded and needed time off." He crossed his arms over his massive chest and scowled. "Or is that something I just imagined and pulled out of my ass?"

Matthew dropped his gaze to the desk—the submissive in him instinctively reacting to the disappointment in the Dom's tone. "No, Sir, you didn't imagine it. I planned to sleep at least eight hours last night, but it was my last clinical rotation in the ER, and a bunch of patients from a bad car accident were brought in, along with two cardiac arrests, and it was all hands on deck. Once I'm done here, I don't have to do anything until tomorrow afternoon but catch up on my sleep. But I swear I'm fine."

It wasn't until he tried to run a hand through his stylish blond hair that he realized Master Del hadn't let go of him. The man's thumb sensually caressed his wrist as he studied the submissive's face. The intense stare turned Matthew on, causing a shiver to race down his spine, while the zephyr-like touch could almost lull him to sleep standing up.

Master Ian sighed and dropped his arms. "Who's your relief tonight, and are they here yet?"

He reluctantly dragged his attention back to his boss. "It's Molly, Sir, and she's inside somewhere."

"Get your things and then ask one of the waitstaff or DMs to find Molly and send her to me. I'll man the desk until she gets here. Let me know if she's in the middle of a scene, and I'll find someone else."

Horrified at the thought of the owner, a Dom and retired Navy SEAL, filling the desk clerk position even for a few moments, Matthew's eyes widened as he shook his head. "Oh, you don't have to do that, Sir, I'm fine, re—"

"That was an order I think you should obey, pup," Master Del interrupted. His tone was low and filled with a warning, and damn, it made Matthew want to sink to his knees. "I look forward to seeing you again when you're well rested, and maybe then we can negotiate some playtime."

Oh, Goddess of Twink submissives, I love you! Not sure what I did to grab this gorgeous man's interest, but if I could, I would kiss your feet right now as a thank you!

He swallowed hard, willing his cock to behave since it wouldn't find any relief tonight unless it were by his own hand. "Um, y-yes, Sir. I-I'd like that very much, Sir."

The Dom smiled, and those dimples appeared again —*swoon!* "Good. Now, do as Master Ian instructed, and then go home and get some sleep."

Chapter Two

After taking his membership card and forcing himself to release Matthew's wrist, Del watched as the beautiful sub gathered a few things. With a last glance at Ian, who shooed him away with an impatient flick of his hand, Matthew hurried toward the wooden double doors leading into the club, giving Del a full view of his body.

He sucked in a breath as his gaze roamed over every visible tanned inch of the twink's smooth skin. The dark red boy shorts he wore molded to his cute tight ass, one Del wanted to take a hand to and spank until it was the same color. The black leather harness highlighted his lean yet toned physique. Del couldn't tear his gaze away until the sub disappeared into the club and the door closed behind him. It'd been a while since someone had piqued his interest to the point that Del already fantasized about what he wanted to do to the younger man without knowing anything about him.

Turning back to the desk, which Ian now stood behind, looking quite bored already, Del said, "Tell me about him."

The other Dom lifted his eyebrows. "Matthew? What do you want to know?"

"The basics." He shrugged, then amended his statement. "Okay, a little more than the basics."

Instead of answering right away, Ian turned around and opened one of the drawers of the horizontal file cabinets lined up against the wall. After a moment of scanning the tabs, he pulled out a folder, flipped it open, and began reading aloud. "Matthew Behan, twenty-six years old. One hundred percent *fabulously* gay." He smirked as his amused gaze met Del's. "He wrote that verbatim, by the way."

Del chuckled as the other man closed the file but continued talking. "Matthew's a good kid: intelligent, trustworthy, responsible. You already heard he's almost done with the paramedic program at the local community college. He's been an EMT for about six or seven years, I think, with Tampa Fire Rescue and helps out here whenever a medical emergency pops up, which isn't often, thank God.

"He's a masochist and has a few sessions each month with one of our Whip Masters. As far as I know, he hasn't been collared in a long time, but I get the feeling he'd like to be. However, he won't settle just to be in a relationship. He can be a brat when he wants, which is often, and has a very protective streak regarding his fellow submissives. While he needs a good Dom to take care of him when he pushes himself too much, like you just saw, he's also strong enough to stand on his own."

Everything the other man said had Del mentally checking off boxes in his head. He couldn't have selected a more perfect submissive to find attractive, especially now that he had time to relax and explore a new relationship—if he got that far with Matthew.

Ian pulled three stapled sheets of paper from the folder and handed them to Del. "Here's his limit list. Every sub has one on file available for the Doms to look at—just ask whoever's working the desk to pull one for you."

As Del scanned the list, a cute brown-haired woman wearing a schoolgirl's outfit and pigtails rushed up to the desk. "Hi, Master Ian. Matthew said you wanted me to take over for him early so he could get some sleep. No worries. I owe him from a swap we did last month anyway."

"Thank you, Molly. Make sure you note on your timecard that I approved it. I'll see that you get an extra break during the shift too." He gave her the folder he still held and then gestured toward Del. "This is Master Del—he's just looking over Matthew's limit list."

The cheerful sub smiled broadly at Del. "It's nice to meet you, Sir. Take your time. Matthew's a really great guy and isn't collared or seeing anyone."

The little imp clearly attempted to play matchmaker, but he let it slide. Apparently, Ian decided to let it go, too, because he rolled his eyes before addressing

Del. "I'll be at the bar having a drink. Come join me when you're done, and I'll introduce you to a few people. My wife, sister-in-law, and goddaughter are in my apartment with the kids, watching some chick flick that's probably going to have them bawling their eyes out—the fuck-twat croaks or something at the end—so I've got about an hour and a half to kill."

A snort escaped Del as the other man walked away, leaving him to read through Matthew's hard and soft limits. He was happy to see they were pretty compatible. Now, he just had to bide his time until the beautiful blond-haired, blue-eyed submissive was available to play.

~

Several days later . . .

Del strode across the parking lot of The Covenant, looking forward to relaxing for a few hours and hoping to run into Matthew again. Since meeting him, he hadn't been able to get the pretty younger man out of his mind when he should have been thinking of an idea for a new app.

Three years ago, he created a fitness app that he recently sold for $650 million, a staggering amount that still shocked the shit out of him. One of the first things he'd done after the money transferred into his bank account was pack up and move from Cincinnati to Clearwater, Florida, out of his greedy father's immediate reach. His deadbeat dad was sorely mistaken if he thought he'd ever see a cent of the money Del earned through blood, sweat, and tears. The bastard had somehow tracked Del down and knocked on the door of his rented apartment the day after the sale was reported by the media. Del had taken one look at his sperm donor's face and slammed the door shut. He then had to call the cops because Ron Gibbons continued pounding on the door for twenty minutes, demanding money and refusing to leave. Del filed for a restraining order the next day.

While there was no way he'd ever give his father a dime, Del regretted his mother was no longer alive because he would've loved to spoil her. She'd spent his entire childhood working two jobs while raising him alone.

Kim Sutton had been kicked out by her strict, God-fearing parents when she got pregnant at nineteen. An unwed mother, she'd somehow managed to make a loving home for her only child despite her boyfriend breaking up with her the same night she told him he'd knocked her up. Del's mother could've given him up for adoption, but as she'd always told him, after the first time she felt him kick in her womb, she wanted to keep him. While money was tight as he grew up, Del always knew his mother loved him and wanted to give him the world. Unfortunately, she passed away from cancer a few years ago before he'd gotten the idea for the new app.

At fourteen, Del started taking whatever jobs he

could find so his mother wouldn't have to work so hard. His father never gave her child support and occasionally came around, asking her for money instead, which she'd refused to do.

Understanding technology always came easy for Del. At twenty, he'd graduated from his local community college with not one but three associate degrees in information technology, computer programming, and computer science. He spent the next fifteen years working as an IT tech for a small corporation while taking odd side jobs. He created several apps over the years, and while a few had done okay, none of them had really taken off. However, that changed when he got the idea for the specialized fitness app while working out in the gym he belonged to. It took him about six months to design, and then a few bugs needed fixing before it finally launched. It was downloaded over two million times within the first ninety days, and the numbers kept increasing. Its revenue from in-app purchases and advertisers, in addition to his freelance clients, had allowed him to quit his full-time job and start his own LLC—DelTech.

A tech giant approached him about purchasing the app almost a year ago. After four months of negotiations, with one of Del's best friends, a corporate lawyer, reviewing everything with a fine-tooth comb, they agreed on a sale price. It took a few more months for everything to be finalized, but Del was now a multi-millionaire with plenty of free time but no one to spoil. Hopefully, that would soon change.

Finding His Forever

The big 4-0 was approaching, and being in a committed relationship was now one of the things left on his long-term bucket list. Before she died, he promised his mother that he wouldn't swear off a chance at love just because she'd been unsuccessful. He knew the reason she hadn't dated much was because she'd spent all her time providing for and loving her son. He'd been lucky to have several teachers, coaches, and neighbors who were good male role models over the years. They took him under their wings, ensuring he knew the difference between right and wrong. He'd stayed in contact with a few, exchanging the occasional email or phone call even though they'd retired or moved away. Because of them and his mom, he wasn't adverse or afraid to have a family someday. He wanted to be the loving husband and father Ron Gibbons had never been.

No one at The Covenant knew who Del was or how wealthy he was, except for the owners and the guy who'd done his background check, because all his business was done through the LLC. Since he was still trying to come to terms with the fact that he was filthy rich, he didn't want to advertise it. The last thing he wanted was for subs or anyone else to be interested in him for his money.

When Del was in Tampa several weeks ago to find a place to rent, while he searched for something to buy, he also checked out several private BDSM clubs. He'd been in the lifestyle for over a decade. After getting a guest pass and a tour of The Covenant, it'd been a no-brainer for him to request membership. The club's owners were wealthy in their own rights. Two of them—Ian and Devon—were retired Navy SEALs who also owned a private security company. During a conversation with them, he'd learned their father was a well-known, self-made real estate billionaire. Their cousin Mitch, the third owner, also had a nose for business and had apparently invested well. As a result, security and privacy were among their top priorities for The Covenant.

During his few times there, Del recognized several other wealthy members, including Gray and Remi Mann, who owned Black Diamond Records, one of the biggest music production companies in the world. The two brothers were in a ménage marriage with their wife, Abigail. Country singer Summer Hayes, A-list actors Keith Gatlin and Clarissa James, and her ex-husband, movie director Landon Ford, also belonged to the club. With big names like those, Del figured a few other notable people were members, even if he hadn't seen or heard about them yet.

Climbing the stairs to the club's second-floor entrance, Del was still amazed by the stark difference between the interior and exterior of the building. The Covenant was located in one of four warehouses on several dozen fenced-in acres in a secluded area of Tampa. He'd been told that the other three buildings housed the Trident Security headquarters, as well as several luxury apartments where Devon and Ian lived with their families. Training areas and a helicopter pad could also be seen from the parking lot. However, an interior security fence separated the club's building from everything else.

When he stepped into the club lobby, its rich decor completely belied the commercial-looking exterior. A lot of money had gone into the renovations, and it showed. Beautiful mahogany wood, burgundy, emerald, and gold fabrics, plush carpeting, elegant but comfortable furnishings, and expensive art all combined to create an appealing and sensual atmosphere. With the elaborate Christmas and Hanukkah decorations that had gone up within the past few days, it was quite festive too.

Three seven-foot Christmas trees lined the wall between the front desk and the double doors leading into the main club. They were currently aglow with strings of miniature white lights but devoid of ornaments. Behind the desk, Devon's and Ian's wives, Kristen and Angie, respectively, stood with a collared male submissive Del hadn't met yet. They were busy doing something he couldn't see over the elevated countertop. He approached them, but before he could say hello, Kristen looked up and grinned when she noticed him. "Master Del! It's great to see you again."

Angie gave him a smile and a little wave of her hand. "Hi, Sir."

He dipped his chin. "Ladies, nice to see you too."

His gaze flickered to the dark-haired male submissive, who now stared at Del with his jaw practically on the floor. He was attractive but not as appealing as Matthew.

Angie rolled her eyes and smacked the young man's arm when she noticed his expression. "Sterling!"

"Huh?" Sterling kept his gaze on Del—a dreamy look falling across his face.

Del managed to suppress his grin, but just barely. It wasn't the first time he garnered that response from both male and female submissives, but he'd gotten used to it over the years. He was graced with good looks through his ancestral genes and wasn't ashamed to admit he knew it.

Angie proceeded with the introductions. "Master Del, this is Sterling, who better put his tongue back in his mouth and his eyes back in their sockets before Master Luis gets here and whoops his ass."

That caught Sterling's attention, and he ripped his gaze from Del to glare at Angie, setting his hands on his hips, which were barely covered by black leather boy shorts. "Oh, come on, girlfriend! How can I not appreciate . . ." He dramatically gestured up and down with his hand toward Del, who couldn't hold back a snicker that time. Sterling was probably a handful for his Master. "You know damn well that Sir lets me look as long as I don't touch. Besides, he's going to beat my ass tonight anyway—I was a bit bratty this morning."

"You're always a brat," Kristen chimed in before winking at Del. "But now you have to tell us what you did."

Sterling's attempt to look innocent failed when he

giggled and snorted. "Nothing *too* bad. I just put glitter in his roll-on deodorant. Now his pits sparkle like diamonds."

Oh, yeah, definitely a handful.

Remembering where he was and his status there, Del crossed his arms and gave the other man a stern scowl. "Hmm. I look forward to meeting your Master, Sterling. As a sadist, I might have to offer my services tonight to ensure you're properly reprimanded." When the sub's eyes widened and he gulped, the corners of Del's mouth twitched upward. He couldn't hide his amusement any longer, and a grin spread across his face. "Glitter? In his deodorant? Seriously?"

The sub's face lit up again. "Yup. I wanted to put it in his favorite body lotion, but he's a judge, and I know better than to do anything that'll embarrass him in court. Sparkling from head to toe on the bench while handing down a prison sentence? That would be a no."

All three subs burst out laughing, and Del shook his head. While his sadistic nature flared within the club, out there in the lobby, he would concede to the lighthearted joking. These weren't his submissives, and unless rudeness or an infraction of the club's rules occurred in his presence, he wouldn't demand high protocols or any punishments for their behavior.

After a moment, his gaze dropped to what they'd been doing when he first arrived. Cutout paper snowflakes were stacked in several piles. "What's all this?"

"Oh, it's for our Secret Santa event," Kristen

announced. "This is the first year we're doing it. Each snowflake will have the name of an uncollared sub on it, along with their sexual orientation, so there are no misunderstandings. We'll hang them on the trees over there, and the single Doms get to pick whomever they want. Then, next Saturday night, the subs will be given three clues about their Secret Santa, and they'll have to figure out who it is within thirty minutes. When the time is up, if they guess right, they get to choose what scene they do with the Dom. If they don't, then the Dom chooses the scene."

"Sounds like fun." And the perfect way to get to know a certain twink. "When will you put them on the trees?"

Kristen grinned smugly as if she was privy to what was going on in his head. "Once we're done putting everyone's names on these. Was there someone you had in mind? I can give you their snowflake now."

He arched his brow. "Wouldn't that be against the rules?"

"Well, since this was our idea," she gestured to her sister-in-law, "and we made up the rules, I don't see why we can't adjust them a little as needed, right, Ange?"

"Right! Besides, we're almost done, so you could just wait while we hang them on the tree. Or we could give you the one you want so you don't have to look through them all." Ian's wife leaned forward and lowered her voice conspiratorially. "So, whose flake do you want?"

Since he didn't want to miss out on being Matthew's Secret Santa, he'd let the two women play matchmakers—there seemed to be quite a few in the club. He eyed the piles in front of them. "Have you written out Matthew's yet?"

"Matthew Behan? Yes! Oh, he's perfect for you!"

All three subs frantically searched through several dozen snowflakes, making a mess of the piles.

"Here it is!" Sterling held up the white filigree paper and waved it high above his head before passing it to Del.

Sure enough, it had Matthew's full name and "100% fabulously gay" written in the center. Del grinned.

"I just need three clues from you by Friday so we can print them out on a card," Kristen said while penciling Del's name next to Matthew's on a checklist.

Angie handed him a small sheet of paper. "Here are some suggestions for the types of clues you can use. You can send them to me or Kristen—our email addresses are at the bottom. We figured that was easier than trying to track us down during the week since we're not always here." Both women had a child under the age of two, so their club time had understandably decreased since giving birth.

After scanning the list, Del folded it and the snowflake twice before sticking them into the back pocket of his black jeans. "I'll make sure you have them before Friday. Thank you very much, subbies."

"You're welcome, Sir," the trio replied in unison.

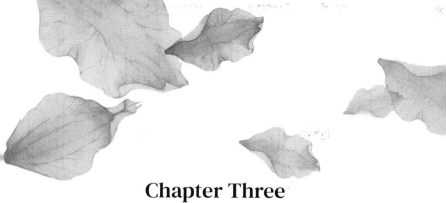

Chapter Three

"Oh, c'mon, Kristen. Tell me who got my snowflake. Please!" Matthew gave her his best puppy-dog eyes with his hands clasped under his chin. He was dying to know who'd chosen him for tonight's Secret Santa. When his friend wouldn't cave and just shook her head, he turned to her sister-in-law. "Pretty please, Angie, with cherries and multiple orgasms on top!"

"Nope. You have to guess like everyone else. Besides, I don't remember who got your name, and Master Mitch has the list now, right, Kristen?"

"Right."

"Bull crap." Scowling, which he didn't often do because he didn't want permanent frown lines before he was eighty—he took pride in his perfect pores and smooth skin—Matthew pointed a freshly manicured finger from one woman to the other and back again. "No wonder you two always get punished by your

Doms—neither of you can bluff. I'd make a killing if we played poker. Master Mitch may have the list, but I'm sure you two memorized it before giving it to him."

Yesterday, he'd taken the last of his final exams. He was positive he passed all the practicals—when the paramedic students role-played how they would treat patients in the field based on different scenarios. The individual tests included running a cardiac arrest, EKG interpretation and subsequent treatment, trauma assessment, and scene management, among others, and he got through them all without any errors. However, as expected, the written exam was rough. Many paramedic students didn't pass their first time and had to retake it. Matthew prayed he didn't fall into that category. After walking out at the end of the test, he repeatedly second-guessed several questions he'd stumbled on.

He couldn't do anything about it now but wait, so he tried to push his worry to the back of his mind and focus on something else—currently wondering which Dom had his snowflake. Hopefully, it was someone compatible, engaging, and deliciously handsome.

He had the night off after swapping shifts with a single mother EMT so she wouldn't have to work on Christmas next week. Many police officers, firefighters, EMTs, and paramedics throughout the city often rearranged their schedules to let coworkers with little ones celebrate the holidays with them. The swap had been a win/win for Matthew anyway, letting him attend the Secret Santa. The Covenant always had fun games and events throughout the year, especially before the winter holidays, and he tried not to miss them. And now that his exams were over, he wanted to *par-tay*!

Several new gay Doms had joined the club over the last few months, but he hadn't played with any of them yet because of his school and work schedules. However, he could now look forward to getting to know them, especially the yummy Master Del.

Now there's a Dom I could seriously get into. Or let him get into me, pun intended!

Many people stood at the bar on the club's second floor, waiting for one of the bartenders to notice them. The place was packed, which wasn't unusual during December. Even though Saturday nights were already the busiest at the club, it appeared as if almost every member was there, probably because of the Secret Santa event.

Last night, Matthew had been too exhausted, mentally and physically, to attend the annual Reindeer Races, which involved Sybians, a grid marked off on the floor, and a pair of big fuzzy dice. Subs rode the ultimate vibrating sex machines, complete with a dildo attachment, while the Doms rolled the dice. Whoever's number came up was pushed forward one space on the grid. If a "reindeer" reached the finish line first, their reward was an orgasm. Any contestant who came before crossing the finish line had to race again. The record so far was four races in a row by a female submissive two years ago, and she'd nearly passed out from the multiple orgasms. Master Mitch finally took pity on her and let her sit out for the remainder of the event.

The Reindeer Races took place in the garden, a domed annex added two years ago. With potted trees, shrubs, flowers, and grassy areas, it was like an indoor hedonistic Eden mixed with BDSM equipment, colorful cabanas, and comfortable seating. When the roof was retracted, it let in the fresh air, and you could see the stars and moon. For security, a thin mesh netting across the opening apparently reflected light when seen from above, so no one could use a drone or helicopter to take photos of the people playing in the garden. From below, you almost couldn't tell the netting was there. It was really cool.

In addition to the bar, the second floor of the main club also had seating areas, offices, stock rooms, and a boutique that offered toys, fet-wear, lingerie, and various other items. A massive opening in the center of the upper floor allowed people to observe the cavernous play area below. A grand staircase led down to the "pit," as the dungeon was dubbed when the club first opened. Under the bar were the locker rooms and lounges for both men and women. At the far end of the pit were twenty-four private playrooms, some with viewing windows.

Since neither woman standing in front of him would give in to his pleading, he sighed dramatically and rolled his eyes. "All right. Fine. I'll play along if I must. How does this go again?"

Finding His Forever

"Once everyone is ready," Kristen explained, "we'll hand all the eligible subs an envelope. It'll have three clues about the Dom who picked you. You have to figure out who it is before time runs out."

"Thirty minutes, right?"

"Yup. If you win, you choose how you'll play for two hours. If you lose, the Dom chooses."

That would've sounded super easy if he knew all the gay Doms well enough, but with the new ones who'd joined recently, he might not be so lucky to guess correctly.

"Okay, how do we know which Doms are involved? I'm not all caught up with the club gossip lately, and some of the Doms I know could be in relationships now. There are also a bunch of new Doms."

Angie gestured toward a group of Doms milling about the bar. "See the necklaces some of them have on?" Several wore either a red or green lanyard with a large pendant of the same color. "They're Christmas bulbs that light up, and all the Doms taking part in the Secret Santa have one and will turn theirs on after we hand out the clues to the subs."

"Does it matter which color they're wearing? Like red for straight and green for LGBTQ?"

"Nope. The store just didn't have enough of one color, so we got both. If you don't know if someone swings your way, you'll have to ask one of the other subs. We'll explain all this and more when we start."

A half-hour later, with a white wine spritzer under his belt, Matthew stood to the left of the pit's oval-shaped center stage, surrounded by other unattached subs whose snowflakes had been picked by a Dom or Domme. He'd dressed extra festively for the evening of holiday fun in red leather shorts, green, gold, and white suspenders over his bare torso, a Santa hat, elfin ears, and red, pointed slippers with tiny gold bells on them. Usually, when he got his bi-weekly mani/pedi, he went with clear polish because of his public service job, but earlier that day, he asked for alternating fingernails of red and green. After a good night's sleep, he was able to forgo the concealer and, instead, wore a little mascara and an eyeliner he saved for special occasions. It was black but with a bit of sparkle. On his lips, he'd opted for a red-tinted gloss.

As the three owners and their significant others took the stage, the music pumping through the club's speakers was turned off. Everyone in the pit and watching from the balcony level turned their attention to the stage. Spotlights fell upon Master Ian, Angie, Master Devon, Kristen, Master Mitch, and his two submissives, his switch husband, Tyler, and their wife, Tori. Master Ian spoke first. "Good evening, everyone. Looks like we have a full house again tonight. Thank you all for joining us, not just tonight but throughout the year. When Master Mitch first approached my brother and me about opening a BDSM club here in Tampa, we didn't foresee our membership growing to almost five hundred kinky people. But here you all are, and we thank you for helping us make The Covenant the premier private lifestyle club on the Florida Gulf Coast."

A thunderous round of applause, accompanied by cheers and whistles, filled the air and echoed off the high ceiling. The Dom-in-Residence handed the microphone to Master Mitch, who had to wait almost a full minute before the din died down enough for him to be heard. "Thanks, everyone. And thank you to my cousins for taking a chance on my crazy idea and making my dream come true.

"Now, as you all know, tonight's Secret Santa event is for our unattached Doms and submissives. I'll hand the microphone over to Kristen and Angie in a moment, and they'll go over the rules, but we also have a holiday surprise for everyone. For those who may not have noticed yet, several ticket booths are set up down here, upstairs on the balcony, and out in the garden. Make sure you stop at one of them to get in on our big raffle. Tonight, we're giving away a few trips to Master Key, our new lifestyle resort in the Florida Keys."

The crowd went wild again, and Master Mitch chuckled. "All right, everyone. Fucking chill out so I can tell you how you can win." He pointed toward the big St. Andrew's cross at the back of the stage. In front of it was a small table with a raffle drum. When it came time, the drum would be spun to mix up the entries before the winning tickets were chosen. "We've already put one ticket per member into the drum—we wanted to make sure everyone had a chance, even if they couldn't be here tonight. If you want to purchase more tickets, they're twenty-five dollars each, five for a hundred dollars, or twenty-five for five hundred dollars. You can use your membership cards to make your purchase, which will be added to next month's invoices. What we raise tonight will go to our favorite charity—Healing Heroes—which my beautiful wife founded several years ago. The money you fork over will help train rescue dogs to be partnered with veterans suffering from PTSD."

There was a brief round of applause before the Dom continued. "We'll draw five lucky winners who can bring one guest with them for a three-night stay of their choice of dates, subject to room availability. You'll have to call the reservation number to see what dates are open. The only other thing you have to arrange is your transportation. The winners will also receive a welcome basket upon their arrival, filled with all sorts of surprises, and dinner for two, prepared by renowned Chef Adley Markham in the resort's five-star restaurant, Decadence. Each trip is valued at over thirty-five hundred dollars. Now, there's plenty of time to get your tickets—the booths will be open for the next three hours, so you don't have to rush—and then at midnight, we'll return to the stage to pull the winners. Your names will be on the tickets, so you don't need to be present. I'll send out emails tomorrow notifying any winners not here with all the paperwork and instructions for claiming the trip.

"And don't forget, in two weeks, we'll be closed on

Friday and Saturday for Christmas. If you plan to join us for our big New Year's Eve party, please visit The Covenant's website and RSVP as soon as possible. It's limited to three hundred members because we're having a catered buffet, a bunch of demonstrations, and fun activities, and our very own Summer Hayes will give us a short performance that night."

Again, the crowd went nuts. Summer was one of the world's hottest country music singers and a submissive in the lifestyle. While she still recovered from injuries received in a motor vehicle accident last year in California and hadn't returned to touring or recording yet, she lived in the nearby Indian Shores. Like many of the club members who'd gotten to know her in the privacy of The Covenant, Matthew adored her. She was the sweetest thing, and everyone had been devastated when she was almost killed in the rollover. Thankfully, she was on the mend.

Mitch passed the microphone to Angie, who immediately gave it to Kristen, although her words faintly came through the speakers. "She's in charge. This was her idea."

Kristen laughed and held the mic in front of her mouth. "It might've been my idea, but you figured out how we should do it. Anyway, here are the rules. When we're ready, Angie, Tori, and I will hand out pens and envelopes with the clues to the eligible subs. Do *not* open them until we tell you to. The participating Dominants are wearing a red or green light-bulb necklace. The Doms will turn on their lights when we tell the subs to open their envelopes." She briefly consulted a piece of paper with the list of things she wanted to mention. "The Doms chose their snowflakes based on the sub's sexual orientation, so you don't have to worry about not being properly matched that way. The Doms were also given a copy of their chosen sub's limit list if requested, and as always, hard limits and safewords will be respected. If any problems arise, speak to a Dungeon Monitor.

"Subs will have thirty minutes to try and figure out who has their snowflake based on the three clues given to them. You *cannot* ask any Doms any questions—participating or not. You also can't ask Angie, Tori, Sterling, or me to help since we know who was matched with whom." She met Matthew's glare and winked at him. "Yeah, we lied, sweetie. Deal with it."

Numerous chuckles reached his ears, and he glared at Kristen as she continued. "Now, you can confer with your fellow submissives—including those collared or not participating for whatever reason—to figure out who your Dom is for the night. You can also use your envelope to jot down notes—*don't* use the card for your notes.

"When the thirty minutes is up, you must write down who you think has your snowflake on the back of your clue card. We'll call the subs up here one by one and announce which Dom you wrote down. If you're right, you can choose the type of play you and your

Dom will do for the next two hours. If you get it wrong, then your Dom gets to decide. Make sure your decision is final before you write it down because if any names are crossed out on your card, it'll be an automatic loss, and your Dom will get to pick your play. That's why I said not to use your card for notes.

"Are there any questions?"

Matthew glanced around. Everyone seemed to understand how the game was played, and the excitement levels had risen as subs whispered about who they hoped had their snowflake. Matthew knew who he wanted, especially after spotting Master Del a little while ago. The Dom looked like sin incarnate tonight, wearing snug black leather pants, motorcycle boots, and a crimson leather vest without a shirt. Unfortunately, Matthew hadn't been able to catch the man's eye. Much to his disappointment, it seemed as if Master Del's attention was on another single gay sub named Branden. The Dom had probably picked his snowflake. *Shit.*

"All right, let's get started!" The four men left the women on the stage as Angie and Tori peeled off from Kristen, heading to the opposite sides of the raised platform. "Subs, if your last name starts with A through H, please see Angie. If your last name starts with I through P, then I'll have your envelopes at center stage." She pointed to her left. "And Tori will have Q through Z over on this side."

Three collared subs, carrying boxes of pens, joined

the women as the eligible submissives moved toward whoever had their envelope. Matthew stayed where he was because it was the perfect spot to get his from Angie. It only took about five minutes for all the participating subs to get their envelopes and a pen.

Kristen picked up the microphone again. "Okay, we're ready to start. Master Mitch has a stopwatch and will give a five-minute warning and then a one-minute warning. You must hand your clue card to Tori, Angie, or me at the end of the thirty minutes.

"Here we go! Doms, please turn on your Christmas bulbs! Subs, please open your clues! Good luck!"

As glowing bulbs of green and red lit up throughout the crowd, Matthew ripped open the top of his envelope and slid the card out. It had a string of colorful Christmas lights bordering it, and the text was laser-printed with red ink.

> **Matthew B., here are the clues your Secret Santa provided.**
>
> **Clue #1: Outside the club, your Secret Santa is tech-savvy.**
>
> **Clue #2: The cane is your Secret Santa's favorite implement inside the club.**
>
> **Clue #3: The one thing your Secret Santa doesn't want is for you to call him Daddy.**

And, of course, no one immediately came to mind.

Damn. Okay, I can do this. Just think!

"Matthew, c'mere!"

He spun around to see his friend Natalia beckoning him over to where she and four other participating subs were huddled together. A collared submissive named Jamal was with them, offering his services to help each one deduce who their Secret Santa was. After Matthew joined them, Natalia was the first to read the clues off her card. "Okay, clue number one—his favorite piece of equipment is the spanking bench. Clue number two—he loves CIA thrillers. And clue number three—he . . . huh? He wants me to sit on his handlebars? What does that mean?"

Matthew only needed two seconds to figure it out, and he grinned. "I know who that is! It's Master Dimitri! Almost every time he plays, it's on a spanking bench. I also heard him talking to Master Marco a few weeks ago about a CIA thriller he'd read, and it sounded good, so I got the e-book to read after my tests were over. And the handlebars are his mustache!" The Dom had one of those long mustaches that curled up at the ends. For some men, it would probably look weird or old-fashioned, but for the handsome Master Dimitri, it worked.

Another female sub named Kristina agreed with a squeal. "*Eep*! That has to be him!"

A smile lit up Natalia's face. "I've wanted to scene with him ever since he uncollared that blond chick— what was her name again?"

"Brenda," Jamal supplied with an eye roll. "The one who thought her shit didn't stink when Master Dimitri wasn't around. I was so glad when they broke up and she stopped coming here." His attitude did a one-eighty as he clapped his hands several times. "Okay, Carly, you're next. Let's do this!"

Carly and then the other three subs—two women and one straight guy—read their clues, but the group could only figure out for certain who Kristina's Secret Santa was—Mistress Odette. The sub was a little leery since the Domme was relatively new to the club, and they'd never played together. Kristina was on the shy side and felt more comfortable with the Dommes the longer she knew them. Matthew and Natalia reassured the other sub that she had nothing to worry about. Mistress Odette wasn't a sadist, and the few female submissives who'd scened with the Domme all had nice things to say about her.

Master Mitch's voice boomed over the speakers and announced, "Five-minute warning. Subs, you have five minutes left."

Jamal's dark eyes rounded, and he rotated his hands frantically. "Shit! Hurry, Matthew, you're the last one! Give us your clues!"

After he read them off, he looked at his friends expectantly but was disappointed when no one appeared to have a light-bulb moment. Everyone took a few seconds to glance around the large crowd, hoping for inspiration.

"Hmm, that's hard," Kristina said. "Maybe Master Alan?"

The Dom was an archaeologist and a college professor in his late fifties. While he liked using the cane during scenes, sex had never been included whenever Matthew played with him, which was fine since there was no attraction between them other than a masochist being drawn to a sadist.

Natalia shook her head. "Nope, it can't be him. He's definitely not tech-savvy. Last week, he picked up a brand-new smartphone right before coming here because his old flip phone finally died. I had to show him how to turn it off before he came inside so he wouldn't have to walk back out and leave it in his car." The only place cell phones were allowed to be used in the club was in the lobby. If they were brought inside, they had to be off and left in the member's locker. Occasionally, if a member was on-call, like one of the doctors or detectives, they could leave their cell phone at the front desk. If it rang or a text came in, whoever was working at the desk would get a message to them immediately so they could return the call.

"Okay, then, who else?" Jamal asked. "Master Victor?"

"I doubt it," Matthew replied, shaking his head in frustration. "The one and only time we scened together, it didn't exactly go well—kinda boring for both of us. That, and I know he looked at Angelo's limit list last week."

"Well, crap. It's gotta be someone."

"One-minute warning!" Master Mitch's announcement came over the speakers, and Matthew and the rest of his group started to panic.

Scanning the room once again, Matthew caught sight of Master Del's profile. He stood toward the other side of the stage, talking to Masters Brody and Marco. "What about Master—"

"Wait! I think I know who it is," Natalia interrupted. "Master Jonah!"

Matthew's eyes narrowed. "Who?"

She rushed to explain. "I've met him a few times while working the front desk. He just joined about a month ago and is kinda geeky in a sexy way, so I'm sure he's computer savvy. I think he's in his forties and has been in the lifestyle for a long time. Last week, I saw him give a demo to a baby Dom who was interested in caning. I'm not sure whether or not he likes to be called Daddy, but two out of three is better than anything else, right?"

Matthew reluctantly agreed. If it was a new Dom, he might've randomly chosen a snowflake, intending to meet a sub he didn't know yet. "Okay, Master Jonah it is."

He jotted down the name on the back of his clue card just as Kristen announced the time was up and the subs had to hand in their guesses. Hopefully, whichever Dom had gotten his snowflake, Master Jonah or someone else, they'd be able to give Matthew the pain he craved. The stress of the last few weeks in the paramedic program had him in need of the release he could only find with a good sadist. Mentally crossing his fingers and toes, he handed his card to Angie before dropping his pen into one of two baskets on the stage floor, with the empty envelope going into the other. Then, he rejoined his little group and waited with bated breath.

Chapter Four

Del watched as Matthew handed his clue card back to Ian's wife and wondered if the twink had correctly guessed who picked his snowflake. It'd taken a lot for the Dom not to stare at the object of his lust over the past hour or so, especially while all the subs taking part in the event tried to figure out who their Secret Santa was. Dressed as an adorable elf, Matthew had caught the attention of many gay men in the club since arriving about an hour ago. As he sashayed past them, their hungry gazes raked over the sub's delectable body. Del wanted to tell every single one of them that he had dibs on the boy tonight and, hopefully, for the foreseeable future.

Mitch retook the stage. "Listen up! We want to get through these quickly, so if you are *not* a participating Dom or sub, please back away from the stage and give them some room. If you are participating, please come closer so you can step right up when we call your name. Doms, once you've claimed your sub, head to wherever you plan to play tonight or at least out of the immediate area." People started moving forward or back out of the way, and Del found himself near the right side of the oval stage, with a perfect view of Matthew on the opposite end. "You have until eleven p.m. to complete your scene. Aftercare can extend past that for as long as you need. If you're participating and haven't had a chance to get your raffle tickets, don't worry. Besides the booths, subs will walk around with tickets from eleven to midnight to ensure everyone can get theirs. Good luck, everyone!"

He passed the microphone to Kristen and then left the stage. "Okay, like Master Mitch said, we're going to try and get through these quickly so you can get started on your scenes. Subs, when I call your name, come up on stage. Doms, please be ready to claim your sub even if they didn't guess correctly." Next to her, Angie randomly shuffled the cards while Tori stood on the other side of Kristen, holding a clipboard with several papers—probably the main list of who was matched to whom. Angie handed Kristen a card. "Here we go! Our first submissive is Carly J.!"

Next to Matthew, the cute sub squeaked before lurching forward and running up the few steps to the stage as Kristen continued. "Carly guessed that Master Cain is her Secret Santa!" Tori pointed to a spot on one of the papers she held and showed it to Kristen, who announced, "And that is incorrect! Master Tristan is your Dom for the night."

Finding His Forever

As the burly, russet-haired Trident Security employee Del met last week climbed the steps to claim his sub, Carly grinned, clearly happy with the results. After the Dom took her hand, he led her from the stage while Kristen announced the next submissive. Surprisingly, despite the large number of entries, the process went smoothly. Del had to chuckle as he watched several participating subs throw their hands up in the air or groan loudly when a Dom was called for someone else, likely because that had been their choice. But Del's primary attention was on Matthew, who glanced nervously in his direction every few seconds. At one point, he whispered something to the female sub standing beside him and jutted his chin toward Del. It was evident the younger man now second-guessed his choice, thrilling the Dom. That meant Del got to choose their play tonight.

He increased the intensity of his stare and felt electricity shoot through him when Matthew gulped but didn't look away. In fact, after a moment, he lifted his chin and licked his lips seductively—*insolent little pup.*

As the crowd of participating members dwindled, the moment Del had waited for finally arrived. "Matthew B.!"

The sub didn't move. It was as if he were caught in a web that Del's gaze had cast over him from the other side of the stage. The Dom reveled in it.

"Matthew B., come on up!"

Not breaking their invisible connection, Del raised his brow and cocked his head toward the stage. At the same time, one of Matthew's friends elbowed him in the side. He jumped in surprise and then ran onto the stage, the pom-pom of his hat bouncing along as Kristen and others laughed at him. "Glad you could join us. Matthew guessed Master Jonah as his Secret Santa, which is incorrect! Master Del, please claim your sub."

He didn't need to be told twice. He'd already started for the steps before she said the other Dom's name. Stopping at the top of the stairs, he crooked a finger at Matthew, silently ordering the sub to come to him. Matthew's blue eyes rounded as his feet seemed to work on autopilot while Kristen moved on to another name. "Our next sub is Molly H.!"

Ignoring everything else going on in the cavernous dungeon, Del held out his hand, and when a gaping Matthew took it, he led him down the steps toward the back of the club where he'd reserved one of the playrooms. While he wasn't sure he'd win and choose their play, he'd been optimistic. The room had a large display window where others could observe what happened inside, yet not disturb the occupants, and was the perfect choice for Del after reviewing Matthew's limit list again earlier in the week. While he wanted the quiet it would provide, his little masochist was also a bit of an exhibitionist, which was fine with the Dom.

Stopping in front of the playroom door with a "15" on it, Del studied the submissive's beautiful face. Matthew's lips had a tinge of red gloss, and his downcast eyes were accented by sparkling black liner and mascara that hopefully weren't waterproof. Del would make the masochist cry tonight, and the sadist in him loved to see a sub's perfect makeup destroyed by the end of a scene. Twisted? Yes, but that was the world they played in.

"Eyes on me, pup." When their gazes met, he asked, "Are you disappointed Master Jonah isn't your Secret Santa?"

A flush spread from Matthew's chest up his neck to his face and ears. "N-no, Sir. Not at all. I, um . . . I don't even know who he is. He's new to the club, and one of the other subs thought he fit the clues."

Del was glad to hear that. He wasn't stupid enough to think Matthew hadn't played with plenty of Doms in the club, but the fact he hadn't written down someone he knew intimately was a tad satisfying.

"Good to know. What's your safeword?"

There was no stuttering this time—in fact, a smug smile spread across his face. "Red or pussy, Sir."

A bark of laughter burst from Del. "Well, okay then. Red or pussy will do. And when you're gagged, you'll be given a bell for your safeword."

"G-gagged, Sir?"

Instead of answering him, Del pushed the door to the playroom open. "Welcome to my temporary lair, pup. Enter if you dare. Not that you have a choice beyond your safeword since you're mine for the next two hours."

Barely a moment's hesitation preceded Matthew

entering the room. Del followed and shut the door behind them.

"As cute as your outfit is, strip completely, then kneel next to the cross while I get a few things ready." He paused, then smirked. "On second thought, leave the pointy ears on, my little Vulcan. Tonight, instead of Master Del, you will call me Captain Del."

Matthew's eyes widened at the *Star Trek* reference before he responded, "Yes, Captain Del," and quickly began to strip—not that he had much on to begin with.

The other night, thanks to a few chatty subs, Del discovered Matthew was a Trekkie, having seen every episode and all the movies multiple times. He was especially fond of the original series, starring William Shatner and Leonard Nimoy, and had gone to several *Star Trek* conventions. It was another way he and Del were compatible. Even though Del never wore a role-play costume to the events, he kind of hoped Matthew did—it might be a way to fulfill a few fantasies in the future.

Since they were both fans of *Star Trek*, Del had chosen a futuristic theme room. The ceiling and walls were covered in a dark, cloudless, midnight-sky mural. It gave the feeling of floating in the far reaches of the universe among trillions of stars. A vast emptiness that begged to be explored by those who dared. When Del flipped a switch, the room's lighting changed from white to black, giving the stars an almost eerie glow. The St. Andrew's cross, a spanking bench, contemporary storage cabinets, a king-size bed with white sheets, and other furnishings were all trimmed with purple paint or fabric that glimmered under the black lights.

Black drapes covered the window, and Del pulled on the cord to open them. The recessed hall lighting was dim enough not to disturb the room's atmosphere. A few people already strolled past, waiting to see which rooms would be available for viewing.

He'd stopped in the playroom earlier and stored his toy bag in one of the cabinets so he wouldn't have to carry it around or retrieve it from his locker or from behind the bar. From what he'd been told since joining the club, the Doms respected each other's property, while the subs were known to play tricks and mess with a Dominant's unattended toy bag. He figured his duffel was safe since no one had seen him leave it there.

Sliding the zipper open, he used the soft glow of a fluorescent light under the upper cabinet to inspect the contents and noted nothing had been disturbed.

After lining up a few items he needed for the scene on the countertop, Del turned to see his submissive kneeling as instructed. The glow from the black lights gave Matthew's smooth, pale skin a lavender hue. The only tan lines were from a thong, and that turned Del on even more. He wondered where the sassy twink sunbathed in a skimpy thong because he wanted to watch next time.

Moving to stand in front of the sub, he placed two fingers from one hand under Matthew's chin and lifted until their gazes met. "Damn, you're so beautiful, pup."

Matthew swallowed before responding. "Thank you, Captain Del. And may I say you're very handsome?"

The corners of his mouth ticked upward. "You may, and thank you as well." He brushed his thumb across Matthew's cheek. "I'm going to use a cane on your sweet ass and thighs tonight. You're going to scream and cry for me, and then I'm going to fuck your ass and make you come harder than you've ever come in your life. If that isn't what you want, say your safeword now."

Lust and need filled the submissive's eyes. His lips parted as he swayed into Del's touch. "That's *exactly* what I want, Master—I mean, Captain Del. I don't want to safeword."

"But you will if it gets to be too much. Promise me." When he didn't get an immediate answer, Del gripped Matthew's chin hard with one hand and twisted the sub's nipple with the other, garnering a satisfying gasp. "Answer me, pup. Promise me you'll safeword if I go too far."

"Y-you won't, Sir. I trust you. But you have my promise—I'll use my safeword if I need to."

Del studied the sub's face, seeing the truth behind his words and feeling humbled. Matthew *did* trust Del to take care of him. To give him what he needed, what he craved. He also trusted Del not to harm him. Hurt him? Yes, that's why the masochist was there. However, the Dom would never *harm* him. There was a stark difference, and they both knew it.

"Thank you. Stand and face the cross." Once Matthew was in position, Del secured his wrists and ankles with fleece-lined leather restraints, ensuring they weren't too tight. Next, a large strap was fastened across his waist, and two more just above his knees, limiting his movements even further.

Striding back to the cabinets, Del grabbed several items before returning to his sub. A decent-sized crowd watched them from the other side of the window. With the room's intercom system set to semi-private, everyone in the hallway could hear the scene inside, but Del and Matthew wouldn't be disturbed by any outside noise. A large man wearing a gold vest, who Del didn't recognize, leaned against the wall on the far-right side of the window. A dungeon monitor. It didn't surprise him since he was the new sadist in the club and hadn't fully proved himself to be a responsible and alert Dom yet. Even though he received a glowing recommendation from his old club in Ohio, he would still be observed until the owners and the DMs were satisfied all his play was safe, sane, and consensual. It was another reason The Covenant had such a stellar reputation in the BDSM community on the Gulf Coast.

The large, white leather X the twink was attached to stood about two and a half feet from the wall, giving Del enough room to move between them and face Matthew. "I'm going to explain a few things before we continue, pup, because then I'm going to take away most of your senses."

He held up one hand, showing off the items he'd

selected hanging from his fingers. "You'll wear noise-canceling headphones, a blindfold, and a ball gag during most of the scene. I want all your attention on the pain I'm going to inflict. Since you won't be able to speak," he showed Matthew the two small brass bells in his other hand, "I'm going to put one of these in each of your hands. Occasionally, I'll lift one side of the headphones, ask if you're still green, and instruct you to ring the bells for me. If you drop both bells, I'll take that to mean you're saying your safeword, and the scene will end. If one falls to the floor, I'll question you to see if it was an accident. If you need me to slow down for a moment or adjust something, just ring the bells, and I'll check in with you. Understand?"

"Yes, Captain Del. Ring the bells if I need you to slow down or adjust. Drop them both to safeword."

"Good. After I prep your hole with some lube, I'll start to warm your ass up with my hand and then the flogger. The cane will come next. How quickly do you usually go into subspace?" He had to ask because, with the starry-eyed expression on Matthew's face, Del had to wonder if just the thought of the cane had the sub halfway to Nirvana already.

"It depends, Sir. Some Doms can get me there pretty quickly. With others, I might not hit it at all."

He smirked. "Well, that gives me something to aim for then. You're not to come until I'm in that fine ass of yours. Then you can climax whenever you need to."

"Yes, Sir. Thank you, Sir."

Chapter Five

A shiver rolled down Matthew's spine as Master Del winked before rounding the cross and stopping behind him. The blindfold went on first, followed by the gag in his mouth, which was strapped in place behind his head. It wasn't the first time he'd been gagged, but it wasn't on his list of fun things to do during a scene. What bothered him the most was the fact that he always ended up slobbering all over the place, like a Mastiff or a St. Bernard.

The noise-canceling headphones went on last. For all intents and purposes, Matthew was blind, mute, and deaf. If there were a loud noise, like the cane hitting his flesh, he'd hear it, but other than that, his entire world would be focused on the forthcoming pain—just as Master Del had said and what Matthew wanted.

He'd been shocked as all hell when Kristen announced that Master Del was his Secret Santa. The sneaky Dom had pulled one over on him, not that Matthew would complain about it.

As far as he knew, Master Del hadn't played with anyone since coming to the club as a full member last week. Surely, if one of the male submissives had scened with the hot new Dom, they wouldn't have kept it a secret. "Don't kiss and tell" was far from being a mantra among The Covenant's subs. Being open about one's sexual experiences and kinks was part of the lifestyle. If Del had played with someone at the club, Matthew would have heard about it by now.

Had he been so interested in me that he waited for an opportunity to play with me first? Goddess, I hope so.

Just the thought of any other male sub sceneing with the Dom made Matthew's inner green-eyed monster roar in envy—which was never a good look on him. For some reason, he felt a connection to Master Del that he never experienced before with anyone else—Dominant or not. He was probably imagining things. Love at first sight happened in the steamy novels Kristen wrote under her maiden name but not in real life. At least, he didn't think it did.

Master Del lined the front of his body up with Matthew's naked back, sending goosebumps dancing across his flesh. Sensual warmth enveloped him. At some point, the Dom removed the vest he'd worn but still had on the leather pants. Matthew wished he could get an eyeful of all that luscious skin, but he'd have to wait until later.

The left headphone was pulled away from his ear,

and Master Del's lips brushed against his lobe. "Wiggle your fingers and toes for me, pup."

The bells jingled a little as he did as ordered, and then his ear was covered again. All he could hear was his own breathing and heartbeat. Large masculine hands squeezed his ass cheeks, making his hard-on pulse between his legs. He had the sudden urge to thrust his hips forward but didn't want to risk whatever punishment that might bring.

The hands disappeared, and then cool liquid dripped into his crack. A thick, calloused finger spread the lubricant over his puckered hole before demanding entry. Matthew relaxed his muscles the best he could, giving the Dom access to the dark depths of his body. Behind the blindfold, his eyes closed as he took pleasure in being prepped so expertly.

A second finger joined the first and then a third. Plunging. Withdrawing. Stroking. Stretching. The friction of skin against sensitive tissue, the burn firing up his nerves, and the sense of being filled to completion were incredible. The gag muffled Matthew's moan, but it was still loud in his own head. When Master Del pulled his fingers out, Matthew whimpered at the loss.

Not being able to use most of his senses, he was startled when the first hand slapped across his ass cheek, but then he settled in for the warm-up. Every smack was in a different spot, bringing his blood to the surface. A sharp sting followed each time the Dom's hand struck his flesh, but it wasn't enough to start easing him into subspace—not that he expected it to.

That would hopefully come with the flogger, but he knew it wouldn't be until the cane left angry red welts on his ass and thighs that he would fall into a sea of bliss. The intense pain that would send most people screaming into the hills was what he needed—what he craved. He could come hard and without effort at that point. Physical stimulation of his cock wasn't necessary, but he had to hold off until Master Del was buried inside him and then he could finally find his release.

Matthew lost count of the number of hand spanks he received before they were replaced with the buttery-soft leather tongues of the flogger. However, soft didn't mean they didn't hurt. With his skin warmed up, his nerve endings were on full alert. He couldn't hear the slaps against his flesh, which heightened his awareness of the burn they brought. He could imagine the dark pink hue that covered his ass cheeks and the backs of his thighs. His cock was long and thick against his abdomen, his balls heavy below. Drool spilled from the corners of his mouth. His eyes watered, but not to the point they overflowed. However, they would soon.

The tendrils of subspace teased the edges of his mind, rising and falling with the rhythmic strikes of the flogger's knotted tails. It felt like he floated on a calm ocean, the waves gently lifting and dropping him as they glided beneath him. A thousand bees buzzed in his ears as every inch of his skin, from head to toe, tingled.

The Dom was good—he'd give him that. Matthew's

endorphin-energized brain began to rush toward subspace faster than usual, and they hadn't even started with the cane yet.

The left headphone was lifted, surprising him since he didn't realize Master Del stopped hitting him with the flogger. The Dom's deep voice rumbled in his ear, "Color, pup. Ring one bell for green. Ring both for yellow. Drop them for red."

It took a herculean effort to move one set of fingers until he heard the jingle of the clapper against brass. He was stoned out of his mind—a high he doubted any drug could duplicate for him, not that he would try to find it outside the realm of the BDSM community. He'd seen a few EMTs, medics, cops, and firefighters tank their careers after falling victim to addiction. Two EMTs he'd known lost their lives to accidental overdoses. No, drugs weren't for him. But this . . . this pain-induced pleasure eased his stress, relaxing him, anchoring him.

The headphone was replaced, returning him to the silence only interrupted by the sounds of his own body. He sniffled, panted, slurped, and gulped—each action as loud as fireworks exploding in the summer sky. With every beat of his heart, he could hear the blood hurtling through his arteries and veins. His pulse thumped in his ears as his cock throbbed in time.

Matthew never heard the swish of the cane, and the slap was barely audible, but oh, how he felt it. It caught him off-guard, causing a grunt to burst from his chest. A white-hot line seared across the middle of his ass, the heat spreading like wildfire up his back and down his legs. The cane was held against his skin, letting his body absorb the sting accompanying the implement. It took a few seconds for the gratifying pain to follow, and Matthew savored it as it took hold and cocooned him.

The next strike landed on his sit-spot, right below his ass. His scream was muffled but undoubtedly loud enough to be heard over the room's intercom by whoever observed the scene in the hallway. Involuntarily, he rolled up onto the balls of his feet but immediately brought his heels back down again. The tears he'd held back until then now flowed in rivulets down his cheeks. His jaw ached from trying to clench down, which the gag prevented him from doing.

Master Del expertly established a rhythm of his own making that soon had Matthew plummeting down a euphoric rabbit hole. The cane bounced off his ass or upper thighs after some of the strokes, while others lingered against his burning flesh. There was no pattern he could discern which was his preference. He liked being kept on edge, not knowing the strength behind the next strike or where it would land.

His tears soaked the blindfold while snot dripped from his upper lip. Saliva rolled off his chin, splashing onto his chest. His cock wept with the need to come as his ass and thighs burned bright. His throat was sore from his stifled screams. He didn't care about any of that because the need for the cathartic release he chased trumped everything.

He clutched the bells tightly in his hands, desperately not wanting them to drop, causing the scene to end far too soon.

Again, he didn't realize Master Del had stopped until the headphones were removed, this time, completely. "You take the cane beautifully, pup. What's your color? One bell for green, two for yellow, drop them for red."

It took all Matthew's concentration to ring the bell in his right hand. A hiss escaped around the curves of the ball gag as the Dom caressed the abused flesh of Matthew's ass. "Mmm. I love seeing my welts on your skin. Can you handle a few more before I fuck you senseless?"

If Matthew could speak, he would've said he was already senseless, but since that wasn't an option, he wiggled his fingers on one hand, letting the bell answer for him.

"Perfect."

The headphones remained off, and Master Del also removed the ball gag, but the blindfold stayed in place. Matthew sensed, more than heard, the Dom step away from him. "Three more. I want you to count the first two out loud for me."

When he tried to respond verbally, it took a moment to get his mouth, tongue, and throat working again. His voice was raspy when he finally croaked, "Yes, Captain Del."

"Good boy."

Despite losing the headphones, he still didn't hear

the swish of the cane before it hit just below his sit-spot. His yelp was followed by, "One, Sir!"

Adrenaline resulting from the pleasure/pain flooded his body. If anything touched his cock right then, he'd go off like a rocket.

Thwack!

That one landed on his upper ass, spiraling him further into subspace. "Yes! Two, Sir!" His mind registered the words he didn't realize he'd spoken.

"Last one, pup. Scream for me. Let them hear you upstairs in the bar."

Thwack!

Just below mid-center, the cane scorched his ass cheeks. A high-pitched screech ripped from his chest. His tortured flesh was consumed by lava, heating the blood rushing to his dick. He couldn't focus on anything else but the need to come.

Matthew cried out again when Master Del's naked body pressed against his. He had no idea when the man had stripped out of his leathers and boots, but he didn't care. "Please, Sir. Please, Captain Del. I need…"

"I know what you need, Matthew, and I'm going to give it to you."

His flaming cheeks were separated, and two fingers coated more lube over his hole. Matthew gasped for air and pleaded for relief. The digits were replaced by the tip of the Dom's condom-covered cock. Matthew's body greedily sucked the other man in. It took two or three thrusts before Master Del bottomed out, his hot skin and the hairs covering his lower abdomen, groin, and thighs abrading the welts he'd left on Matthew. The contact was a welcome torture to the masochist.

Master Del growled in his ear. "Fuck, baby. So tight. You got me so worked up, I won't last long."

"M-me either, Sir. Please."

"Come whenever you need to."

The Dom retreated and thrust forward—hard. Again. And again, rubbing against Matthew's prostate. Each plunge brought him closer to the edge until his orgasm hit him with the strength of a tsunami. The wave catapulted him into the star-filled galaxy surrounding them, spinning weightlessly through space. His mind went completely blank as streams of cum painted his abdomen. Behind him, Master Del stiffened and roared his own release.

Matthew's legs gave out—the only things still holding him up were the restraints and being sandwiched between Master Del's delicious form and the leather-covered padded cross. He sucked in lungfuls of air, trying to sate his body's need to replenish the oxygen it was suddenly lacking. The Dom's heavy gasps near Matthew's ear said he was trying to recover from the intense experience as well.

Time seemed to speed up and slow down simultaneously—like they were in some wormhole in the space-time continuum. Matthew wasn't sure how many seconds, minutes, or even hours passed before Master Del pulled out, took the bells away, and began releasing the restraints. The strap across Matthew's waist was the last to go, and before he could step away from the cross, Master Del swept him up in his arms and carried him across the room to the large bed. Setting him on his feet again, Master Del instructed, "Lay on your stomach, pup."

He didn't have to be told twice. The Dom helped Matthew ease onto the clean sheets and get into position. Through slits in his eyes, the sub watched Master Del close the curtains to give them privacy before grabbing and pulling on his leather pants, leaving the fly undone. He retrieved a tube of arnica gel from his toy bag and returned to the bed, taking a seat beside Matthew's thighs. "How're you feeling?"

He hissed when the first drop of cool gel landed on his right butt cheek. "Phenomenal—that was incredible. Thank you." His words were slurred as sleep tried its best to pull him under.

"You're very welcome. Rest now while I take care of you. We'll talk more later."

"Yes, Sir."

Chapter Six

Del spent the next forty-five minutes tending to the submissive and watching him sleep. After applying arnica gel to the welts up and down Matthew's ass and upper thighs, Del turned him onto his side and covered him with a clean, warm blanket. Next, he grabbed a package of baby wipes he'd seen in one of the cabinets and used several to remove Matthew's ruined makeup—something he'd never done with a sub after a scene.

Something about the younger man caused Del's protective nature to override his sadistic streak. He loved making Matthew cry and seeing the remnants of the sparkly eyeliner and mascara streaming down his cheeks. Usually, he let the submissives he played with walk through the club after recovering from subspace to clean up in the bathroom or locker room, letting everyone see how the Dom had brought the masochist to tears. But for some reason, he hadn't wanted to share the results with anyone else this time.

He knew several sadists who liked to cuddle with their subs after giving them the pain they craved, but Del always did it out of his obligation as a responsible Dom in the lifestyle. Others he knew would pawn a sub's aftercare onto someone else. If that was part of their negotiations, then Del could be tolerant, even if he disagreed with it. But what he couldn't stand was a sadist who didn't fulfill their duty to a masochist, ensuring they were safe and had recovered after a scene before leaving them alone. Del always waited until he was confident his D/s partners were stable and in the right state of mind before letting them go after sending them into subspace—whether it took thirty minutes or three hours for them to recover. Many times, he escorted a submissive home and then called them the next day to make sure they were okay.

However, when it came to the beautiful twink he now had wrapped in his arms, Del wanted to take him home and wake up with him in the morning. That was something he'd never done before, either. There was an attraction . . . a draw to Matthew that he had never experienced with any other man, and they barely knew each other. But that was something Del wanted to fix. He tried to remember the last time he went out on a date. Like a *date*-date. Dinner at a nice restaurant or somewhere they both enjoyed while talking, holding hands, and laughing. Thinking back, it had to have been several years. His only sexual encounters of late had been in a club.

What would Matthew say if I asked him out? Would he be interested in me for more than just a giver of pleasure/pain?

A sexy moan came from the man in his arms. Matthew's head rested on Del's bare chest. His breaths, gentle puffs of air across Del's skin, left goosebumps in their wake. Unable to help himself, Del dipped his chin and swept his lips across Matthew's forehead. "Wake up, pup."

The sub blinked several times before his eyes stayed open, still filled with post-orgasmic drowsiness. "Hi, Sir."

Del grinned and flicked one of the pointy ears the younger man still wore. "Hi back, my sexy, little Vulcan. Since you're still recovering, you can relax on protocol until we leave this room. How're you feeling?"

"Mmm. Like I was ridden hard and put away wet—just how I like it."

"Ha! Glad to hear it." He brushed a few strands of Matthew's blond hair, no longer damp from sweat, off his forehead. "You take the cane beautifully."

Matthew blushed. "You handle it beautifully. I fell into subspace almost as fast as I do with the bullwhip."

"Really? Hmm. We'll have to try that after I've been cleared to play with the whip." Before allowing certain types of intense play, The Covenant's owners demanded new Doms take classes and demonstrate they could keep the subs they played with safe. "It's my second favorite implement."

The mere thought of sceneing again with the other man had the Dom's blood rushing to his cock, but he ignored the stirring in his groin. The submissive was in no condition for a second round of sex any time soon. Del grabbed a bottle of water he'd set on a bedside table, cracked it open, and handed it to Matthew. "Drink up."

When his order was obeyed, he said, "They're going to draw the raffle winners soon. Do you want to get tickets?"

Del bought tickets earlier after inquiring about the booths scattered around the club. Since it was going to a worthy cause, he bought a hundred of them and asked the woman at the booth to help him put the names of all the club's employees, including Matthew, on three tickets each. He knew many submissives worked off part of their membership fees. Once the employees were taken care of, he scribbled his own name on the remaining tickets. Later, he wanted to talk to Mitch's wife about making a sizable donation to her charity. While he hadn't gone into the military, he deeply respected those who signed up to defend their country. In addition to helping veterans, the charity also rescued dogs—a win/win in his book.

Matthew shook his head after swallowing half of the water in the bottle. "No, Sir. I bought a few when I first got here. But I'd like to be there for the drawing."

A wicked grin spread across his face. "I'm feeling lucky tonight."

"You are, huh?"

"Well, I got lucky when you picked my snowflake." He took another sip of water, and his gaze dropped to his lap. "Um, can I ask you something, Sir?"

"Sure. If you look me in the eye when you ask. What would you like to know?"

That blush he loved was back and deeper this time as Matthew met his gaze. "Did you . . . uh, did you purposefully pick me for the Secret Santa, or was it random?"

Del ran two fingers down the younger man's cheek, his gaze trailing after them. "Do you honestly believe I wouldn't be first in line to get your snowflake after meeting you? You had me spellbound that first night, pup. I've been waiting ever since to scene with you."

"Really?"

"Really." Leaning down, he brushed their lips together. "I just hope I don't have to wait two more weeks to see you again."

Matthew practically melted in Del's arms. "Have mercy, Sir." His eyes lit up. "No, scratch that. Don't have mercy, Sir."

Del laughed before retaking the submissive's mouth. He'd have to thank Kristen and Angie later for letting him get Matthew's snowflake before they put the others up on the trees. For now, he would enjoy the rest of the evening with his pretty little sub.

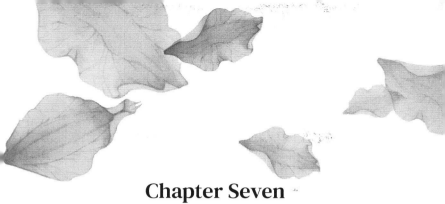

Chapter Seven

Matthew regretted wearing his snug, red leather shorts because they chafed the welts the cane had left on his tender bottom. It probably wouldn't be as irritating if he were standing. After he was allowed to scrub his face clean of the last of his ruined makeup, Master Del led him out to the pit. Once there, the Dom found an oversized, plush chair with an ottoman and pulled Matthew onto his lap. Snuggling with the Dom, who'd given Matthew one of the best scenes of his life, was more than enough to make up for any discomfort he experienced.

When Matthew shivered, despite the warm air in the club, Master Del asked one of the servers, Cassandra, to bring a blanket for him, which he then wrapped around Matthew's torso. "Better?"

"Yes, Sir. Thank you." He rested his head on Master Del's shoulder, his eyes closing as the remnants of subspace taunted him.

They had another ten minutes or so before the raffle winners were drawn. More and more D/s couples settled into the many seating areas situated around the pit or looked down from above on the second floor. Some were the Doms and subs paired up through the Secret Santa, while others were in established relationships. Many of the submissives appeared to be still recovering from their scenes. Matthew spotted Natalia with a dreamy, satisfied look on her face, sitting on Master Dimitri's lap in an area closer to the stage. He was happy his friend seemed to have had fun with the Dom. She would probably call Matthew on the phone sometime tomorrow to chat about their scenes, as they often did, so he'd get all the details then.

"Here you go, Sir."

Matthew opened his eyes to see Cassandra had returned with three drinks—what looked like an appletini and a whiskey on the rocks, and a cold bottle of water. The pretty sub used to work at the club, like other submissives, to pay off part of her membership, but since being permanently collared by Master Stefan and going back to school for nursing, she only filled in on occasion. Matthew knew Kristen and Angie had asked the collared subs to swap out with the single ones who were supposed to work that evening so they could participate in the Secret Santa. That included the waitstaff, the front desk personnel, boutique clerks, and the sitters at the child-care center on the other side of the parking lot from the club.

Cassandra handed the green drink to Master Del,

who held it out for Matthew to take. The Dom then took the short tumbler and water bottle from the woman before she left them.

"I didn't even hear you order these, Sir," Matthew said as Master Del clinked their glasses together. "Thank you."

"You were dozing again, pup. No worries. Is the appletini okay? The waitress said it was one of your favorites."

"It's perfect, Sir. Thank you." Holding the drink with both hands so he wouldn't accidentally spill any of it, he took a sip and sighed in delight as the sweet taste of apples with a kick of vodka tantalized his taste buds.

Master Del smiled. "That's the only drink you're allowed tonight, though. It'll take you a few more hours to recover from our scene."

"Yes, Sir."

After tasting his drink, the Dom said, "I understand you had your final exams yesterday. How did you do? Have you gotten the results yet?"

"No, Sir. I won't find out until probably after Christmas, but I *think* I did really well. I know I was spot-on for my practicals, so it's the written exam I'm worried about. That's what candidates usually have problems with and have to retake it if they fail."

"Well, from what people in the club say, I'm sure you aced both the practicals and the written."

Sitting up quickly, Matthew winced as his tortured

ass and thighs protested. "People have been talking about my exams?"

Nodding, Master Del swallowed another sip of the amber liquid in his glass. "Uh-huh. Doms, subs, your bosses, and fellow employees—apparently, everyone's had their fingers crossed this week but didn't want to say anything to you. They figured you were nervous enough as it was. You have a lot of supporters here who are immensely proud of you, pup, and they're certain you'll go far in your career. Does that surprise you?"

"A little, I guess." He snuggled against the Dom's chest when he was pulled closer again. "I have a bunch of friends here, but I didn't realize so many members were interested in my job or that they knew me beyond working the front desk."

"You light up any room you walk into, Matthew. How could they not know or want to know you?" He paused as an announcement came over the sound system stating that the ticket booths were closing and asking all subs who sold tickets to bring them to the stage. Masters Mitch, Ian, and Devon were already up there, bringing the raffle drum front and center.

Master Del ran a hand up Matthew's arm. "When can I see you again? I want to take you to dinner and get to know you better."

His eyes widened. *Oh, be still my heart!* "Really?"

"Really. That is if you'd like to go on a date with me. If you'd rather we keep our relationship to the club for now—"

"No! I mean, yes, Sir! No! I mean—crap." Frustrated,

he took a deep breath and let it out, grateful to see an amused smile spreading across Master Del's handsome face. *Is this truly happening?* "Can I start over, Sir?"

"I really wish you would. Please."

"Sir, I would love to go on a date with you. I have to look at my schedule before I commit to a day and time, though. Some of my shifts have been switched around with the upcoming holiday. We try to make sure the medics and EMTs with kids can be off on Christmas. I also picked up a few overtime split shifts over the next two weeks—it's a busy time of year. And on Christmas Eve, my folks and I always volunteer to help cook and serve dinner at a homeless shelter."

The Dom chuckled. "I might have to stop calling you 'pup' and call you busy bee instead. But I have a better idea. You check your schedule and let me know when you're free for lunch or dinner. It doesn't matter to me as long as I can see you again. As for Christmas Eve, my mother and I used to volunteer at a women's shelter whenever we could—which wasn't often, but we tried to put in some time to help. Would I be able to come with you on Christmas Eve?"

Matthew fell a little bit in love with the man right then and there. "Um, if you want to, Sir, we could always use an extra set of hands. That would be great."

"Then it's a date. But, hopefully, we'll have plenty more before that," he said with a wink.

His head spun, but before Matthew could say anything more, Master Ian's voice boomed over the club's speakers, "Listen up! It's time to pull the winners of the raffle. If your name is called, please come up, and Master Mitch will give you an envelope with all the information you need to plan your trip to the Master Key Resort. If a winner isn't present, we'll contact them tomorrow, but feel free to blow up their phone tonight and let them know they won. Also, club employees, make sure you thank Master Del for buying a few tickets in each of your names. Thanks for the donation, Del."

Matthew gasped and stared at the Dom whose lap he sat on, while thunderous applause came from the other members. Master Del squeezed Matthew's waist and held up his almost empty glass to acknowledge everyone else. With pinkened cheeks, he appeared a little embarrassed at the attention and the fact that his charitable act was announced.

Oh, Goddess of Twink submissives everywhere, I could fall hard for this man. Please don't let him break my heart!

On the stage, Master Devon rotated the big raffle drum, and the crowd's excitement seemed to vibrate the walls. When Matthew finished his appletini with a gulp, Master Del took the glass from him and swapped it for the bottle of water sitting on a little table beside their chair. "Drink all of that—we have to rehydrate you."

As he did as he was told, Master Mitch drew the first ticket from the drum and handed it to Master Ian, who looked at it, then groaned and rolled his eyes. "Master Brody, come up and get your bloody ticket. As if you haven't spent enough fucking time at the resort already."

A loud *hoo-yah* echoed off the ceiling, and everyone laughed, cheered, and clapped. Brody Evans was a major computer geek and a retired Navy SEAL who co-owned Trident Security. He and his wife, Fancy, had a little boy named Zane, who was just over a year old and absolutely adorable.

Once the Dom retrieved a manila envelope from Master Mitch and thrust his hands in the air, bellowing out another *hoo-yah,* the exuberant crowd was ready for another name to be announced. The following three winners were Cassandra, Sterling, and Mistress Roxy, whose submissive wife, Kayla, yelled louder than Master Brody had.

The barrel was spun for the final time, and Matthew held his breath. It would be so cool to win a trip to the resort he'd heard all about from the owners and their wives. He glanced furtively at Master Del.

Would he want to go with me if I won?

He couldn't help but think something was building between them in the short time they'd known each other. Something special. Something he'd hoped to find someday—the man who would be his forever.

Master Mitch handed the final ticket to Master Ian, who, surprisingly, smiled broadly this time. "Well, I can't think of anyone more deserving than this person. He's worked his ass off for the past year, and I, for one, am proud of him. I know, without a doubt, he'll make an amazing paramedic soon. Matthew Behan, get your one-hundred percent fabulously gay ass up here!"

He froze when the head Dom said the word "paramedic" because, as far as Matthew knew, no other members were paramedics or EMTs taking the course. When his name was finally announced, his jaw dropped, and his eyes grew to the size of saucers as the crowd whistled and yelled out their congratulations. Matthew didn't move until Master Del stood, letting the sub slide down his thighs to a standing position. The Dom kissed him on the cheek. "Go on, pup! Get your prize. Congratulations."

When the reality hit him, Matthew covered his mouth and jumped up and down before running toward the stage. He'd never won anything that big in his life and still couldn't believe it happened this time. Masters Ian, Devon, and Mitch shook his hand before the latter gave him a large envelope. Matthew turned and waved it in the air. As the cheers rose and then dwindled, he hurried down the steps and back over to Master Del, who grinned at him. Matthew threw his arms around him as the taller man laughed and hugged him back. "Congratulations. As Ian said, it's well deserved."

Matthew was on cloud nine. It felt like he'd won a million-dollar lottery—a fantastic trip, a Dom he was already falling for, and hopefully, a new career as a paramedic. He couldn't wait to see what the New Year would bring. If it were anything like tonight, it would be awesome.

Chapter Eight

Tuesday night, Del held out a chair for Matthew at their table at Tuscany and then sat across from him. Although Matthew had once been inside the upscale Italian restaurant near the Riverwalk in Tampa for a patient who choked on a piece of veal, he'd never eaten there. Thankfully, the victim survived. Otherwise, Matthew might've been uncomfortable having dinner at the place.

Now, he could take in his surroundings and enjoy the pleasant atmosphere. Beautiful strains of instrumental music floated through the air, but it was muted enough to accommodate conversations. The decor was rich and elegant but not ostentatious. It was what Matthew imagined inviting restaurants in Italy looked like. Florence, the capital of Tuscany, was on his bucket list ever since his cousin raved about it after honeymooning with her husband there a few years ago. Someday, he'd get there.

With the unopened menu the hostess had left on the table in front of him, he was a little nervous about finding out what the meals cost. When they discussed where to go on a date, Del made it clear that dinner would be his treat. Matthew then realized he didn't know much about what Del did for a living other than he was a computer programmer or something like that. While the man could obviously afford The Covenant's club membership, it didn't mean he had an abundance of wealth. Regardless, Matthew would find one of the cheaper entrees to order. He didn't want to come across as greedy and high-maintenance. Money wasn't what he found attractive in a man, and he would never date someone because they were rich or not date someone because they were poor. He just wanted to find someone to love and have the man love him back for no reason other than they were meant to be together.

It was their second date since the night of the Secret Santa when they exchanged cell phone numbers before parting. Matthew was thrilled to receive a text from Del the following day, thanking him for a fantastic evening. They texted each other on and off for several hours before making plans to see each other again.

They met for lunch at the Sand Key Park in Clearwater yesterday, several hours before Matthew's 7:00 p.m. split shift. Del picked up sandwiches at a deli, and since it was raining, they ate them in Matthew's truck while discussing various topics. Several times, he missed things that Del said because he'd been too busy silently undressing the man in his mind—which he seemed to be doing again right then.

Yesterday, Del wore jeans, sneakers, and a Cincinnati Bengals T-shirt molded to his fine physique. Tonight, he was dressed all in black—dress pants, a leather belt, a silk shirt with the top two buttons undone, and a pair of oxfords on his feet that were shined to perfection. The attire was more suitable for the fancy restaurant and The Covenant, where they planned to go for dessert later. And yes, that was a euphemism for a scene involving sex.

Matthew had spent over an hour trying on different shirts and pants, wanting to look fabulous and alluring to his date without coming across as a hooker in a gay version of *Pretty Woman*. He'd finally settled on skinny black dress pants with ankle boots and a shiny, satin teal button-down shirt with a built-in tie instead of lapels that hung loosely from his neck. He'd topped it off with a black, waist-length bolero jacket with a lacy teal handkerchief square in the left breast pocket.

Before they could look at their menus, a tall, young waiter approached and stopped beside their table. His brown-eyed gaze zeroed in on Del, making Matthew want to stand up and slap the man silly.

Feeling possessive and jealous? Why, yes, I am. Thank you very much!

"Hi, my name is Josh, and I'll be your server tonight. Can I get you a drink *or* . . . anything else, sir?" the blond himbo asked, never taking his eyes off Del or acknowledging Matthew's presence.

The come-fuck-me drawl in his voice was also hard to miss, and Matthew huffed loudly, drawing Del's full attention. The Dom winked at him as if he knew Matthew was annoyed as fuck. "*Sweetheart*, what would you like to drink?"

He nearly melted at the endearment. Instead, he gave Del a sultry gaze and licked his upper lip before shifting his eyes to stare at the waiter, whose face showed his disappointment that the hottest guy in the place was most definitely taken. "I'll have an orange margarita with sugar instead of salt since I'm already so sweet and delicious." His gaze returned to Del. "Aren't I, *Sir*?"

Across the table, Del hid a smirk behind his fist before clearing his throat. "Absolutely," he said before murmuring, "Little brat."

Del stared at Matthew's grin for several heartbeats before addressing the server, still waiting for his order. "And I'll have a glass of merlot, please."

"Of course."

After giving Matthew a sideways stink-eye, the guy left to get their drinks. It was then an awful thought popped into Matthew's mind. He leaned forward and lowered his voice. "Oh, crap. I hope he doesn't spit in my food later!"

Del barked out a soft laugh. "I'll make it clear that we're sharing our meals. Hopefully, that will deter any wayward and unhygienic ideas he might have."

He picked up his menu and gestured for Matthew

to do the same. "Let's decide what to eat, and then there are a few things I want to discuss with you."

"Uh-oh. That sounds ominous."

Another chuckle erupted from Del's throat. "Not at all. Despite our previous conversations, I realized we haven't negotiated a contract or talked about whether you want one with me."

"I do!" he proclaimed a bit too loudly. Several nearby patrons glanced in their direction, and a blush stole across his cheeks. *Eager much?* He brought the volume of his voice down a level or two. "I mean, I'd be honored to negotiate a contract with you, Sir."

"I'm glad. It'll be my honor as well." Del's gaze dropped to the menu. "What looks good to you?"

Matthew licked his lips as he studied the dark chest hair peeking out from the V of Del's shirt. He remembered what it felt like against his back while strapped to the St. Andrew's cross during their Secret Santa scene. The thought had his cock hardening. He'd jacked off to that memory every morning and night since, but nothing came close to the real thing.

"Matthew."

"Hmm?"

"I asked what you wanted to eat."

"You, Sir." His eyes widened when he realized he said that aloud, and their server had returned in time to hear it. Matthew's drink was placed a little too hard on the table in front of him, almost causing the liquid to splash over the top. He gave the man a brief glare and then focused on the menu. While the prices were slightly higher than at the more casual restaurants he usually frequented, they weren't exorbitant, thank goodness. "Um . . . What are you getting? Everything looks so good."

"Why don't we pick two entrees and share them?"

Damn, the man was smooth and hadn't forgotten Matthew's fear. Once confident he wouldn't giggle out loud, he replied, "Oooh. That's a great idea. Uh, let's see." He quickly scanned the list of entrees and their descriptions. "The chicken alla Milanese looks yummy."

"It does. How about that and the wild mushroom ravioli?"

Matthew found it on the menu and then nodded. "Sounds absolutely *scrumptious*."

Okay, he was laying it on a little thick, for Josh's sake, but so what? He was in a bratty mood and never one to back down from the competition.

"Good."

Del took Matthew's menu and added it to his own to hand to the server when the man was done jotting down their order. "What dressing would you like on your salad, sir?"

Again, he only addressed Del, and Matthew knew he wasn't the only one who noticed because the Dom's jaw tightened for a moment before he asked, "Matthew, what would you like on your salad?"

With an all-too-sweet cheeky grin, he placed his elbows on the table, tucked his clasped hands under his chin, and batted his eyes at the server. "Bleu cheese, please."

"Make that two," Del added dismissively.

Once the server left them alone again, Matthew tilted his head. "Thank you."

Del took a sip of his wine. "For what?"

"For letting me know you were annoyed at him and not making a scene about it."

"He was rude, pup." He reached across the table and took Matthew's hand. "Everyone here can probably tell we're on a date, and even if we weren't, his forwardness was unwanted and uncalled for, especially since he's here to do a job. I doubt the restaurant's owner approves of his servers flirting with the clientele."

Del glanced down to where his thumb caressed the back of Matthew's hand before meeting his gaze again. "I'm very attracted to you, Matthew. As it sometimes happens in the lifestyle, we started backward—sceneing and having sex before our first date. I want to continue seeing you in and out of the club, and if you say yes to that, it'll be exclusive. We'll sign a contract, and you'll wear my collar at the club and be committed to a relationship with me outside of it. I don't share. I also don't cheat or lead someone on, and I expect the same respect in return."

For a moment, he was speechless. He hadn't expected Del to want to be exclusive after knowing each other for only a few days. "I don't do any of that either, Sir. And I would really love to wear your collar and date you."

Del squeezed his hand. "Thank you."

"Does this mean I can call you my boyfriend?"

"Do you want to?"

"Uh, *yeah*." He dramatically pointed in Josh's direction as he attended to another table. "I mean, it'll be easier to get rid of waiters who drool all over you."

Laughing, Del shook his head. "Permission granted, for that reason alone." He shrugged. "Or for any other reason."

Throughout the rest of the meal, they discussed each other's hard and soft limits and the protocols Del expected Matthew to follow while in the club. They were compatible with their limits, and no protocols were red flags for Matthew, for which he thanked the Goddess of Twink submissives. They agreed to play at the club that evening but put off officially signing a contract until after Christmas. Del said it was because Matthew had too much on his mind between the upcoming holidays and waiting for his test results. The man seemed to know him so well already, and that made Matthew's heart swell.

It'd been a long time since he was so enamored with a Dom, and not just for sex or to satisfy his masochistic needs. In less than a week, he'd fallen for Del—hard. He just hoped it wasn't one-sided. Just because Del wanted to be exclusive didn't mean the relationship wouldn't end at some point.

Matthew couldn't wait to get to the club by the time their dinner was over. While his stomach's hunger was sated, he couldn't say the same for the rest of his body.

His cock was hard, and his ass ached to be filled. The cane marks on his skin had faded since Del expertly put them there. They both knew that a second caning only a few days later would not be wise, so Del planned another form of torture to send the submissive into subspace tonight. However, he refused to tell Matthew what it was until they were at The Covenant, making his anticipation and need spike. Heaven help him.

Chapter Nine

Del took Matthew's hand and laced their fingers together as they exited the restaurant. He couldn't remember the last time he'd romantically held hands with a man while on a date. At least two or three years. Despite his EMS career, which undoubtedly required a lot of soap, water, and sanitizer, Matthew's hands were baby-soft, as if he slathered them with lotion several times daily.

He steered them toward where Matthew's white Tacoma was parked next to his blue BMW M4 convertible. While the luxury vehicle wasn't a top-of-the-line model, it was still one of the few extravagant indulgences he'd allowed himself after moving to Florida. He did want to buy a house eventually, but for now, he rented a nice two-bedroom condo in a secure building overlooking Tampa Bay. The last person he wanted to be was someone who spent a massive windfall, writing checks left and right, without any thought about the future, until they were flat broke again.

He squeezed Matthew's hand. "Would you like to ride with me to the club, pup? We can come back for your truck later."

"That's fine, Sir."

Reluctantly releasing him, Del unlocked and opened the passenger door. The sub smiled and kissed Del's cheek before sliding into the leather seat. "I do love a gentleman."

Before shutting the door, he leaned down and whispered, "But I'm not always a *gentle* man, pup. In the club, I won't be gentle at all."

"Rowr!" Matthew made a claw with his hand, pawed the air, and wiggled his eyebrows. "That's what I'm counting on, Master Del."

"Brat." Without waiting for a reply, he shut the door, walked around to the driver's side, climbed in, and started the vehicle. He caressed the steering wheel momentarily, thinking he'd never get tired of hearing the purr of the exemplary engine. All his life, he'd bought used vehicles that always sounded like they needed a tune-up, even after getting one. Those days were in his past, and now he looked forward to his future. Would Matthew be a big part of that? Del wasn't sure yet, but for once, he was optimistic that a longtime relationship with a sub might work.

It didn't take long to reach The Covenant, and after retrieving his toy bag from the trunk, Del held Matthew's hand again as they walked up the steps leading to the second-floor entrance. "What are you wearing under your clothes, pup?"

"Just a thong, Sir."

Del's cock stirred. Damn. Just four little words from the sweet submissive, and he was ready to strip him down to said thong, push it aside, bend him over, and fuck him silly before they even got through the club's front door. Taking a deep breath, he willed his dick to behave—at least until it was playtime.

"Go to the lockers and take off everything but the thong. Then meet me at the shop."

"Yes, Sir."

After they strode through the lobby and the massive double doors to the main club, Matthew hurried toward the stairwell leading to the men's and women's lounges. Meanwhile, Del said hello to a few people on his way to the club's boutique on the far side, opposite the bar and grand staircase. While he had a simple leather dog collar in his toy bag for whenever he temporarily claimed a sub, he'd decided over dinner that it wasn't good enough for Matthew. The shop carried a wide variety of fet-wear, sex toys, and supplies. Pretty much anything a Dom needed, they had.

Entering the shop, Del was greeted by a pretty male submissive in his mid-twenties, wearing black pants and a gold and red bowtie without a shirt. He was skinnier than Matthew but seemed to have a similar flirtatious and flamboyant nature. "Good evening, Sir. You must be new to the club because I would never have forgotten meeting you. I'm Aldo, the boutique's manager. What can I get for you? Hopefully, me."

"Down, Aldo." Del's tone was stern and filled with an unspoken warning. While he loved Matthew's sass and forwardness, he didn't appreciate it from most subs, especially one he only met fifteen seconds ago.

The younger man's gaze dropped to the floor, his demeanor doing an about-face as his tone changed to one of submission. "Sorry, Sir. Forgive me. How may I help you?"

"I'd like to see what collars you have available."

Now thoroughly professional, Aldo gestured to a long glass display case. "We have plenty for you to choose from over here, Sir. Did you have something specific in mind?"

He didn't, hoping something would catch his eye. He scanned the large assortment of collars—leather, gold, silver, jeweled, metal, ropes, and more. A wide, black leather one grabbed his attention. A row of blue gems that reminded him of Matthew's eyes were encrusted in the center of the strap. The collar would look beautiful on his sub.

He was about to point to it when Matthew entered the shop, causing Del's breath to catch. The white thong left nothing to the imagination and had blood rushing to Del's cock. He swallowed hard, trying to control his body's response to the gorgeous man. It wasn't just physical since he was mentally and emotionally drawn to the younger man too. Even when sex wasn't a part of their time together, he enjoyed being with him.

Clearing his throat, he forced his gaze to focus on Matthew's face. "Kneel beside me, pup."

After Matthew gracefully did as instructed, Del turned back to Aldo, who waited patiently behind the display case. He pointed to the collar he wanted. "I'll take that one, please."

Aldo opened the back of the display case and removed the collar, handing it to Del. "If you have your membership card, Sir, I can scan it to your account."

Not looking at the price tag—he didn't care what it cost—Del removed it and tossed it onto the counter. He pulled his wallet from his pants pocket, found his membership card, and gave it to Aldo. While the manager processed the sale, Del undid the collar's clasp and held the leather strap taut in both hands so Matthew could see it. "Do you like it?"

Matthew's eyes widened as he looked at the collar. "It's beautiful, Sir. I love it."

"Good." Stepping behind the sub, he wrapped the collar around his slender neck and fastened it before returning to his previous spot. "Look at me." When Matthew obeyed, Del smiled as he compared the blue gems to the submissive's eyes. "I was right. They're the same color as your eyes—stunning."

Matthew's face lit up at the compliment. "Thank you, Sir."

"You're welcome." Taking his membership card back from Aldo, along with a receipt, Del stuffed them into his wallet and put it back in his pocket. He then held out his hand to help Matthew stand. "Come, pup. Let's go play."

As they headed for the door, Del could've sworn he heard a dramatic yet wistful sigh from behind them but didn't turn around. Aldo would have to find another Dom because Del was most definitely taken.

They descended a wrought iron circular staircase near the boutique into the pit. Del strolled around with his sub, stopping to watch the occasional scene or make small talk with a few other Dominants. He smiled every time he noticed Matthew finger his new collar and how he glowed whenever someone complimented him on it. Del recalled Ian saying it had been a while since Matthew had worn a Dom's collar. A wave of possessive jealousy came over him as he glanced around the dungeon. Were there any Doms there who'd collared the sub before? Del wasn't sure he wanted to know.

After breaking away from a group as they observed Mistress China whip a female submissive, Del found an unoccupied play area. "Stand in a present position, pup, facing away from the wall. Hands clasping your forearms behind your back."

"Yes, Sir."

While Matthew got into position, Del set his toy bag on a nearby shelf. He always kept it organized so he could find things quickly and easily. After selecting what he needed and lining them up on the shelf, he zipped up the bag and placed it on the floor, out of his way. Picking up a wide leather and Velcro strap, he stepped behind Matthew. He wrapped the strap around the sub's forearms and ran his fingers underneath to ensure it wasn't too tight that it cut off circulation. Grabbing the next items, he moved to stand in front of his sub. "Ready for some pain, pup?"

"Oh, yes, Sir."

"Good boy."

Bending, Del licked one of Matthew's nipples several times, stimulating it until it engorged enough that he could bite and tug on it.

"Oh, Goddess, yes!"

Del released the nipple and smirked. "Oh, I have only begun, pup." Without further explanation, he quickly attached an alligator claw clamp to the stiff peak.

As the sub groaned, Del repeated the process on his other nipple. By the time he was done, they had drawn a small crowd, and Matthew's cock strained against the scrap of fabric barely covering it. Del grabbed the thong's thin strings at the sub's hips and pulled until they ripped. "I'll buy you new ones."

Tossing the ruined garment on top of his duffel bag, he picked up the next toy he would use to torture the masochist. This one needed to be plugged in, and he found an available outlet in a convenient spot on the wall. After plugging it in, he held it behind Matthew's left ear, close enough for him to hear when it was turned on but not enough that it would make contact.

Del hit the on button, and the violet wand crackled

to life. Matthew's body jerked at the electric sound, but he managed not to move from where he stood.

"That's my good pup. You know what that is, and you want it. Do your best not to move, and you'll be rewarded."

"Yes, Sir."

Del lowered the wand and ran it over Matthew's ass cheek, causing the muscles to twitch and the sub to moan. He alternated, touching the wand to the skin of Matthew's ass, hips, and thighs and then removing it. Matthew gasped, begged, and shook with the pleasure/pain shooting through his body.

Grabbing one cheek, Del pulled it to the side to expose the hidden puckered hole. Matthew hissed, knowing what was coming next. Del smirked as he turned the wand off and settled it into the crack of the sub's ass. He counted to five before flipping the switch on again. Matthew yelped and went up on his toes but remained glued to that spot. Del was proud of how well he took the wand. But he was far from done yet.

Circling around, Del glanced down at Matthew's long, thick, hard cock, weeping with pre-cum. The sadist in him silently roared in satisfaction. He stroked the cock with the wand, sending tiny jolts of electricity through it. "Do you need more, pup? Give me a color."

"Oh, green, Sir! So green! Please!"

He moved the wand down to Matthew's balls. The sub hissed, and tears filled his eyes. More pre-cum leaked from his cock, and Del couldn't resist. Dropping to his knees, he took the stiff shaft in his mouth and caressed Matthew's inner thighs with the wand, not leaving it in any single spot. He laved the dick with his tongue, reveling in the taste of this beautiful man.

Matthew squirmed, and his pleading grew louder. Del took him to the back of his throat and swallowed.

"Oh, please! Sir, I'm going to come!"

Pulling back, Del looked up at his sub's naked body. The clamps still tormented his nipples, and the tears now rolled down his cheeks. "Come down my throat, pup. Give me everything you have."

Without waiting for a response, he dropped the wand, grasped the base of Matthew's cock, and sucked the rest back into his mouth.

"Oh, Goddess! Harder, Sir!"

The sub was nearly topping from the bottom but probably too far gone to realize it. At that point, Del didn't care either—maybe he would if he wasn't so out of his mind with lust. He swallowed around the tip and simultaneously tugged on Matthew's balls. That sent the sub over the edge, and he screamed his release, filling Del's mouth with the most delicious salty cum he'd ever tasted. He swallowed rapidly, not wanting to lose a single drop.

When Matthew was finally spent, Del stood, grabbed him by his nape, and crushed their mouths together. He thrust his tongue deep, letting Matthew taste himself. All Del could think about was that this man was his. Who he'd been waiting for all his life. This masochist submissive was his perfect match in every way. And he never wanted to let him go.

Chapter Ten

The Day Before Christmas Eve ...

Matthew's hand shook as it hovered above his smartphone while he stared at the screen. In the middle of numerous emails from friends and family, newsletters, ads, and spam was one from the community college he'd been waiting for all week. Somehow, the subject line appeared bigger than all the others, nearly leaping off the screen at him.

Paramedic Program: Final Exam Results

Nervous energy coursed through him. The email's contents would tell him if he was now a full-fledged, certified paramedic or a complete failure. Okay, maybe not a *complete* failure, but a failure nonetheless.

If he hadn't passed, there would be one more opportunity to retake the test. A second failure would mean repeating an entire year's worth of classes, including clinical rotations and practicals, before getting a third chance.

He hadn't expected the results to come in until after Christmas, but the email had been sent at 9:42 last night, about an hour after he last looked at his inbox. He'd shut his computer down when Del had called to say hello. The conversation quickly advanced to some of the hottest phone sex Matthew had ever experienced in his life.

"Well, are you going to open the damn thing or stare at the screen all day?" his regular partner, Paramedic Adam Zimmerman, asked from over Matthew's shoulder.

They were only an hour into their shift. After ensuring their ambulance was fully stocked and their gear was in working order, they grabbed coffee and egg sandwiches at a nearby bagel shop and returned to the fire station to await their first call. While eating breakfast, Matthew scrolled through his social media accounts, liking and commenting on several posts, before opening his email app. Now, he couldn't decide whether to tap on the one from the college or wait until after Christmas. If he failed, he'd be miserable for days—not exactly how he wanted to spend the holidays, especially since he would see Del tonight at the homeless shelter, where they would serve food and hand out donated gifts.

The past two weeks with Del had been magical. They'd gone on a couple of dates, played at the club, talked on the phone, and texted whenever they could. Del was a combination of a perfect gentleman, a caring and fun partner, and a sadistic Dom, and Matthew couldn't get enough of him. As far as he could tell, everyone who met Del liked the man. He'd already become friends with several Dominants at the club and joined a few of them for drinks at Donovan's Pub the other night while Matthew was at work.

He was glad that Del would join him and his parents tomorrow night. From their conversations, Matthew knew the other man was also an only child whose mother passed away a few years ago, and he wasn't close to his father. Matthew didn't know why but figured Del would tell him if and when he wanted.

Matthew had always been an open book, but many people weren't. Being a masochistic submissive in the BDSM lifestyle was the only aspect of his life he hid from anyone since coming out to his family and friends during his sophomore year of high school. The only reason for that was most of the vanilla people he knew wouldn't understand it and would assume he was in an abusive relationship with someone. He kept no deep, dark secrets from his friends at The Covenant—nothing he was ashamed of or felt wasn't any of their business.

While he didn't feel Del was hiding something about himself that he was ashamed of, Matthew didn't know everything about him. Okay, they'd only known each other for a short amount of time, so he couldn't have learned *everything* yet. But it appeared Del wasn't as open as Matthew, which was fine since their relationship was new. Hopefully, the man would share all his secrets with him someday.

Adam nudged Matthew's shoulder. "Come on, Behan. Open it. Or do you want me to?"

The two had been partners for the past four years, ever since Matthew's previous partner was promoted, and they became good friends almost immediately. After knowing Adam for six months, Matthew introduced him to his cousin, Pia. He'd been confident they would be perfect for each other, and he was right. Last year, he was a groomsman at their wedding, and now, their first child was due in March.

"I'll do it. Just give me a minute, Zim." He glanced around. They were the only two people in the kitchen/dining room combo on the station's second floor. The firemen were all downstairs, cleaning the engine and ladder truck, inspecting the equipment, exercising in the gym, or doing whatever.

Taking a deep breath, he let it out slowly, then tapped on the email that would reveal his fate. Of course, his scores didn't immediately appear on the phone's small screen, nor did any indication of whether he passed the entire program or not, and he had to scroll down a bit to find the information.

"Ninety-six!" Adam bellowed and grabbed Matthew's shoulders, shaking them hard, before the number registered in his mind. "I fucking told you! I knew you passed! I goddamn knew it!" He released

Matthew and ran to the nearby half-wall overlooking the garage. "Behan passed with a fucking ninety-six!"

Cheers, whistles, and applause erupted from below.

"Way to go, Behan!"

"Nice job, man!"

"Congratulations!"

"Drinks are on you next time!"

"Fucking awesome!"

They were a great bunch of men and two women, and if any of them had an issue with his twinkness or sexual orientation, they never showed it. He was always invited to parties and nights out with everyone else. After working with most of them for over five years, he'd earned their respect and even treated several when they'd gotten injured on calls. Two years ago, there'd been one guy who made numerous derogatory statements about Matthew to the others, and a few reported him to the captain, who booted his ass out of the station. The captain's college-aged interracial daughter was a lesbian, and he refused to allow any bullies or bigots on his crew.

Matthew's grin spread, and he couldn't take his gaze off the scores for the written exam and the practicals, which he'd aced as he suspected, afraid they would change if he looked away. He raised his voice to be heard downstairs. "Thanks, everyone!" After a few moments, his shock wore off, and joy and triumph kicked in. He jumped up and danced around the room like a lunatic on speed. "Holy shit, holy shit, holy shit! I did it!"

Adam laughed. "I know!"

"I gotta call . . ." Before he could finish with "my parents and Del," the station's alarm blared, and his and Adam's radios squawked to life with a dispatcher assigning them to a possible heart attack. Well, damn. Work first, then there would be time to celebrate.

Chapter Eleven

Christmas Eve . . .

Del jumped out of his car and ran toward Matthew as he exited his apartment building. The younger man wore skinny blue jeans, red Converse sneakers, and a Rudolph the Red-Nosed Reindeer T-shirt with the nose lit up somehow. His blond hair looked like he'd just run his hands through it several times, messy yet stylish, which fit him. Clear lip gloss and a bit of black eyeliner enhanced his beautiful facial features. Damn. How had Del gotten so lucky to have found this sweet submissive?

Grabbing him around the waist, Del picked him up and swung him around, loving the feel of the slender, hard body against his larger one. He inhaled Matthew's unique scent, savoring it. "I'm so happy for you, baby. I didn't doubt that you would pass, but I kept my fingers crossed all week as extra insurance."

"So . . . did . . . I," Matthew said in between giggling

in delight. He wrapped his legs and arms around Del's hips and neck.

After three back-to-back medical calls yesterday morning, he finally had a few minutes of downtime to call his parents and Del to tell them the good news. They hadn't been able to celebrate until now since Matthew had worked a hectic twenty-four hours before going home to sleep for most of the day.

Del was thrilled about his new boyfriend's achievement and couldn't be prouder. After looking up the paramedic program on the college's website, he realized just how hard Matthew had worked over the past two years to get his certification. In addition to three semesters concentrating specifically on emergency medicine classes, practicals, and clinical rotations at local hospitals or in the field with certified paramedics, other courses were also needed to get his associate's degree in Health Sciences.

During their lunch by the beach the other day, Matthew explained the difference in skills and training between basic EMTs and paramedics, and Del was blown away. Under the guidance and orders of ER doctors, paramedics could almost bring the emergency room to a scene. Advanced life support, as it's called, includes analyzing EKGs, starting IVs, administering medications, cardiac defibrillation, emergency tracheotomies, and inserting an endotracheal tube to help with respiration. Matthew had learned how to do all of that and more. And that was on top of treating trauma victims and preparing them for transport.

While he assumed many TV shows exaggerated what paramedics could do in the field, Del never realized the extent of training that real paramedics had. He was in awe of Matthew for becoming one.

Setting him back on his feet, Del dipped and kissed him, not caring who might be watching them. If it was one thing he'd already learned about his submissive, it was that he was out and proud and didn't give a damn if it bothered anyone—something that Del loved about him since he shared the same viewpoint.

Yes, he used the "L" word. To anyone else, it might be too soon to think like that, but Del had never met a man as charismatic and adorable as Matthew. Everything about him—his looks, fashion sense, intelligence, adventurism, empathy, courage, brattiness, humor, and more—drew Del in like a moth to a flame. Even when they were apart, Del's mind conjured up the other man several times an hour, no matter what he tried to concentrate on.

Plunging his tongue into Matthew's mouth, he laid claim to it, just as he'd done every time they kissed. It may have been lust at first sight for Del when they met at The Covenant, but it quickly bloomed into something more. Something he'd never experienced before with another man. He wanted this relationship to work. Since he was now financially stable and no longer interested in one-night stands or short-term relationships, he was ready to find his forever love, and the man in his arms might very well be him. When they sat down to discuss their BDSM contract in a few days, he didn't want to put an end date on it. He would if Matthew insisted, but that space could remain permanently blank from Del's point of view.

A horn blared from the other side of the small apartment complex's parking lot, and Del reluctantly ended the blazing kiss and set a breathless Matthew upright. "Merry Christmas Eve, pup. I think I just licked off all your lip gloss."

Matthew reached up and brushed his thumb across Del's lips, presumably to wipe off the remnants of said gloss. "That's okay. It was worth it. Plus, I can put more on in the car."

"Ready to go?"

"We better." He furtively palmed his erection, and Del smirked as he took his hand.

"Don't do that. Otherwise, I'll drag you back into your apartment and have my way with you. I don't think the people at the shelter would appreciate their dinner being late."

They walked hand-in-hand to Matthew's truck, which was a few years old but still in good condition. Earlier on the phone, he offered to drive tonight, saying that where they were going, Del's new luxury vehicle would stand out as an invitation to steal it or, at least, break into it. Del agreed since he was still learning about the city and suburbs.

When they reached the truck, he opened the driver's door for Matthew, earning him a surprised look. After the sub climbed in, Del leaned forward and kissed his temple. "Chivalry isn't dead, pup," he whispered in his ear, causing Matthew to shiver. Smiling, Del shut the door and circled to the passenger side.

It had been ages since he wanted to be both a gentleman *and* a sadist toward someone. Usually, the courteous parts of him occurred outside the club with regular everyday people, while his sadistic side was reserved for the BDSM lifestyle. Occasionally, they crossed over, but rarely. That is, until he met Matthew. He wanted to satisfy the man's masochistic hunger and then pamper him for hours on end afterward, as he'd done after playing at the club the other night. The submissive had floated in subspace for longer than expected, and Del drove him home and accepted an invite to sleep over—something he hadn't done with another man in quite a while. He loved how Matthew cuddled into his side before sleep overtook them.

As they drove toward the homeless shelter, Del's anxiety rose—a rarity for him. The last time he'd experienced butterflies in his stomach was as he signed on the dotted line to sell his app. He couldn't remember when his nerves had gotten the best of him before that. He would meet Matthew's parents for the first time tonight and hoped he made a good impression on them. It'd been years since he met a boyfriend's parents. Either his relationships never got to that point, the parents weren't in the picture, as Del's weren't, or there'd been no reason since a contract with an end date had been signed. He wanted Mr. and Mrs. Behan to like him because he certainly liked their son. While they'd only been together for two weeks, Del realized how dull his life was before Matthew's bright sunshine became a part of it.

He hadn't told the younger man about his wealth. Del was still trying to wrap his own brain around the number of zeroes in his bank account. He doubted it would make a difference to Matthew—he didn't seem like the type of guy who'd expect Del to pay for everything on their dates and buy him expensive things because he could. But exposing that part of his life to anyone made him uneasy, especially after what he went through with his father. Money made some people greedy or, as in his father's case, greedier. Very few knew about Del's fortune—mainly his accountant, his new investment broker, the company that bought the app from him, the Sawyers because of The Covenant's background check, and two longtime friends he trusted with his life.

Both Brian Hendrix and Randy Driscoll had done well in their careers and didn't lack money either. Brian decided to retire two years ago after playing centerfield in the Major Leagues for sixteen years, with three World Series rings among his many achievements. He lived in San Diego with his wife and three children, where he was now a hitting coach for the Padres.

Meanwhile, Randy recently took over the helm of the corporate law firm his father had founded and presided over in Morrison, Ohio, before retiring after thirty-five years. Randy had also been Del's lawyer for the app sale. He and his husband of five years adopted their second child a few months ago.

Both sets of kids called him Uncle Del, which he loved since he would never have any blood-related nieces and nephews. He may have gone overboard with all the Christmas presents he sent them this year, but it was the first time he hadn't needed to stay on a budget.

Del had never been jealous of his friends' successes in their professional and personal lives, and the three stayed in touch between visits by talking on the phone and Skyping weekly.

They met in first grade and quickly became thick as thieves. Although Del technically had lived in a different school district, their city's socioeconomic integration program bussed him to another district. His friends were never ashamed or embarrassed by Del's lower social status and didn't allow him to be either. They stood up to anyone who tried to bully him.

It wasn't until fifth grade that he realized how often Randy and Brian loaned him clothes and toys and then *conveniently* forgot to get them back from him for months, and he loved his friends for it. After that, though, he drew the line whenever they tried to give him anything valuable or part of their allowances for the movies or arcades. He started finding ways to make some cash by doing errands for his neighbors and the local business owners before he was old enough for a job. Whenever he had a little extra, he'd sneak it into the plastic pink box his mother kept her waitress tips hidden in before she could bring them to the bank.

Years later, he realized she noticed the additional funds because his birthday and Christmas presents had become more expensive. Not by much, but it was her way of repaying him without making a fuss.

Hmm. A thought just occurred to him. When he called Randy and Brian to wish them and their families a Merry Christmas, he should mention he was dating someone special. Their significant others had tried to hook him up with their gay friends for years. He knew Amy and David meant well, but their version of the perfect man for him was far different than his. None of the men they'd introduced him to had been in the lifestyle—not that either of his friends or their spouses knew he was a Dominant in the lifestyle. He'd never felt the need to announce it to them.

Matthew pulled the truck into a dilapidated strip mall parking lot that'd seen better days. It must have been years since it was last paved, and litter was scattered around. While the few businesses—a liquor store, a dry cleaner, a ninety-nine-cent store, and a local pharmacy—appeared occupied, their signs were old and outdated, with two missing some of their lights. It wasn't a well-kept area, but Del wasn't surprised. The shelters he and his mother had volunteered at back in Ohio were always in the same poor section of the city where they lived in a small, two-bedroom apartment at the top of a three-floor walk-up.

"It's across the street," Matthew said as he pulled into a parking spot near seven or eight other vehicles. "It's an old firehouse that was converted after a new one was built two blocks over." He tilted his head toward the sedan next to him. "That's my dad's Camry, so they're already here."

At a brick building on the other side of the street, people waited in a long line that started by the front door. The disheveled men, women, and several children looked worse for wear in dirty, ill-fitting clothes and carried what was probably their only possessions in shopping or garbage bags. The sight of the little ones caused Del's heart to clench. He thought of his nieces and nephews and was grateful they had roofs over their heads, healthy food in their stomachs, and soft, clean beds to sleep in.

Matthew opened the driver's door, but Del gently grabbed the back of his neck before he could exit, pulled him closer, and sweetly kissed him. "Put some more lip gloss on. I like it."

Once Matthew's lips shined brightly again, they climbed out of the truck and hurried across the two-lane street during a break in traffic. Instead of going in through a front entrance, Matthew led the way to a side alley where a door was propped open with a brick. Del followed him inside to an industrial-size kitchen that buzzed with activity. Matthew introduced Del to several men and women wearing white aprons, latex gloves, and hair nets as they prepped dozens of trays filled with food, but none were his parents.

A swinging door to another room flew open, and a woman who appeared to be in her late fifties bustled in. She was slender and about five feet five, and Del knew instinctively she was Matthew's mother. He'd gotten her attractive looks—from her blonde hair, which was pulled up into a ponytail, to her beautiful blue eyes and high cheekbones.

Her face lit up the moment she saw them. "Matthew, there you are! I was getting worried." She kissed his cheek and hugged him. "Hi, honey. Congratulations again on passing your test. Dad and I are so proud of you."

"Thanks, Mom."

When she released Matthew, her gaze shifted to Del. "Who's this?"

"Del, this is my mom, Carla Behan. Mom, this is Delmar Sutton, my—my, um, boyfriend," he added as pink tinged his cheeks.

"Boyfriend? You didn't tell me you were dating anyone." She held out her hand. "It's a pleasure to meet you, Del. I hope you realize what an honor it is since it's been a long time since my son introduced me to someone he was seeing."

Del gently took her hand in both of his. "It's an honor for me no matter what. I'm grateful he's given me the opportunity to get to know him. You've raised an amazing son, Mrs. Behan."

She blushed almost as much as Matthew. "Thank you. And it's Carla, please. Are you here to help us, too, or do you have somewhere you need to be with family tonight?"

"I'm here to help. My mother's been gone for a while now, and she was my only family. I just moved to

Florida a couple of months ago, so I didn't really have any plans for the holidays." Ever since his mother's death, Randy and Brian both invited him to join one of them for Christmas each year, but he always turned them down, not wanting to intrude on their family time. This year, he was glad he had. "When Matthew told me about you all volunteering here, I offered to come with him. My mom and I volunteered at a shelter whenever we could while I was growing up."

Carla clasped her hands to her chest. "Oh, I'm sorry for your loss, dear. She sounds like she was a wonderful mother."

"She was," Del agreed wistfully. Although it had been years since his mother died, his chest still ached whenever he remembered how full she made his life, despite what little they had. He glanced at Matthew. Maybe his mother had sent him someone to fill the hole in his heart. The corners of his mouth pulled upward at the thought. She would've loved Matthew.

"Well, thank you for coming. We can use all the help we can get." Carla gestured toward the door behind her. "Let's introduce you to my husband and then put you both to work. There's still a lot to do in the dining room before we open the front door."

Del braced for impact. One parent down. One to go.

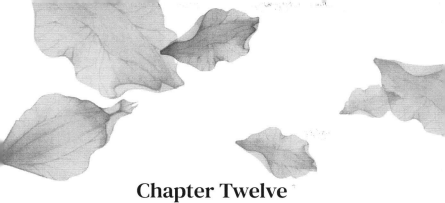

Chapter Twelve

After meeting Evan Behan, Del spent the next half hour helping set up tables and chairs while being grilled by the man about various inquiries, including Del's intentions toward his son, who'd groaned and begged his father to back off. Del hadn't minded the interrogation, especially when Evan finally seemed to approve of the two men dating.

The two-story former firehouse was now a sizeable shelter. The truck and engine bays had been converted into the new kitchen and a cafeteria-style dining room that doubled as the men's sleeping area when cots were laid out. Showers and bathrooms were also on the first floor. Offices and sleeping areas for women and children were upstairs where the original kitchen, bunk room, and living spaces had been. As far as shelters went, Del had seen worse.

Two hours later, the dining room was filled with

people of all ages, and the buffet's dozens of assorted food trays were empty. As Del helped with the cleanup, Matthew was across the room with an older gentleman dressed as Santa Claus, playing with the children and the small toys they'd received as presents. Meanwhile, Carla and several other volunteers handed out new clothing, toiletries, and non-perishable food that had been donated to the adults. Del made a mental note to speak to the shelter's director about making a monetary donation before they left for the night.

It took another ninety minutes to clean the kitchen and exchange the dining room tables and chairs for folding cots. Once everything was in order, the volunteers said their goodbyes as the shelter staff took over for the night.

Carla surprised Del when she linked their arms together as they walked across the street with Evan and Matthew. "Del, since Matthew usually works on Christmas to give his coworkers with children the day off, we've been celebrating on the twenty-sixth for the past few years. We would love for you to join us on Sunday if you don't have plans. My sister and brother-in-law, their kids, and a few grandkids will be there."

A glance in Matthew's direction told Del the younger man wasn't surprised about the invitation. His mother probably asked him if it was all right before approaching Del. Matthew gave him a little nod in encouragement. He wanted Del to meet his extended family, and the knowledge had warmth coursing through Del's body. "Thank you, Carla. I would love to join you. Just tell me what I can bring."

"We have all the food planned already, and beer, wine, and soda. If you want anything special to drink, you can bring that. And my son, of course."

"Of course," he said, opening the Camry passenger door for her after Evan used a fob to unlock it. "I couldn't leave out the best part of my day."

She grinned at him. "Now I see how Matthew fell for you so quickly." She kissed his cheek and then Matthew's before climbing into the car. "We'll see you on Sunday. Be safe tomorrow, dear."

"I will, Mom. Bye, Dad."

Evan hugged Matthew. "Bye, Son. Be safe." He turned to Del and held out his hand. "It was great to meet you. Thanks for helping out tonight."

Del shook his hand. "It was my pleasure and nice to meet you too."

"See you on Sunday. Fair warning, though, you'll probably be the only Cinnci Bengal fan there."

He laughed because the Bengals were scheduled to play the Tampa Bay Buccaneers that day. "That's okay. I can hold my own."

The older man winked. "I'm sure you can."

Del and Matthew waited until Evan started the car and pulled out of the parking lot. They waved goodbye to the couple, and then Del glanced around. It was overcast and dark, the only light coming from the street lamps and the neon signs in the windows of a convenience store next door to the shelter.

When Matthew wrapped his arms around Del's neck, Del grabbed his hips and pulled him closer. "I had a good time tonight, pup. Thank you for inviting me. It felt good to volunteer again. It's been a long time—since before my mom died."

Matthew laid his head on Del's shoulder. "I bet she's looking down on you right now, smiling."

"I wouldn't be surprised. She probably sees how happy I am."

"Happy?"

"Mm-hmm. You, pup. You've made me happier than I've been since . . . well, since I don't know when. Maybe I've never been this happy in my life. Let me stay with you tonight? I'd invite you to my place, but my car is at yours, and you probably need your uniform for tom—"

"Yes!" Matthew lifted his head, and their gazes met. "I want you to stay with me. I was going to ask, but I didn't want to come across as too needy or—or . . . I don't know. I mean, a lot has happened in the past week. Am I pushing you? Between dinner, and you staying over, and meeting my parents, and now, Sunday?"

Del let him babble momentarily, trying to comprehend his fears before reassuring him. He wanted to be certain Matthew wasn't feeling pressure from him. "No, you're not pushy, sweetheart. Hell, if I had my way, you wouldn't work at all. Instead, you'd spend all your time with me."

Matthew snorted. "As if we could afford not to work."

Biting his bottom lip, Del closed his eyes for a moment. What he said in the next few minutes could make or break their budding relationship. "What if you hit the lottery tomorrow and were suddenly a millionaire? Would you quit your job?"

His brow furrowed. "Huh? What are you talking about? The odds of winning the lottery are—"

"Humor me. If you suddenly had more money than you knew what to do with, would you go to work tomorrow?"

Matthew tilted his head as though seriously pondering the question. It was a few moments before he responded, "Yeah. I would. I'd miss what I do. I love being an EMT and know I'll love being a paramedic even more. Would I drive a nicer car, get a bigger apartment or a house, and travel more? Hell yeah! But quit doing what I love?" He shook his head. "Nope, I wouldn't.

"What about you?" Matthew asked. "Would you give up . . . whatever it is you do?"

He grinned and chuckled. "You don't remember what I told you I do?"

"Um, I may have been imagining you naked when you told me." The sheepish expression on his face was endearing and so fucking sexy. "In fact, I imagine you naked a lot, and it's very distracting."

"I know the feeling. I imagine you naked all the time

too. I prefer it when you're naked in real life, though." Okay, now that he was hard as granite, maybe his confession could wait a little while. "Get in the truck, pup. Now."

Matthew's eyes lit up. "Yes, Captain Del, Sir!"

Chapter Thirteen

Matthew lay on his side in post-orgasmic bliss, cuddled against Del's strong body with his head resting on the man's shoulder. His breathing and heart rate had finally returned to normal, but the remnants of subspace made him feel drugged as endorphins still flooded his system.

After walking into Matthew's apartment and shutting the door, they hadn't gone any further before Del pinned him against the wall and kissed him until his toes curled in his shoes. The Dom had quickly stripped them both, then pushed Matthew to his knees so he could fuck his mouth. It hadn't taken long for Del to blow his load down Matthew's throat. The sub liked to think that was due to a combination of the man being so hard and hot for him, his talented tongue, and his ability to deep-throat without choking.

Before Matthew was able to gloat, Del had dragged him into the shower, where he tortured the submissive. He'd grabbed his toy bag from his car after Matthew had parked next to it in the lot. While water pelted Matthew, clamps pinched his nipples and balls. A cock ring went on next, followed by a prostate massager being shoved up his ass. Del had edged him over and over, until Matthew was a babbling and begging mess, before finally allowing him to come. Matthew didn't think he'd ever climaxed as hard as he did then.

Once he was strong enough to stand without help, Del cleaned him up and toweled them dry before steering Matthew into the bedroom. As exhausted as he was, Matthew couldn't fall asleep. Honestly, he didn't want to. Not when the most incredible man he ever met was in his bed.

Tracing random shapes on Del's chest with a single finger, Matthew lifted a leg and draped it over the other man's thighs. They fit together perfectly as if they'd been made for each other. Everything had happened so fast that Matthew was afraid to say the words that were on the tip of his tongue. He was in love with this man. He had to be since he'd never felt like this before. Images of the two of them sharing new experiences, having kids someday, growing old together, and more flashed through his mind. Del was the yin to Matthew's yang, the sun to his moon, the cream to his coffee, the peanut butter to his jelly. Okay, subspace still scattered his thoughts a little, but despite that, he knew Del was the man, *the Dom*, he'd waited for all his life.

Del ran his hand over Matthew's hip. "There's something we need to talk about, pup."

"Uh-oh. That sounds ominous." He felt, rather than heard, Del's soft snort.

"You like that word, don't you?"

He pushed onto his elbow and stared down at Del. "When you use that serious but sexy voice and say we have to talk about something? Uh, yeah, that's the only word that comes to mind. I don't know if whatever you're about to say is something good or if you're about to tell me this thing between us was fun while it lasted and then kick me to the curb."

Before the last syllable was out of his mouth, Matthew found himself flat on his back with Del's bigger body on top of him. The Dom scowled. "I have no intention of kicking you to the curb, pup."

It occurred to Matthew to retort that since they were in *his* apartment, that was probably the wrong idiom to use, but Del didn't give him a chance to say anything, crushing their mouths together in a searing kiss. Seconds, minutes, hours, or maybe even eons later, Matthew panted for oxygen when Del pulled away. "I love you, Matthew. I know that sounds crazy because we've only known each other for a short time, but I've never felt this way. And I've never said those words to anyone in my life other than my mother. I can't imagine my life without you. Can't remember what it was like before I met you. You're mine for as long as you'll have me. I'm hoping it'll be forever."

Gaping, Matthew stared at him. His brain had

short-circuited just as it'd done during his earlier orgasm. "L-love? You love me? D-did I hear you right, or am I dreaming?" He pinched his own nipple hard and yelped. "Nope! Not dreaming."

Del laughed. "No, you're not dreaming or hearing things, pup. Maybe my timing is wro—"

"No! I mean, I—I love you too. I think I fell in love with you the first night we met when you grabbed my wrist and brushed your thumb over it." He could still remember the shiver that went down his spine and the tingles he'd felt all over. Then again, those things happened every time Del touched him.

Leaning down, Del kissed him again, then rolled onto his back, taking Matthew with him until they were in their original position. "Okay, now. About that thing I wanted to talk about—"

"You mean it wasn't the fact that you love me?" He tilted his chin so he could see Del's face.

"While that was an important side subject, and it makes what I have to say a little easier, I hope—"

"Sir, you're scaring me now." Matthew had never heard his Dom sound so unsure of himself, and worry flooded him. They'd just said "I love you" to each other, so why did it feel like a bomb would explode in the room?

Del took a deep breath and let it out slowly. "I told you I create apps and do coding for a living through my own company."

"Right. While I wasn't paying attention." When Del growled and pinched Matthew's side, he squealed and tried to shift away. "Sorry! I'm paying attention now. I promise."

"Good." Pulling Matthew closer again, Del brushed his lips across the younger man's forehead. "So, about three years ago, I created a fitness app. It gained popularity, and another company approached me last year to buy it. I was surprised, but after months of negotiations, we completed the sale. That was right before I moved here."

"Wow, that's great." Matthew didn't know what else to say. Other than using apps, he had no clue what went into creating them. "But why didn't you keep it? I mean, don't you make money through in-app purchases and advertisers?"

After a few heartbeats, Del responded, "Matthew, I sold it for six hundred fifty million dollars."

A deafening silence descended over the room. Matthew tried to comprehend what Del had said and thought he was hearing things again. Maybe he should make an appointment to see an audiologist.

"Pup?"

Confused, he sat up, his gaze darting around Del's face. "I'm sorry. It sounded like you said s-six hundred fifty . . . m-million dollars."

"Yeah, that was pretty much my reaction at first too."

Matthew's eyes widened. "You're a . . . a . . . a . . ." He gulped, unable to say the word on the tip of his tongue.

"A millionaire. Yes. Actually, a multi-millionaire."

Del ran a hand down his face. "God, it's still so weird to say out loud or even think about."

"Whoooooa." Dumbfounded, he sat stock still and tried to think of something to say. His brain was fried from the shock. "I—I—I think I'm speechless for the first time in my life."

A bark of laughter erupted from Del. "Well, if that's the case, I'm honored to be the cause of it." He pulled Matthew back down to rest against his side. "Very few people know. My two best friends, Randy and Brian, the owners of The Covenant, whoever did my background check for the club, and people at the company that bought it from me. Oh, and my fucking father knows."

"How did he find out?" From what little he'd heard about Del's sperm donor, there was no love there—just well-deserved hate. He couldn't imagine Del telling the man he was now a millionaire.

"I'm not sure. The only thing I can think of is he somehow discovered that DelTech is my company and heard about the sale when it was announced to the media. Showed up at my apartment in Ohio the next day, demanding five million dollars. Said he deserved it since the only reason I was alive was because he got my mother knocked up."

"What a fucking asshole! I hope you kicked his ass!"

Del smirked. "In hindsight, I wish I did. Instead, I slammed the door in his face and called the cops when he wouldn't leave. Got a restraining order the next day and decided to move."

"What made you pick Tampa?"

"One of my best friends was a Major League baseball player, and I came down here almost every year to watch the pre-season games. I liked the area, so I decided to move here."

Matthew popped back up into a sitting position again. "Wait a minute. You're good friends with a Major League player? Who?"

"He's retired now, but Brian Hendrix."

This time, he jumped off the bed, ran his hands through his hair, and paced the room. "Okay. I'm not asleep, so that means I'm in some sort of parallel universe where my perfect Dom just told me, A—he loves me. B—he's a goddessdamn multi-millionaire. And C—he's best friends with Brian Fucking Hendrix! *The* Brian Hendrix who won three World Series rings, Most Valuable Player in two of them, played in eight All-Star games, and was Rookie of the Year in his first MLB season."

Del chuckled. "Do you know his stats off the top of your head too?"

He stopped short, put his hands on his hips, and glared at Del. "If you want me to, I can rattle them off. Oh, my goddess!" He pointed at the man laughing in his bed. "If you ever introduce me to him, you'll have to pick me up when I faint. He was my favorite player for years. I cried when he announced his retirement."

"If you tell me you had a crush on him, I'll never introduce you."

Climbing onto the bed, he crawled over Del's naked

body and kissed him. "Can I add something to our contract?"

"What?" Del asked warily.

"You don't tell me about your past crushes, and I don't tell you about mine?"

Del swatted Matthew's ass. "Brat."

"But I'm your brat."

Flipping their positions, Del ground his erection against Matthew's. "Damn right, you are."

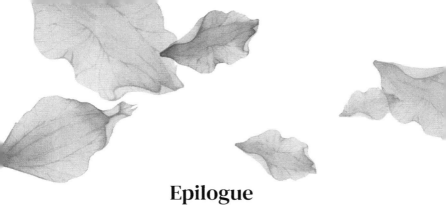

Epilogue

Five months later...

"Ahhh. This is the life, Sir." Matthew took another sip of his key lime martini, swallowed, and then smacked his lips. The drink was a specialty at the Master Key Resort and a nice change of pace from his usual appletini. "I could get used to this."

Between his vacation options on the schedule and the resort's room availability, it had taken a few months before he and Del could use the trip he won at the Secret Santa event. Since being officially promoted to a paramedic, he became the low man on the totem pole again for scheduling time off. While he was assigned to the same firehouse he'd worked at for the past few years, after another paramedic was promoted to an administrative position, he acquired a new partner—a female EMT named Delilah Shore, who he adored. She was friendly and fun, knew her

EMS shit, and had no qualms about getting her hands dirty and diving in to help whenever needed. Matthew lucked out with her since Zim's new EMT was a slacker. Behind-the-scenes bets had been made at the firehouse on when the guy would eventually get fired or, at least, transferred. Their captain's patience was clearly running thin, and Zim constantly bitched to Matthew that he was about to lose his mind.

As of six weeks ago, Del and Matthew lived together in a two-thousand-six-hundred-square-foot, three-bedroom house in a gated community in Palm Harbor, just north of Tampa, not far from Matthew's station. Neither had wanted an ostentatious mansion or penthouse apartment, although Del could afford that. Coming from lower- and middle-class families, those didn't suit them. Their new house had more space than they were used to, but they'd fallen in love with it at first sight. While searching for the perfect place, they both wanted to find a pleasant, safe area where neighbors knew and looked out for each other. The single-level ranch sat on almost an acre of land. It had a pool and a fenced-in backyard, perfect for parties and the two dogs they adopted last month. After realizing the bonded pair couldn't be separated, Tori Sawyer, Mitch's and Ty's wife, facilitated the adoption through her charity that trained rescue dogs for veterans with PTSD. Nip was a corgi mix, while Tuck was a cockapoo. They were approximately four years old and had been spoiled rotten since finding their forever home. Tori was dog-sitting them while their dads were away for the long weekend.

Before agreeing to move in with Del, Matthew made several demands. First, since Del paid cash for the $899,000 home, Matthew insisted on paying the utilities. They split other expenses such as groceries and a landscaper, a pool cleaning guy, and a housekeeper, who each came once a week. Second, they'd signed the equivalent of a prenup that stated if they went their separate ways, the house belonged to Del even though Matthew's name was also on the deed. If something happened to Del, he didn't want Matthew to lose the home for any reason, so both their names were listed. Third, after discussing them first, Del was allowed to make large purchases that benefitted both of them, but gifts to Matthew couldn't be more extravagant than something he might buy for himself. So, the new fancier truck Del had wanted to get him was a no-go. Matthew would trade in his pickup soon for a newer model that he could afford on his increased salary.

While Del had resisted Matthew's terms, he finally relented. Matthew never wanted his Dom to think he loved him for his money. Stability was more important than the number of zeroes on the man's bank statement. Over the past few months, Matthew learned Del was both generous and shrewd with his wealth. Donations were made to Tori's Healing Heroes charity and the homeless shelter, where they volunteered twice a month now. Del also considered his purchases before making them instead of just throwing his money around. He valued quality over what was most popular or expensive and did his research.

Matthew's parents and extended family loved Del. While they knew the man owned a technology company and worked from home as a computer coding contractor and app developer, they didn't know about the one he'd sold for millions. Matthew respected his wishes to keep that to themselves and understood the man's reasoning since his deadbeat dad attempted to get his hands on Del's money.

Next month, Matthew would meet Del's best friends and their families on a joint trip to Disney World. He knew them from the trio's weekly Skype sessions and phone calls. Apparently, their children couldn't wait to meet their new "Uncle Matty." No one had called him anything other than Matthew since grade school by his choice, but he already loved the name the kids had picked for him.

Del leaned forward and licked Matthew's lips. "That tastes good on you, but not as good as how that thong bathing suit looks on you, pup. I should be jealous of the men staring at you, but then I remember you're mine. They can look all they want at my exhibitionist sub as long as they don't touch. Then I'll have to break their hands."

Matthew didn't care who expressed interest in him at the resort—he only had eyes for Del. Okay, maybe he checked out their current waiter, Hector, a few times in the last half hour. With dark hair and eyes, a well-toned and tanned body, swoon-worthy dimples, and a tight ass you could bounce quarters off of, both men agreed he was a fine specimen of the male gender. He was also attentive but not flirtatious, which would garner him a hefty tip later, but nothing more since Del and Matthew established early in their relationship that neither had any desire to share or cheat. According to Del, he couldn't handle more than Matthew and didn't want to try, which the submissive loved.

He adjusted the shoulder of the mesh top he wore, which was the same color as his peach thong, and shifted on the towel-covered chair he sat on. Thongs were his favorite choice for swimwear whenever they weren't inappropriate, but he hated sitting or laying on any outdoor furniture that an unhygienic person may have used before him. Meanwhile, Del was shirtless and wore a pair of short white swim trunks that molded to his hips, ass, and groin spectacularly. Matthew wasn't the only one attracting attention as they sat in the shade of an umbrella at a table by the pool, waiting for Hector to return with the appetizers they ordered for lunch.

They didn't want to overeat because they had dinner plans later with the resort's manager, Master Cordell Roberts, and the assistant manager, his submissive fiancée, Tiffany Armstrong. Tiffany was Tori's cousin, and Matthew had met the couple once before when they'd attended Tori, Ty, and Mitch's collaring ceremony at The Covenant. Tiffany was no longer the timid woman she'd once been, and Matthew was happy for her. She'd blossomed during her relationship with her new Dom.

The resort was even better than everyone had described. Their room was spacious and comfortable, the private island was gorgeous, and the food and drinks were delicious. They'd gone windsurfing that morning, and Del wanted to try snorkeling tomorrow. Being from Ohio, he'd never done either, and Matthew loved teaching his Dom things he grew up doing while living so close to the Gulf of Mexico.

Because they were only there for three nights, Del had booked them on a flight from Tampa to the Florida Keys Marathon International Airport, where they rented a car to drive to the resort. They probably could've just taken a ride-share or taxi since Master Key was only about twenty minutes away, but Del wanted a vehicle available in case they wanted to do some sightseeing. However, the resort was beautiful, with plenty to do and see, and Matthew doubted they would leave until it was time to return to the airport.

They arrived just before noon yesterday and were able to check in early. By two, they were sipping cocktails and relaxing in a cabana on the beach, overlooking the clear, blue water of the Atlantic Ocean. Later, a fantastic dinner at Decadence was followed by a fun evening of playing and socializing in both the dungeon and Club 69, a nightclub where they met several lovely couples and a few single guests. Also available were a Dominants-only lounge, another one for submissives, a cigar bar, a boutique, a day spa, more water sports, and a hiking/biking trail that took them around the island. As far as Matthew was concerned, it was paradise as long as Del was by his side.

Matthew's cell phone chimed with an incoming text. He opened it to find Tori had sent him a cute picture of Nip and Tuck sleeping together on a dog bed. Smiling, he showed it to Del as the waiter arrived with their food. "Can I get you anything else, gentlemen?"

Del eyed Matthew's nearly empty martini glass and his own bottle of beer. "Another round of drinks, please, Hector."

"Certainly."

Both men smiled and stared at the server's fine ass as he walked away from them. After a moment, Del chuckled, lifted his beer, and gestured for Matthew to pick up his martini. Del gently clicked his bottle against the glass. "Cheers, pup."

"Cheers, Sir."

They sipped their drinks and then dove into the nachos and an antipasto platter. "I was thinking." Del said. "Your parents' anniversary is next month. What do you think about taking them to Florence for a week or two when you can get some more time off?"

Surprised, Matthew choked on an olive and coughed. He covered his mouth with a napkin until he could talk again. "Florence? As in Florence, Italy? Or Florence, Alabama?"

Del narrowed his eyes and tilted his head. "What do

you think? Of course, Florence, Italy. I overheard you and your mom talking with your cousin about it a few weeks ago. She went there on her honeymoon, and they want to go back, right?"

"Y-yeah. Are you serious?"

"Yes, I'm serious. It would be an excellent present for their anniversary—your mom said they've never been to Italy, but it's on her bucket list. I get the feeling it's on yours too. Am I right?"

Still stunned, Matthew nodded. Del reached over and clasped his hand. "Look. I know this falls under your definition of big gifts, so I asked instead of surprising you and them. But I'd really like to treat everyone to a trip. Will you let me spoil you just this once?"

He pursed his lips and glared at Del. "Why do I get the feeling that 'just this once,'" he made air quotes with his free hand, "will become a phrase you'll use *more* than once?"

Del laughed. "Okay, so maybe I'm getting used to the fact I'm stinkin' rich and can splurge on things I never could before. Maybe we can take one big trip a year to treat ourselves. Besides, I have good news. That new app I've been working on? It looks like I may have a buyer for it. I won't get as much money for this one as I did with the fitness app, but it's a significant offer. Randy has already started negotiating a counteroffer and is reviewing the contract. If all goes well, it might be sold by September or October, giving us another reason to celebrate."

"Oh, wow! That's great, Del. I'm so proud of you."

"Thanks. So, what do you think? A trip to Italy with your folks?"

He relaxed into his chair again. "They would love that, especially my mom. So, yes, that would be an amazing present for their thirtieth anniversary. Thank you."

"It's my pleasure." Del squeezed his hand. "You know, I like to think your mom and mine would've been good friends. And your dad has been more than a dad to me these past few months than my sperm donor ever was. I never thought I'd find love so soon after moving to Tampa, but I did. I love you, pup, and your family. And having that love returned is the best thing that's ever happened to me. I came to Florida to start a new life. What I found was my forever."

Oh, Goddess of Twinks everywhere. He says the most beautiful things!

"You're my forever, too, Sir."

I hope you enjoyed Del & Matthew's story. To receive a
BONUS EPILOGUE, sign up for my newsletter -
BookHip.com/QXTAJBZ

Other Books by Samantha Cole

**Denotes titles/series that are only available on select digital sites. Paperbacks and audiobooks are available on most book sites.

TRIDENT SECURITY SERIES

Leather & Lace

His Angel

Waiting For Him

Not Negotiable: A Novella

Topping The Alpha

Watching From the Shadows

Whiskey Tribute: A Novella

Tickle His Fancy

No Way in Hell: A Steel Corp/Trident Security Crossover (co-authored with J.B. Havens)

Absolving His Sins

Option Number Three: A Novella

Salvaging His Soul

Trident Security Field Manual

Torn In Half: A Novella

HEELS, RHYMES, & NURSERY CRIMES SERIES

(WITH 13 OTHER AUTHORS)

Jack Be Nimble: A Trident Security-Related Short Story

***DEIMOS SERIES

Handling Haven: Special Forces: Operation Alpha

Cheating the Devil: Special Forces: Operation Alpha

TRIDENT SECURITY OMEGA TEAM SERIES

Mountain of Evil

A Dead Man's Pulse

Forty Days & One Knight

DOMS OF THE COVENANT SERIES

Double Down & Dirty

Entertaining Distraction

Knot a Chance

Finding His Forever

BLACKHAWK SECURITY SERIES

Tuff Enough

Blood Bound

MASTER KEY SERIES

Master Key Resort

Master Cordell

HAZARD FALLS SERIES

Don't Fight It

Don't Shoot the Messenger

COCK & BULL SERIES
Scout

Rico

MALONE BROTHERS SERIES
Her Secret

Her Sleuth

LARGO RIDGE SERIES
Cold Feet

ANTELOPE ROCK SERIES
(CO-AUTHORED WITH J.B. HAVENS)
Wannabe in Wyoming

Wistful in Wyoming

AWARD-WINNING STANDALONE BOOKS
The Road to Solace

Scattered Moments in Time: A Collection of Short Stories & More

Standalone Books
Sweet Revenge (A Novella)

The Sugarplum Fairy (A Novella)

***THE BID ON LOVE SERIES
(WITH 7 OTHER AUTHORS!)
Going, Going, Gone: Book 2

***THE COLLECTIVE: SEASON TWO
(WITH 7 OTHER AUTHORS!)

Angst: Book 7

***SPECIAL COLLECTIONS

Trident Security Series: Volume I

Trident Security Series: Volume II

Trident Security Series: Volume III

Trident Security Series: Volume IV

Trident Security Series: Volume V

Trident Security Series: Volume VI

About Samantha Cole

USA Today Bestselling Author and Award-Winning Author Samantha Cole is a retired policewoman and former paramedic. Using her life experiences and training, she strives to find the perfect mix of suspense and romance for her readers to enjoy.

Awards:

Wannabe in Wyoming (co-authored by J.B. Havens) won the bronze medal in the 2021 Readers' Favorite Awards in the General Romance category.

Scattered Moments in Time, won the gold medal in the 2020 Readers' Favorite Awards in the Fiction Anthology category.

The Road to Solace (formerly *The Friar*), won the silver medal in the 2017 Readers' Favorite Awards in the Contemporary Romance category.

Samantha has over thirty-five books published throughout several different series as well as a few standalone novels. A full list can be found on her website.

Sexy Six-Pack's Sirens Group on Facebook
Website: www.samanthacoleauthor.com
Newsletter: www.samanthacoleauthor.com/newsletter-signup

- facebook.com/SamanthaColeAuthor
- instagram.com/samanthacoleauthor
- bookbub.com/profile/samantha-a-cole
- goodreads.com/SamanthaCole
- amazon.com/Samantha-A-Cole/e/B00X53K3X8

Made in the USA
Middletown, DE
30 July 2025